MURDER NEVER DIES

Ian Borrett

Mill Place Books

Copyright © 2024 Ian Borrett

All rights reserved

The characters and events portrayed in this book are fictitious. Any similarity to real persons, living or dead, is coincidental and not intended by the author.

No part of this book may be reproduced, or stored in a retrieval system, or transmitted in any form or by any means, electronic, mechanical, photocopying, recording, or otherwise, without express written permission of the publisher.

ISBN-13: 9781234567890
ISBN-10: 1477123456

Cover design by: Art Painter
Library of Congress Control Number: 2018675309
Printed in the United States of America

CONTENTS

Title Page
Copyright
Chapter One - 2012   1
Chapter Two   9
Chapter Three   17
Chapter Four   22
Chapter Five - 2012   31
Chapter Six - 2024   36
Chapter Seven - 2012   39
Chapter Eight - 2024   48
Chapter Nine   56
Chapter Ten   66
Chapter Eleven   73
Chapter Twelve   81
Chapter Thirteen   86
Chapter Fourteen   91
Chapter Fifteen   97

Chapter Sixteen	104
Chapter Seventeen	108
Chapter Eighteen	116
Chapter Nineteen	123
Chapter Twenty	128
Chapter Twenty One	138
Chapter Twenty Two	144
Chapter Twenty Three	153
Chapter Twenty Four	159
Chapter Twenty Five	164
Chapter Twenty Six	171
Chapter Twenty Seven	175
Chapter Twenty Eight	185
Chapter Twenty Nine	194
Chapter Thirty	202
Chapter Thirty One	209
Chapter Thirty Two	215
Chapter Thirty Three	222
Chapter Thirty Four	229
Chapter Thirty Five	239
Chapter Thirty Six	243
Chapter Thirty Seven	249
Chapter Thirty Eight	256
Chapter Thirty Nine	261

Chapter Forty	264
Chapter Forty One	270
Chapter Forty Two	274
Chapter Forty Three	279
Chapter Forty Four	285
Chapter Forty Five	293
Chapter Forty Six	300
Chapter Forty Seven	309
Chapter Forty Eight	316
Chapter Forty Nine	319
Chapter Fifty	325
Chapter Fifty One	329
Chapter Fifty Two	336
Chapter Fifty Three	341
Acknowledgements	345
Jake Stone Investigations	347

CHAPTER ONE - 2012

She checked her new Garmin wristwatch, ten miles done, one more to go to reach her target, with two months left until the London Marathon. The days were starting to get noticeably longer but the gloom was gathering on a drizzly February late afternoon. Not for the first time she wondered what the hell she was doing, running three times a week through a wet, miserable winter when most people would be hunkering down at home and keeping warm. But still, she's through the worst of it now, and after April she may never put running shoes on again. She knew that wasn't true, it was 2012 and Parkrun's were really starting to get going up and down the country, and the London Olympics was just around the corner.

The gravel crunched melodically under her feet as she glimpsed the lights of the village of Brockenhurst ahead. Commuters were driving home along the main road and she started to hear the distant hum of tyre on tarmac. The gravel ended and she was mostly running on moss, springy and squelchy underfoot. The trees were now closing in as she came across quite a dense copse before the first houses of the village appeared. It was a lonely spot and not inviting in the half-light, it seemed someone was gradually turning the dimmer down on the day.

Suddenly, there was a crack which knocked her out of her stride pattern. Then a thud, something hit the ground ahead of her. She felt a chill despite sweating from the run, was it a New Forest pony wandering into her path? Or something, or someone more dangerous? She stopped and peered ahead, screwing her eyes up, thinking it would help her focus better. There was no further sound. Was somebody waiting for her? No, something was lying across her path about twenty metres ahead and she was sure it wasn't an animal, so tentatively she walked forward as it clearly wasn't moving. Her heart was leaping into her throat as she realised this was a man, lying on his back, eyes closed, looking peaceful. He was clearly dead.

An absolute stillness seemed to settle around her. There was not a sound. She glanced all around to try and make sense of what she was looking at. There was a large branch on the ground just a few feet away which appeared to have just broken off a nearby tree. Was the body on the branch and they both just fell to the ground? It would explain the crack followed by the thud. She tentatively reached out to touch the body, it was cold. Her limited knowledge of forensics told her that he'd been dead for a while.

Was it murder? If so, hopefully that meant the killer was not hanging around, lurking in the shadows watching her. She wished an innocent looking person would come by so she could share her discovery, like an old lady just taking her dog for a walk. There again, any unexpected human appearance would not be welcome. She felt so alone and exposed. The light was fading rapidly so she fumbled for her phone and dialled 999. She got through to the police control room where an exhausted sounding operative asked her what she wanted. The tone changed when she explained that she'd found a dead body, and she was alone in near darkness. Karen was told to stay on the line, and someone would be out to see her as soon as possible.

It was the longest ten minutes of her life, and every sound she heard seemed to be magnified, making her jump constantly. She was thankful there was another person she could talk to in the control room while she waited. At that moment Vicky became her new best friend.

Suddenly, there was a scream from about fifty metres away, she backed herself up against the tree, struggling to breathe, hearing her rapid heartbeat as if it was trying to break out from her chest. Then another scream and the flutter of wings which, to her relief confirmed it was not human, but a crow, or something like it.

Looking to her right she could just about make out a flashing blue light which stopped alongside the main road, about one hundred and fifty metres away. She let out a huge sigh and started to move towards it as a torchlight also started to come into view, pointed in her direction.

'Hello,' a voice called out to her. 'It's the police.' A male voice. She started slowly walking towards the voice, although she was wary. She'd read too many crime detective novels to be confident she would now be safe. Then a fresh-faced young man appeared in front of her. 'It's ok madam, I'm PC Joe Attwood, from Lyndhurst Police Station.'

'Oh, thank god, I don't think I've ever been so scared in all my life.' She'd forgotten that Vicky was still hanging on, so she quickly let her know that a policeman had arrived. 'At least you were here pretty quickly.'

Joe had a grim look on his face as he glanced across at the body lying prostrate on the damp, mossy ground. He carried on looking while he spoke.

'A detective constable will be out shortly to take a look, and a pathologist has also been called.' He seemed to snap back into consciousness and looked at her.

'Is he dead?'

'I'd say so, I just quickly touched him and he's cold.'

'Probably a stupid question, but do you know him?'

'No.' She explained that she'd been running through the forest, heard a crack and a thud, and there he was.

'Do you think he fell out of the tree here?'

'He may have done, but I didn't really see him fall.' She was starting to feel very cold, which PC Attwood noticed.

'Here,' he said, 'take my jacket,' as he took his regulation police jacket off and handed it to her, mindful not to put it around her shoulders himself in case it caused offence. 'I have to admit this is the first time I've seen a dead body, only been in the force two months.' He hesitated and glanced at her. 'If I'm honest, and I probably shouldn't say this, it's just a little bit exciting, and to be first on the scene.'

'Well, I suppose something like this doesn't happen every day in rural Hampshire.' She was a little amused by his naivety.

'Not in my experience. So far anyway.' Joe raised his eyebrows with a half-smile.

'Well, now you're here PC Attwood, I think so too. It is a little bit exciting.' She started to relax.

'Call me Joe. You've had a shock.' He wandered a bit closer to the body and peered over to take a good look, shining his torch up and down. He seemed to be intrigued.

'Not much older than me,' he muttered, 'short, dark hair, hoodie and jeans, Adidas trainers.'

'Now then,' he said, taking out a notepad and pen. 'You say you touched the body, but did you move it at all?' Karen shook her head. 'Good. I need to take down some details then.' Joe was looking more confident as he wrote down Karen's address.

'You're sounding like a detective, Joe.'

'One day,' he smiled back at her.

Karen warmed to the young policeman, and she hoped he wouldn't soon become cynical and overly judgmental in his approach to the general public, but it was probably inevitable.

'He must have been dead a while before he fell out of the tree.'

'I'm no expert but I'd guess so.' Joe said, then looked up and tensed slightly. Another car had arrived, and two more torches were coming towards them. Karen's relief was now complete as a female detective introduced herself, DCI Amey Lorimer, clearly a no-nonsense type, she was ordering her colleague, DS Matthew Boyle around as if he was an obedient dog. PC Joe Attwood backed away allowing the detectives to take over.

'Now then love, what's your name?' DCI Amey Lorimer said.

'Karen Carpenter. As in the singer.'

'Well, she's been dead for a while, it's a wonder you remember her.'

'Thank my parents for that.' Karen said, screwing her face up. Amey just nodded, then approached the body looking carefully at his face and the angle he was laying. She looked up with an annoyed look on her face.

'DS Boyle, take some details off this young lady. You know the drill and then we can probably let her go home and get warm.' Karen was about to say she'd already done that but decided against it.

'Yes ma'am,' he replied, but he looked a little nervous. 'Ma'am did you see where that plod went? He seems to have disappeared.' Amey looked around.

'Well did you not speak to him first of all?'

'No, ma'am, I was planning to.'

'Fool,' she muttered and turned back to the prostrate body.'

'Did you not know him?' Karen asked DS Boyle.

'Didn't get a good look at him to be honest, but we only speak to uniform when we have to.' Karen looked puzzled. Matthew added, 'It's the way we are in the force, very hierarchical.' He raised his eyebrows.

After a few minutes, DCI Lorimer wandered over to where they were sitting, on a big branch that would have fallen to the ground a few years ago. The pathologist had arrived, and she'd got an initial update, but as always he didn't like to commit until he'd got him 'on the slab.'

'Well, there's no gunshot wounds, no

marks that indicate foul play at this stage. Maybe he was climbing the tree and the branch broke.' Although Karen thought this was unlikely. 'Can you report to Lyndhurst Police Station tomorrow morning, and we'll take a full statement?' Karen nodded. She handed the jacket that PC Attwood had given her to Matthew.

'Did the uniform give this to you?' DS Boyle asked.

'Yes, he was really kind. Only a young lad.'

DS Boyle looked at the jacket and frowned, then turned to Karen.

'Do you need a lift somewhere?'

'Yes please, if you don't mind, my car's on the other side of the village.'

CHAPTER TWO

2023 had been an eventful year for Jake, especially for a rookie private investigator which he now was. But that was last year, and he was smiling, he put his hands on his new desk which was in his new office, above a bakers in Lymford High Street. That made him worry about his waistline, the smell of fresh bread and pastries permeated the floorboards, and he'd already discovered a taste for the cheese and bacon turnovers they made fresh each morning.

His investigations had started to do quite well and kept him busy. He'd just discovered the whereabouts of twenty-four-year-old Ross Gilmore. Ross had received some media coverage two years ago when he was seen walking across the river bridge at Christchurch, but then never arrived at his girlfriend's flat two miles away. She'd been tracking him on her phone when suddenly it seemed to be turned off. Ross had had trouble with alcohol a year before but seemed to have cleaned himself up and got a new job working as a lifeguard on the beach at Southbourne. Police efforts to find him drew a blank, and the investigation was gradually wound down. Charlotte, his girlfriend, was always convinced he was dead. Although there was no indication why he would have been killed, Jake discovered that the police were suspicious Charlotte knew more than she ever let on and wasn't as cooperative as they'd expected. She'd shown little emotion, however she had a cast iron alibi for the time he seemed to disappear, being with reliable friends who could corroborate that she was with them.

The police seemed to be sure that he was probably still alive but had wanted to go off the radar. His parents, naturally, couldn't give up and they contacted Jake two months ago. Eventually, through one of Ross's fellow lifeguards, Jake learnt that he'd changed his name and gone to Dinard in France. Ross had sworn the lifeguard to secrecy so said nothing when the police questioned him.

So, Jake caught the ferry to St Malo and found, the now called Ben Stevens, lifeguarding on the beach. Over a coffee and a croissant Ross explained that Charlotte had been handy with her fists, and he'd become scared and intimidated by her. It wouldn't have been easy just to break off their relationship. He thought it was time for a fresh start, although he'd always felt guilty not contacting his parents. Jake brought him back to England to an emotional reunion with his parents. This had been Jake's most satisfying investigation so far.

He sat back in his chair, ran his hand

through his hair and smiled again. His phone then vibrated on the desk and a picture of Milly eating an ice cream flashed up.

'How's my favourite radio presenter doing?'

'Living the dream my little Teletubby,' Milly replied. This was a new nickname she'd given him after patting his stomach one morning. For the first time in his life, he'd grown a little paunch. He put it down to contentment and reaching his mid-thirties.

Jake chuckled.

'Well, how would you feel about appearing in a podcast?' Milly continued.

'Podcast.' Jake tensed, because he had a good idea what was coming. 'About what?'

'I've been talking to Elias,' Milly went on, 'the station's branching out into podcasts and we thought...well, one about what happened to you last year would be great.'

'About what happened? You mean, finding out I was adopted, and my biological father was a North London gangster who abandoned me and fled abroad. Oh, and his daughter posed as one of my clients and took out a contract on me to get her hands on his money. You want me to talk about that on a podcast?'

'I thought it might help, that's all. You've sorted things out with Isabella, and found you've got another half-sister - a whole new family, in fact. Maybe it would help draw a line under what happened in Menorca?' Jake didn't answer, and she sighed. 'Just think about it for now, okay? We'll talk later.'

Jake grunted. 'I'm not sure I'm ready for the world to hear my back story.'

'I get that, but you have to admit it's an interesting one.'

'I'll give you that,' Jake pondered.

'Look, I've got football practice tonight, so I'll see you tomorrow.'

Jake wandered back to the window and first of all thought about Milly playing football. Now she was in her thirties she was playing for Lymford Veterans which he enjoyed taking the mickey out of her for. She was trying to get him to play in a new mixed team they were setting up. He knew he would as his competitive edge would take over and want to impress her with his silky Messi-like skills, or that's how he perceived them, but he knew he was alone in that impression and his Messi-like skills ended in a y not an i. The podcast deserved serious consideration. Luke had said he could write a book about last year. 'Maybe when I'm sixty!' was his response. He decided to put his running gear on and pound the Lymford shoreline to get his thoughts in order.

The next day was a good one. Jake had two more enquiries to do some sleuthing. One was from a chap called Greg Jones, who he was meeting the following day and sounded intriguing, although he was a little elusive with details, and the other a woman who wanted her husband followed. She was sure he was having an affair. Textbook PI work.

Jake left the office and went straight to Milly's. She was in the shower but heard him come in as she turned the water off, so she shouted through the bathroom door. 'Get me a glass of wine, will you?'

'Shall I join you in there?'

'No. I'm clean and I've had a traumatic day, no offence but I want alcohol rather than you right now.'

Jake opened the door. 'Well, I've got something in my hand for you.' Milly gave him a pitying look as he handed her a glass of Sauvignon Blanc. She gulped a large mouthful down and smiled at Jake. 'Now go and do something interesting while I get dressed.'

Milly was on the phone to Elias at her radio station as she came into the living room of her apartment. The Crunch was now a rebranded station, but so far nothing much had changed, only two presenters had been replaced, although there were rumours of sharing their output with another station in Kent.

'I'm bloody well not doing that.' Jake heard Milly say. He looked up and raised his eyebrows. Milly had a three-seater cream sofa and a matching chair. She threw the phone down on the chair, clearly not happy.

'Crisis at The Crunch?' Jake asked, seriously.

'Idiotic new management wants to start running afternoon community events, like me going to a village hall and interviewing notable people of the village. I thought that was left to community radio, not big brands like us!'

'Oh.' Jake said, trying very hard not to find that amusing. 'Is it time to think again about that place?'

'It's tough though. The radio market is getting swallowed up by big companies who then network shows, and that leads to presenters having broadcasts from Cornwall to Aberdeen, from umpteen different stations. The localness is disappearing. Although we have more stations, the presenters are less.'

Jake tickled the back of her neck. 'But you're good. You could do something else in the media.' He tried to sound reassuring.

'You need another haircut,' Milly said, turning a scowl into a smile, lightening the mood.

His phone rang and an unknown number came up. He answered, 'Jake Stone.' Milly watched his face turn from curiosity into something far more serious, but he said little. Finally, she heard him say goodbye and he turned to her with an incredulous look on his face.

'What was that all about?' she asked,

frowning.

'It's the council, about the houseboat, they want to redevelop that part of the harbour, and someone wants to invest in it.'

'What does that mean, you're being turfed out?'

'Must be.' Jake mused. As he was still renting the houseboat he was surprised the landlord hadn't been in touch. 'I need to get hold of Andy and find out a bit more about what's going on. I love that houseboat, it's my own little haven.'

Milly was frowning again. The subject of them moving in together had been put on the back burner, and she knew Jake wasn't keen on it, at least for now. This might force the issue. She watched Jake dial up Andy Clements, who owned the three houseboats where Jake lived.

'It's gone to voicemail.' Jake threw his phone down onto the sofa and let out an exasperated shout, 'arghhh.'

'Well, phone him back and leave a message.' Milly couldn't help a slightly patronising tone. 'Sorry, I sounded like your mother, didn't I?' She reached out and adjusted his fringe. Hair having fallen down to his nose, in his frustration.

'Maybe it's time to think about what I do next.' Jake said. This came out as if he was making a huge life decision. He didn't look at Milly as he said, 'maybe I now look to buy a place of my own, rent somewhere…or we talk about living together.'

He looked at her, but Milly's face wasn't giving anything away. She pulled her legs up onto the sofa and smacked her lips. She leant into Jake and said. 'What do you want to do?'

Jake sighed, 'I wish I knew.'

CHAPTER THREE

Janice hated her job. Cleaning up people's mess, some human beings were absolutely filthy and had no pride in the way they behaved or cared about their environment. Trouble is she lived in a seaside town, and virtually all the employment was centred around the tourist trade and making the visitors happy. There was little choice for a fifty-four-year-old with few qualifications, lacking a sunny disposition, and riddled with all sorts of ailments brought on by drug abuse when she was younger. No, her cleaning job at the Big Lake Holiday Park in Hayling Island would probably have to last her until retirement, which seemed a long way off. She'd been married to Derek for thirty-four years, you married young in Hayling in those days. He was away during the week working in sales for a plumbing company. This suited Janice just fine. They had one adopted son, Keith, who was now living in Spain with his much older girlfriend.

There were six hundred static caravans at Big Lake, and she worked in an area of the park called 'Paradise.' These were mostly let out to holidaymakers through the owners of the park on a regular one or two-week turnover, but a few had been bought outright and owned. You did get to know these people a little, but Janice couldn't really be bothered to waste her time talking to them. A forced cheery good morning was enough. The park had opened early this year to try and cash in on the half term holiday trade, so this was the second week where it wasn't just owners occupying the site. During the winter season she would still help out with maintenance, so was always around. 2012 was going to be a busy year, she was told people from abroad were booking so they could be in London for the Olympics. Big Lake was only an hour or so from the city.

There was a woman at number forty-three she'd seen her a few times, quite tall and rather hard faced. She was probably in her thirties with dark hair, down to her shoulders, and a very narrow nose. Janice had called her Pinocchio when talking to her colleagues.

Janice was sure she'd seen this woman go into the caravan last week. Her car was outside, alongside the caravan. It was an Audi, big one, so quite expensive. Janice didn't really know much about cars, but her boss had an Audi. Her little Honda Jazz had served her well for years. Anyway, since then she'd not seen her and, as she walked past the caravan every day, she hadn't detected any lights on, or any movement inside. She'd finished her round so decided to have a peek in through the large living room area at the front. She tutted at the mess she could see inside. Clothes, books, pots and pans strewn all over the place. She could see a phone on the floor, half hidden under a chair, and as she squinted and put her hand up to her forehead, to shield the reflection from the low sun, she could see one of the dining area chairs seemed to be smeared and flecked a darker colour than the others. She then saw a similar stain on the door frame which led through to the bedrooms. Something was not right, so Janice called her supervisor, Agu.

Agu, who told Janice meant Leopard in Nigerian, someone full of agility, had spare keys and arrived about ten minutes later. Janice once confessed she'd like to get agile with him when she was four glasses of wine down at the Christmas party. He had politely declined. She stood behind Agu as he opened the door and immediately they were hit by a sickly sweet stench. He turned to Janice and advised her to stay where she was.

Agu looked around him, she noticed he was bracing himself for something unpleasant. The stain on the chair looked like blood. Janice knew that he'd seen a lot of blood back home in Nigeria before he'd emigrated to the UK five years ago.

She watched him walk through the door to the bedroom, then heard a stifled scream of sorts, more like he was being strangled. Five seconds later he came back out again, and Janice was sure his black face looked immeasurably paler. He pushed her aside and proceeded to throw up over the side of the steps that led up to the front door. Janice looked at him and considered going in herself. 'Do not go inside.' Agu shouted at her, as he wiped his mouth. The smell of Agu's vomit was now mixing with the stench from inside, and Janice could feel her own stomach heave.

'There's blood everywhere,' Agu's voice was strained, 'she's standing up but she's cut open,' he blubbered, 'ring the police Janice, that's murder.'

The police had the caravan cordoned off and word had spread around the holiday park as soon as police cars came screeching in. There was a captive audience, and crowds were gathered around the area of the park the caravan was situated, so a larger cordon was being put into place. Police were questioning those staying in the adjacent homes for any suspicious activity they may have seen. They were starting to feel trapped in their own homes.

Several policemen were standing around the cordon. They were joined by another who was keeping his head down as he approached. He saw Janice, who was sitting down with a cup of tea and a big coat draped around her. He then looked up at Agu who was talking to a detective.

The young policeman then tried to peer inside the caravan, as if he was looking for something. His hand went up to the glass which was a small side window to the living area, shading the light creating a glare. A couple of other PC's frowned at each other but didn't say anything. Police had been called in from various stations, so they didn't all know each other. The young PC looked away, biting his lip and frowning. He looked towards the door as if he was going in.

DCI Amey Lorimer arrived; her face hardly visible under a large brown cowboy hat she'd bought on holiday in Houston five years ago. She had a large brown mac to match, which came down to her ankles.

'Right, get out of my way young man.' She didn't look at him as she spoke and the young PC realised he was drawing a little bit of attention to himself. 'What do you think you're doing? Shouldn't you be back at the cordon over there?' He nodded and sloped off. Amey tutted and climbed the three steps to enter the van, with her sidekick, DS Matthew Boyle hot on her heels. Immediately her voice became audible to all outside as she surveyed the scene inside.

CHAPTER FOUR

It was 11.30am by the time Jake climbed into his Audi A3, manoeuvred out of Milly's parking space, down Millstream Avenue, and on to the main road to Southampton. It was early March, and the first daffodils were glowing in the sunshine. Jake loved spring. He was meeting Greg Jones at the Trago Lounge in Southampton, a comfortable bar at noon. He was putting thoughts of losing his houseboat to the back of his mind for now.

Jake parked up just after midday and walked a short distance to the bar. He'd never been there before but liked the look of it as he pushed the door open and looked around. There was a wooden floor with colourful tables and chairs, and more comfortable armchairs and sofas scattered around. As soon as he walked in he heard loud giggling from a couple in the corner. Both had what looked like espresso martinis, one was being very expressive with his hands and shouted. 'It's true, 110% it's true.' It seemed a bit early for them to have drunk much, so that must be their natural behaviour. He felt a pang of guilt for being a little judgemental that people could only be so extroverted from drinking alcohol. Sometimes he wished he was more like that.

He looked to his left and saw this rather gaunt looking man sitting at a table caressing a beer. The man put his hand up and gestured him to the table. He stood up and held out his hand as Jake approached, a rather weak handshake as he introduced himself. His voice was deep which betrayed a frail looking man, probably about the same age as Jake but his short dark hair already showed signs of grey around the temples. His face was thin, brown eyes, and he looked like he could do with a shave. If he was growing a beard, Jake thought, he needed to tidy it up. However, he was dressed quite smartly in dark blue chinos and a light blue Gant polo shirt, buttoned up to the neck.

Greg ordered Jake a drink and came back and sat down, staring nervously at him. Jake could tell he didn't know where to start with the reasons why he'd contacted him. In his fledgling life as an investigator this moment still intrigued him, when a potential client was preparing to describe their concerns and the reason they contacted him. You never really knew what was going to come out. Jake decided to get things going.

'So, what can I do for you?' Greg raised a half smile which changed to a look of annoyance, if not defiance.

'It's my brother. He was killed exactly

twelve years ago, and the killer has never been found.' Jake nodded. 'Don't get me wrong he wasn't a good person, was caught up in all sorts of shit that I probably don't know the half of.' Greg took a sip and looked down at his beer. 'He was found dead in the New Forest, fell out of a tree, injected with cyanide.'

Jake frowned. 'But the police investigated?'

'Not very well. I think they thought he was a wrong 'un, got mixed up in some gangland stuff that went wrong, and decided not to waste too much resource looking for the killer.' Jake could already hear echoes of Dave Constantinou in his head.

'What was his name?'

'Layton. Layton Jones.'

'Did it receive much publicity at the time?'

'Only a little. And for a very short space of time.' Greg looked upset.

'So, what did they conclude?'

'Well, nothing. They basically gave up,' Greg stuttered and looked down at his glass, 'and as far as I'm concerned justice has not yet been served.'

'And you'd like me to do my own investigations?' Jake asked.

Greg nodded. Jake could sense a mix of anger and pleading on his face.

'OK. Tell me more about your brother?'

'Well, he was a couple of years older than me. Good kid, we come from a good home.

Our parents lived in Chilworth, a nice part of Southampton.' Jake knew it was more than nice, one million pound plus houses. 'When he was in his early twenties he rebelled a bit against our upbringing. My parents were snobs, they had no reason to be, but I think he wanted to do the classic thing of shocking our parents. He came back from university and decided not to follow the family business.'

'Which is?' Jake asked.

'Was.' Greg replied. 'Remember the coffee shops called Brendon's? All over the place. Went bankrupt just before the pandemic.'

Jake murmured, recalling their cinnamon buns, which he loved. There was one outside his office when he worked in London. He also knew there were some theories around at the time that Brendon's were involved in some controversy, although he couldn't recall what exactly.

Greg carried on. 'He did a bit of shoplifting, took drugs and generally spiralled downwards. Then after about six months he disappeared. We didn't have a clue what happened to him. The good thing was we knew he was alive though. Every week he'd send our mum a short text, and very occasionally give her a quick call. I think he wanted her to know he was still around, but he never told her anything of what he was doing.'

'So, how did you find out about his death?'

'The texts and calls stopped in February 2012, and then in April we got the knock on the door after we finally reported him missing.'

'So, the police never found out who killed him?'

'Nope. And here we are twelve years later.'

'And your parents?'

'Moved to Perth, Western Australia. They'd planned to go in 2020 as they'd given up hope, and I think they needed to get away from this country. They had to delay it due to Covid, but they've got a nice beachside home in a place called Hillary's. It was their idea to look up a private investigator as a final throw of the dice.'

Jake sat back and considered what Greg had just told him. He ran his hand through his hair and leaned forward again, looking Greg in the eyes.

'You know more than you're telling me. I'm not buying this at the moment.'

Greg looked shocked, but then an element of guilt spread across his face.

'Look, that's the nuts and bolts of it. The police stopped looking and we still need some closure.' Jake stood up. 'I've no doubt you do, but what were you doing as a family to press the police more? Your own investigations? If that was my brother, and son, I wouldn't have waited twelve years!' Greg didn't respond but just stared at Jake, who tapped the table and looked down at the ground. He looked around and could see the couple in the corner were on another cocktail, and definitely getting louder. They were enjoying themselves.

'Do you want to give me anymore?' Jake asked him.

'Well, will you take it on? Do some investigating yourself?'

'I won't deny it's interesting,' he said, looking back at Greg, 'but you need to think about giving me all the details. You've got my number so think about it. It's the only way I can do a proper investigation.' Jake turned and made for the door. He could feel Greg's eyes fixed on him. Jake had done this before and learnt the tactic from an online training session. Don't make it easy for them when you know they're holding back. The nerves show in their eyes. Show that you're happy to walk away and are not desperate for their business. If he hears from Greg again then that will show he's serious, and he wouldn't be wasting his time.

Jake was conscious of his other meeting by the time he got into his car, the straying husband, but checking his messages he saw that she wanted to reschedule to tomorrow, which was something of a relief. Jake got back to his office and finally spoke to Andy Clements. It was he who wanted to develop the harbour area with additional moorings for expensive yachts. The three houseboats were to be sold on to somebody who was keen to move them to Guildford. Not a lot Jake could do. He ran his hand through his hair and looked around his spartan office. He needed to get some more filing cabinets, and he'd seen a sofa in the second hand shop up the road. He needed to get that delivered, and a couple of chairs for his consultations with clients. He wandered over to the window which was about fifteen feet in front of his desk at the back of the office. There was a small cloakroom to the right as he looked out from where he sat, and then another door which led down the stairs towards his own private entrance to the outside.

He was deep in thought as he looked at the street below. The weather had turned, it was cold outside. Further north they were apparently being battered by snow, but here on the coast it was sleety rain, which was quite depressing. He had six months to vacate the houseboat, but he may as well make some decisions sooner rather than later. Does he move in with Milly? Does he buy on his own? Does he buy with her? The latter was slightly scary, and he wasn't sure why. He couldn't imagine life without her, but if it didn't work out between them that would have to be untangled. On the other hand, he was lucky, he didn't need to get a mortgage, and he suspected that Milly may feel uncomfortable if he paid outright for a house that was in joint names. He reflected that it wasn't a bad problem to have. He could, of course, just buy and then maybe Milly moved in at the right time. He turned on the radio and the conflict in Ukraine had no sign of ending. He then felt a pang of conscience that he was so financially affluent while others had no homes, and little future to look forward to.

He needed a beer. He looked at his watch, as it was 5.30pm he knew his mate Luke would be in the Seafarers having an after-work drink. He texted him to check. Luke confirmed he was there with a text reply almost before Jake had even sent his own. He smiled, put everything away and went down the stairs and locked the door. It was a short walk down the road to the pub. Luke had become his sounding board, and he needed to chew his ear right now.

Jake woke with a head that was desperately trying to break out of his skull, and a stomach that was churning like Niagara Falls. He lay there, trying to recall his conversation from the previous evening. An evening with Luke usually ended badly, or at least the following morning was bad. But it was also good fun. Luke was talking a lot about commitment, and it was time that Jake decided that he should make the leap with Milly and properly move in together, but still those doubts crept in. Jake wanted to be convinced, but he wasn't there yet.

He got up, turned on the tap and filled the kettle. He looked at his face in the mirror and felt sure his skin looked green. It then came back to him that he started talking to a woman in the pub he'd seen before. She worked as an estate agent further up the High Street from his own office. They started talking about property, but it wasn't long before she was touching the back of his neck and suggested going back to her place. Jake cringed a little as he thought about it. He recalled Luke coming up to him and reminding him he was a happily taken man. Jenna, that was her name, she then walked away, but not before giving him her phone number which he remembered entering into his phone. He turned around and looked for his phone, which was on charge next to his bed. He scrolled through his contacts and deleted her. He looked again at himself in the mirror iand he decided to have a shower first. Coffee after.

Jake got to the office at 11am. His meeting with Natalie, the one with the straying husband was at 11.30am. He tidied up a bit and then went down to get a packet of Hobnobs from the small Tesco nearby. He also thought he had come to his decision about Milly, whether they should live together. Or at least last night he was sure, this morning his indecision had returned.

CHAPTER FIVE - 2012

PC Joe Attwood was in trouble. He couldn't get to the phone that was left in the holiday home in Hayling Island. His job was quite clear, find out what was happening, clear up where necessary, and report back. He'd hoped that the clear up part wasn't going to be needed, but in this case it was, and a tough challenge to sort out the mistake the killer had made. He thought he could have retrieved the phone if that bloody detective had not arrived on the scene, just as he was about to enter the caravan.

Pretending to be someone else was something he was good at, he'd always known that, and he'd enjoyed playing PC Joe Attwood. He'd needed the money, and that was the truth, and the first job had gone smoothly enough, even if he'd got a bit carried away and said too much to that pretty woman who'd found the body. But authenticity was important, wasn't it? The police were trained to be caring, to show compassion. And being PC Joe Attwood had felt good. It let him step outside the real reason he was there, at least for a while. And when he needed to get away, he didn't hesitate. He'd seen his opportunity and grabbed it. Because timing

…timing was everything.

It was 2pm and he was flicking through TV channels trying to find something to take his mind off things. Nothing was working. He tried watching Friends again, but he just got restless, waiting for the phone to ring. Waiting to know how much trouble he might be in, waiting to be summoned to the bar. His understanding was his 'alternative' job would be needed one more time, and then he should get a handsome payout. His phone rang, he knew the number. He breathed deeply and tried not to sound scared when he spoke.

The Green Room was a smart bar and kitchen located in the heart of Winchester, along one of the main streets in the small city. You walked in and got a sense of class and sophistication. Lots of brass, wood panelling and staff that were all dressed in a combination of black and white. They had a few tables out the front of the building on the pavement, well used in the sunny summer months, otherwise mainly for the hardy, and smokers. The Green Room was long and narrow with a bar to the left as you walked in. One end of the bar was stuffed with homemade cakes, and it was renowned for its food during the day. In the evening it became more of a drinking establishment, and its narrowness could make it very lively. He'd loved the place on a Friday or Saturday evening, but now it had different connotations for him.

He stood outside for a second. Today was sunny, but with the relatively low sun it illuminated the inside of the bar. He could see it was quiet, and James appeared to be fiddling with the optics. The man known as PC Joe Attwood took a deep breath and walked in.

James looked up and his expression was not welcoming. Joe nodded at him, and James indicated that he should go up the stairs to a private room at the back. James followed him a minute or two later, his steps coming up sounded ominous as Joe nervously waited. The room was sparse with just a couple of chairs, a desk and a shelf that held big tubs of mayonnaise, ketchup and mustard. It was two weeks ago since he was last here getting his instructions. James shut the door firmly behind them, and indicated for him to sit down while he pulled a chair up and sat down opposite him.

'So, what happened?' James was talking barely above a whisper.

'It was too risky; the detectives were already there. I did what I could but by then I couldn't get in.' Joe was almost pleading.

'But what the fuck took you so long to get there?'

'I'm sorry. I went to the wrong holiday park at first.' Joe looked down. He was feeling scared now. 'There's two right next to each other.

I went to the wrong one, and by the time I realised everyone else was starting to arrive.'

'Look, it's not your fault that fucking idiot dropped his phone in the first place. I've told them that. Believe me, he's going to regret it. The police are going to find the WhatsApp group on there but hopefully they won't get much further than that. We may be in the clear. The numbers listed won't be registered to anyone so it will be just a series of messages. I don't know what they've said to each other but I'm sure no real names will be mentioned.'

Joe looked up at James, thankful he wasn't getting the grilling he thought he would get. He then thought, naively, that James was just as much a friend as an accomplice in this business. That was how he got involved in the first place.

'What happens next?' he asked tentatively.

'The third one.'

'And the last?'

'Yep. Retribution will be complete.'

'When is it?'

'Three days' time. Slightly different this time, no uniform needed. You'll be a member of the public who's just being a bit nosy.'

Joe was more than a little relieved. This sounded easier. He'd already been briefed on the type of killing and where it was going to be. He just needed to be in the right place at the right time.

'Am I still Joe Attwood?'

'Yep, but drop the PC.' James said, and then stood up, indicating it was time to go. 'Look, you did a great job with the first one, and I'll take the flak for not being able to get the phone back. The next one should be straightforward. I'll give you a call when that's done, and then it'll all be over for you.'

Joe looked at him doubtfully.

'But will it?'

James hesitated for a moment. 'I can't promise you that, but I think it will be. You're involved, but after that I think you can wait for your handsome payout and let the bigger boys make sure nothing comes back to bite you…or me come to that.' James smiled at him, but Joe could see it was a weary smile and maybe this was getting to him as well.

They went back downstairs in silence, and he left The Green Room, just as snow started to drift down from a now black sky. The light was surreal, as if he was living in a parallel universe.

CHAPTER SIX - 2024

Jake checked the time as he watched Natalie descend the stairs and out into Lymford High Street. Lymford was not a big town, and since he'd arrived fifteen months ago, he'd found out if you're a local, then most people at least know of each other. During the summer the town swelled with visitors and yachty types so there's a lot more strangers about. Natalie was married to a local boatyard owner, who was well known, and something of a local celebrity. He'd competed for the UK in the Olympics twelve years ago in Weymouth, having won a gold medal. She suspected him of having an affair with a woman who was a waitress in a popular restaurant just outside of town. Natalie was sure his Tuesday evening meetings with clients in Bournemouth were no such thing, and she wanted Jake to do the dirty work to prove it. He knew his next Tuesday would be spent staking out the husband with his camera.

His phone rang as he sat down at his desk with his feet up on the table. It was Greg Jones. He hadn't expected to hear from him so soon, but knew he would, once he was ready.

'Want to tell me more Greg?'

'Hello Mr Stone. Yes. Can we meet again?'

'Look Greg, I'm not the police. I can't arrest you for anything.'

'Can I just ask you something though?'

Jake agreed.

'Do you do any civil investigation work for Hampshire Police?' Jake was slightly taken aback. This was something that DCI Steve Crumpler had suggested to Jake several months ago. They basically do the same work as an officer but can't arrest. They're employed by the local police force.

'No, but I know what you're talking about.'

'The thing is,' Greg hesitated, 'I'd be wanting you to investigate them as much as anything, so I wanted to make sure you're not biassed.'

'I guessed as much, but you don't need to worry about that.'

'OK, can we set up another meeting....like tomorrow?'

Jake checked his calendar quickly. It would be Friday, normally a very easy day for him. He liked to avoid work if he could on a Friday, but curiosity got the better of him. This was new business.

'Yep. Can you come here? To my office in Lymford?'

'Give me the address and I'll be there for 11am?'

'OK then. See you at 11.' Jake rang off and

found himself smiling for the first time today.

He wandered over to the window. He was beginning to love this window, a window on the Lymford world. You could just see the balcony of Milly's apartment, and there was a good view up and down the High Street, peer to your right you could see across the river and railway line to the east side of Lymford. Jake determinedly strode back to his laptop and clicked on the EasyJet website. He was going to finally give Milly a proper break in Menorca, hopefully without drama this time. He booked the flight for a month's time, for both of them, and then sent a copy of the confirmation email across to her, without mentioning it. He hoped she'd be pleased, and they could have a nice romantic Thursday evening. Their relationship had grown in the last six months. They'd recently passed the anniversary of their first date and Jake had organised a romantic weekend in Rome, which was, in the words of Milly herself, 'perfect.'

CHAPTER SEVEN - 2012

Joe Attwood drove into Andover having had the call the night before. It had been a few days since he saw James in The Green Room. Days of torment for him, and this was going to be a little more complicated than James made out. He just wanted this all to be over with now. He was both relieved and scared when he got the call yesterday. Andover was a place he didn't know very well, despite having grown up only fifteen miles away. You had to have a reason to go there, it wasn't a tourist town, it wasn't a commercial town, and it wasn't known for its shopping or restaurant facilities. You might stop off here if you were on your way to the West Country from London, but you'd have to ask yourself why? Having said that, it was pleasant enough if you wanted a quiet life. Today it may make some headlines, but only if it all went wrong.

He turned off the A303 and headed towards an office complex which belonged to a large UK bank. His instructions were to go to Security and ask for Dan Dennis. They would be expecting him. This he did and a friendly security guard appeared who he detected had a German accent. She directed him to a car park space nearby. He walked back to the Security Gate and waited for Dan to appear. Joe's nerves were now frayed, he just wanted to go home. He noticed the name badge on the security guard, it was Helga, she started to make small talk which he just didn't want to do. Joe wanted to be largely unnoticed, and so kept conversation to a minimum. She was telling him they were expecting quite a few more visitors shortly, and she was clearly excited by the prospect. He couldn't share the enthusiasm.

After a very long five minutes Dan appeared. He was short and squat, shaved head, glasses, pock marked face and a mouth that seemed barely wide enough to be able to open. Apart from James this was the only other person he'd met who was part of this gang, if that's what you called it, and he looked like he had the archetypal look for one.

Helga handed Joe a pass to get into the building, and he and Dan walked off towards the front entrance.

'So, you're the bloke known as Joe Attwood, or is it PC Joe Attwood?' Dan said this with a sneer. 'Just do everything I tell you, try and look natural, and above all keep your wits about you.' Dan's tone was now threatening.

'Yes,' Joe replied rather meekly. Dan looked at him.

'Don't fuck it up you little shit. Alright!' Joe summoned up some courage. 'I won't. I know what to do and I'll do a good job.' They walked through the front doors and took the lift to the second floor. They turned to the left and into a room which Dan had clearly been using. He was on site as an alleged contractor for a project, put in place by someone he didn't know, but obviously someone who had connections with the Bank. This just made him think again who exactly was involved in this plan, or rather crime. Joe felt a small shudder go through him.

Joe was supposedly a potential new contractor who would help Dan, and today Dan was just interviewing him. They sat down.

'So, you know what's happening here today?' Dan asked.

'Yeah, they've got a meeting about the Olympics as this bank is a main sponsor. One of the visitors is the target in his capacity as a respectable businessman. I don't know any more than that.' The truth was Joe didn't want to know more than that, just what he had to do.

'Correct. What's going to happen is that the target will have a heart attack, brought on by something I give him in his water. The meeting is downstairs, and I've volunteered to help, or rather I was asked to help. People have their place settings, and I will add something to his water bottle. In the mayhem that follows I will grab the bottle and dispose of it. I will then disappear. You just need to hang around a bit and report back on what actually happens. If it all goes to plan it won't be a police matter, just paramedics saying he had a fatal heart attack.'

'Is that like the first one?'

'Not exactly. That was cyanide. This is from a foxglove, and it could be up to two hours before the effects kick in, so it's a bit of a waiting game. I will be long gone, and you will be a curious visitor.'

'Fuck.' Joe was hoping he would be out quicker than that.

'Just keep your fucking nerve OK. Nobody will have any reason to suspect you of anything.'

Joe just nodded.

Outside people were starting to arrive for the meeting so Dan had his job to do. 'Just stay here and play with your phone. There's a laptop there so you can look busy if anyone passes by or asks you what you're doing. Then, just wait for the commotion and go and investigate.

Dan shut the door and Joe felt an overwhelming need to go to the toilet. He sat and prayed for the first time in years. He prayed that his life in the future would be so much better than this.

Time had never moved so slowly. Joe opened the laptop and turned it on. There was an excel spreadsheet which he was told to open which could be cover if anyone came in to see what he was doing. Suddenly, the door opened and he knew he looked startled. A woman in her late fifties looked at him.

'Who are you then?' She had a northern accent and was carrying three mugs of tea in one hand. He didn't want to give his name out to anyone else.

'I'm just here waiting for someone.'

She frowned. 'Are you with that Dan fellow then?'

Joe nodded. 'He's going to be interviewing me in a while.'

'Oh yeah. No offence, but he looks a bit chuffing dodgy to me. Tried to tell me to make him a cup of tea earlier, needless to say he made it himself. I'm Elaine by the way, I'll stop wittering and wish you good luck.'

'Oh, thank you.' Joe said, feeling a bit bemused, as well as relieved she wasn't going to question him further. She shut the door, and he could see her toddle off down the hallway through the glass panels which acted as walls to the room.

It was another hour before he heard movement in the reception area below. He went to the window just in time to see Dan getting in a Mini, or rather struggling to get into a Mini, and then drive off past the security gates. A few minutes later he heard the ambulance siren before it pulled into the entrance. The German woman was waving it through and pulled up outside the reception area. Joe left his room and peered over the balcony into the reception area. His first thought was why had it taken Dan so long to leave? This raised his anxiety level. Now he was on his own. Two paramedics came racing in and disappeared below him, there were four other people looking anxious, just standing in the foyer. He would now need to summon up his skills once again. He went down in the lift and met the mild chaos on the ground floor.

Joe got as close to the room where the meeting was being held as he could. There was another security guard outside, so he asked what had happened.

'I don't know,' came the reply. Joe could see the paramedics surrounding a body and using CPR. 'Can you move away please, sir,' the security guard was asking.

'I'm a medical student,' Joe said, looking him directly in the face. The guard seemed to waver. 'Maybe I can help.'

'Well, the police will be here in a minute.' Joe certainly didn't want to draw attention to himself in front of the police. Then he heard the ping of a text message.

'Get the water bottle that's on the floor.' It was from Dan. He looked again at the security guard, 'I specialise in heart conditions.' He pushed past the guard who decided not to object. The paramedics ignored him as he entered the room, they were still working hard on resuscitation. There was one other person,

a man, in the room who glanced up at him and frowned. 'I'm a medical student,' he said confidently. The man looked back down at the body, the paramedics seemed to be losing hope. Joe saw the bottle about five feet from the body. Fortunately, it was behind the people in the room, so he edged round, bent down looking at the paramedics, as if ready to help if he could. He put his left hand out and scooped the bottle up. One of the paramedics suddenly looked at him.

'Who are you, what are you doing?'

'I'm a medical student,' Joe replied again, 'just wondered if I could help. Is it a cardiac arrest?' He wanted to quickly deflect any more questions at him. The paramedic was a young woman, not much older than him, she looked sad as well as confused. Joe wasn't convinced she believed him, but she replied anyway.

'Yep. We've done what we can. Is that your bottle of water?' She was now frowning, looking at the Hildon Water now in Joe's hand.

'Yep,' he said with assurance, 'dropped it as I bent down.' She nodded. 'Well, we didn't manage to revive him.'

Joe had his good looks, which he knew could work in his favour. The paramedic gave him a slight smile and didn't seem to want to question him further. Out the corner of his eye he could see two uniform police arrive. Now was the time to mingle into the background.

'So sad,' he said as he got up and made for

the door.

'Wait.'

Joe actually thought she was going to ask for his phone number. He looked around and she spoke. 'Where are you training?' He detected some doubt in her voice. Joe's mind swirled for a moment. 'Cardiff,' he blurted out, knowing there was a university hospital there. 'OK,' she replied. Joe turned away and walked back out of the room. He heard her mutter, 'Fucking liar.' He felt a cold sweat creep over him. His mind turned to thoughts of the police questioning him. He needed to get out.

There was quite a throng of people down the corridor now, curious office workers, word having spread. The police barged through ignoring Joe and then he heard a voice behind him.

'By 'eck, you chose the right day for an interview.' It was Elaine again. Joe smiled, feeling more comfortable that he could soon disappear and get on the road home, and this whole thing would be over. No more jobs and a nice little pay packet.

'Yep, Dan's had to cancel so Joe here can go home.'

'Joe? That's your name then?'

'Oh...oh it is.' He kicked himself for stupidly saying his name in the third person. He hated people who did that, so why do it?

Elaine looked at him quizzically, 'Well, stupid name if you ask me. Sounds like a parrot.' Joe raised his eyebrows and realised he must now quietly leave. He backed out into the reception area, walked briskly to his car, and drove round to the security gate. He gave Helga his pass, who was looking flustered, and drove out onto the main road. Once on the A303 he stopped at the services for fuel. He texted Dan to say he had the water bottle and received instructions how to dispose of it. He then put a Black Eyed Peas CD on in the car, turned it up and vowed never to commit another crime in his whole life.

CHAPTER EIGHT - 2024

Jake immediately detected that Milly was in an odd mood when he turned up at her apartment, for what he hoped would be a really nice evening. She barely managed a smile when she opened the door. He had a key but still felt a bit uncomfortable just walking in her apartment. He smiled at her.

'Are you okay?'

'Sure, just a bit tired.' She put on a fake cheerfulness which seemed like a real effort.

'I've got Chinese and lots of wine, so hopefully that will help.' Jake said, trying his best to seem upbeat.

'That's lovely. I'm not that hungry to be honest but give me that wine.' Milly grabbed the bottle and marched into the kitchen. Jake followed and watched her clatter two glasses onto the speckled worktop and literally splash the Merlot in before sighing and turning to look at Jake. It was more of a glare than a look, but she didn't speak.

'Any chance I could have that other glass?' he said, sensing he may have done something wrong. Milly pushed it along the worktop so he could reach out for it. There were a few further seconds of silence.

'Come on, what's up?' Jake asked. Milly looked tearful so he moved towards her, but she brushed him away. Jake couldn't guess whether this was just a bad day at the office, or he was the problem. He suspected the latter.

'So, how is the estate agency business?' The sarcastic tone left Jake in no doubt he was in trouble, and Milly had something to say. He thought it best to let her finish.

'This is a small town, and everyone knows that tart is anyone's for a cheese and onion crisp. Jenna the Jumper she's known as, and it sounds like you were ready to be her soft landing if Luke hadn't intervened.' Jake could feel himself getting defensive but decided to let Milly finish. 'I thought you had better taste than that, she's bedded half the men in Lymford so I suppose it was only a matter of time before she hooked you in.' Milly took another swig of wine which seemed to calm her down a bit. Jake turned around and started taking the Chinese boxes out of the carrier bag. Mostly to compose himself so he could wait his turn to speak.

He turned back and looked at her. Milly was looking at the kitchen floor.

'Look, this isn't you. You know there's no chance I would be interested in Jenna, especially as I'm with you,' Jake said, managing a soothing tone. 'If you really want me to explain myself then I will, but you know me better than that.'

Milly twisted her head and he could tell it was probably something she'd been waiting to say to him all day.

'I thought I did,' she mumbled. Jake moved towards her again, but she put her arms up as if to say, "stay away."

'I don't know why you're being like this. It was absolutely nothing. Yes, I talked to her but that was just being polite. Hey, I'm a nice guy, I realised what was going on and gave Luke a nod to come in and rescue me from her.' Jake remained calm, and he paused to see if Milly would come back at him.

"There was no way I was ever going to be sleeping with her. Why would I when I'm in love with someone as wonderful as you.' Milly looked at him and her face visibly softened, she was struggling to remain angry.

'I'm sorry, I do know you better than that,' she said, shaking her head. 'Get that food on the plates.' Milly managed to raise a half smile and Jake nodded. 'Go and sit down and I'll bring you a plate of Lemon Chicken and rice.' She kissed him quickly on the cheek and dutifully walked through to the sofa.

Once settled down and eating, Milly spoke again. She put her plate down on the floor and picked up Jake's hand, turning to him.

'Uh oh,' he said, 'what's coming?' A nervous smirk on his face.

'Well,' Milly said, squeezing his hand a bit

harder, 'it was lovely that you booked flights to Menorca, and I really want to go at some point, but can we go and visit Isabella instead?'

'Umm...yes, I suppose so. Why?'

'I dunno. I'd just like to talk to her again. See a bit more of Italy. Where she's moved to. We can go to Menorca any time.'

'When are you thinking? I can ask her. Pretty sure she'd be happy to see us.'

'The station can do without me for a week or so. Can we go pretty soon?'

Although the little drama when he arrived had passed Jake knew there was still something not quite right.

'Leave it with me, I'll try and speak with her tomorrow.' There was a little more silence and Jake reached for the remote, to turn the TV on.

'Has there been more development in radio land?' He asked.

'Nothing really new,' Milly replied, 'but I still don't like the way it's going. I'm pretty enthusiastic about the podcast idea though, and Elias is right behind it.'

'What ideas have you got?' Jake asked, 'apart from my little adventure.'

'We're open to anything to be honest. We want to keep it local.'

'I've a thought. You know I mentioned this potential client, Greg Jones, and the death of his brother?' Milly nodded, 'well, the family ran that chain of bakeries called Brendons. They went out of business and I'm sure there was something not quite right about it. Maybe a little bit of investigative work?'

Milly pondered. 'That's the sort of thing Elias would love to delve into. I'll mention it to him tomorrow.'

The rest of the evening was pleasant enough but not the romantic one Jake had hoped for. He knew that Milly had still not been totally open with him. He decided that she would tell him in her own good time. He knew there was something else, but he decided not to stay, and she didn't ask him to. A tactical retreat.

The doorbell rang at eleven am on the dot. Jake liked punctuality. He went down the stairs and opened the front door. Greg was standing there with a nervous smile on his face.

'Hello Greg, come on in.'

'Thank you, Jake, thank you for seeing me again.' They both climbed the stairs. Jake looked back at him, 'let's hope it's a more productive meeting this time.' Greg didn't respond. Coffee was already on the go, so he offered Greg a cup, he didn't have any tea bags. Greg had black, no milk, no sugar. Jake took it white with one sugar. He pulled his chair out from behind his desk, and they sat down facing each other.

'So, tell me more?' Greg took a sip, swallowed and then a big intake of breath.

'Well. Brendons was a successful business but back in 2010 the competition was getting pretty hot. As you may remember there was an explosion in the expansion of these types of businesses. We were starting to come out of the financial downturn and there was a new coalition government in charge. There was a lot of talk about austerity, but coffee shops were massively growing.' Greg took another sip of coffee. 'My father asked Layton about his connections. Did he know any strings that could be pulled which would prevent planning permission being given to some of these up-and-coming shops. It seems he did. He indicated there was a network of councillors who would say yes or no to anything for a few bucks. It was almost a club, like the Masons.'

Jake smirked, 'that doesn't surprise me. So, I take it that Layton and your family got involved in this? Bribery?'

'I'm afraid so. We're not proud of it.'

'Do you think this has anything to do with your brother's death?'

'No, and that's the point, but it's not something that we want to come out now. We'd like to keep that history, for obvious reasons. I think Layton was mixed up in much darker stuff than that.'

Jake looked at him, thinking about his conversation with Milly the previous evening. He got up and walked over to his biscuit barrel. He took the top off and offered Greg a Hobnob. He declined. Jake sat back down thinking to himself, thinking this could be a very juicy case, and already relishing the thought of it. He looked again at Greg.

'But that's a risk you may have to take if you want me to investigate his death?'

'I know. We stopped all that when he died, and maybe with the passing of time it's not so important now.'

'So that's why you didn't kick up a fuss when the police stopped investigating?'

Greg just nodded.

'Well then, you better tell me about the investigation and what stuff Layton was involved in.'

'You will investigate then?' Greg asked, the relief on his face made him look like a different person. It was like darkness transformed into light. Jake thought how the gauntness almost disappeared, and he looked a lot healthier.

'Sure.'

'Thank you so much Jake. My parents will be happy.'

'Look, I'm going to need all the info about who the investigating officers were, all the people he knew, that you know of, and what he was up to. I'll trawl the internet for the public stories and find a starting point.'

'Absolutely brilliant. I'll email you a whole host of stuff, we've kept a file of it, and I'll see what my parents can add.' Greg replied looking happy.

They both stood up and shook hands, and Jake showed him down the stairs. As he left, Greg turned and spoke. 'I know there's some sort of Menorca connection.' Jake noticed a chill run down his spine, and he felt knocked sideways. He dreaded some connection with his biological father, but that was highly unlikely surely.

Jake waved Greg off and walked slowly back up the stairs. Did he really want another case which had a Menorca connection? He wanted Menorca to be his happy holiday place, not somewhere he was investigating crime. Then again the monkey was already out of the bag in that respect. He could have died there, and he'd never forget what happened. He looked around his office and paced up and down. By the time he slumped into his chair he'd decided to see how it goes.

CHAPTER NINE

It was a few days before Greg's email dropped into Jake's mailbox. Included were press cuttings, general notes which the family had made for him, and pictures of Layton. He noticed that he wasn't smiling in any of them. He flicked the switch to turn the printer on, pressed print and waited. The chug of the printer indicated it was warming up and started churning the paper out. He felt more comfortable with the physical paper in front of him, which he always believed was much easier to deal with when trying to assess what's going on. Jake got up and made a coffee, took the papers off the printer and sat down with his laptop ready. He barely moved for the next two hours, switching between searching the internet and reading Greg's papers. At noon, he looked up and stretched, and could feel his stomach crying out for some food, so got up and went down the stairs, and stepped onto Lymford High Street.

His thoughts had overtaken him, and he literally walked into a lamp post, stubbing his toe which sent a shot of pain through his right foot. He managed to stop himself swearing but the embarrassment made him cross the road as quickly as possible, away from the sniggers of a group of young lads who'd been approaching him. Once he was across the road, he was able to see the funny side and smiled to himself.

He dived into Greggs, picked up a Mexican Chicken roll and ordered a coffee. It was a beautiful spring day, so he grabbed a seat just outside and pondered over the case. He had a lot of questions for Greg, so he phoned him to arrange another meeting. It went to voicemail, so he left a message to call him back.

He was halfway through his roll when Greg returned his call.

'Hi, Jake, how's it going?'

'Fine Greg. I've spent most of the morning going through the stuff in your email. We need to arrange another meeting, but first of all can you tell me, is DCI Amey Lorimer still around?'

'My understanding is she retired about five years ago,' he replied, 'still lives in the area though I believe.'

'Have you got an address?'

'Not exactly. I'm pretty sure it's Salisbury somewhere.'

'OK, I'll be able to track her down. How helpful was she?'

Greg coughed and he lowered his voice as he answered. 'We didn't really hear much from her. She spoke to us about twice, but we sensed she was not spending much time on it. Then we were told by some anonymous DS that Amey was on another investigation, and they would update us when they had news. It was pretty upsetting to be honest. Then the excuse was that resources had got stretched with the London Olympics approaching and the police were being redeployed all over the place. Apparently, someone had taken over as the Senior Investigating Officer, but we could never get to speak to him. Pat Tweddle was his name. Later on, somebody told us that Amey was actually on sick leave.'

'So, did they actually close the investigation?'

'We've always been told that it's still open, I think they call it inactive, but if you ever ask then no one has been working on the case for a few years. They said there were no leads. That's what prompted us to call you in the end. I know it seems like a long time to stay pretty passive about it, but we tried to trust them.'

Jake leant back in his chair so he could feel the sun on his face.

'Umm.... I think that's going to be my starting point. Track down Ms Lorimer and see what she's got to say for herself.' Jake paused to see if Greg would say anymore, but he remained silent. 'Right when can we meet again? I need to know about this Menorca connection.'

'Tomorrow?' Greg offered up.

'Save you coming through the New Forest, I'll meet you at Rownhams Services, say

10.30am?'

Greg seemed hesitant but agreed. Jake knew this was the moment when clients felt they were committing themselves, and it wasn't unusual for them to get cold feet. He wouldn't be surprised if Greg didn't turn up, but on the other hand he felt that he'd made that leap now and had a need for answers.

As he finished his coffee, his thoughts turned to Milly. She hadn't been herself for the last few days. A bit distant. He was sure there was something on her mind, but he hadn't really asked her. Surely, it couldn't still be his encounter with the estate agent? He hadn't got round to telling her that he'd decided he'd like them both to get a place together. Their own place, not for him to move into her apartment. He'd spoken to Isabella yesterday and she'd seemed really excited about them coming to visit, so he wanted to sit down with Milly this evening and decide when, and to get on and book the flights. He casually looked up flights to Florence for two weeks on his iPhone. He was tempted to book there and then, maybe they could have a couple of days in Florence before driving down to Isabella's house. He better discuss it with Milly first. They were a team now. Or at least he hoped so.

Jake got up putting his jacket on, now that the sun had dived behind a low dark cloud.

Rather than going back to the office he decided to go for a walk first, to think about what he could do to cheer Milly up, he decided to keep it simple and pop into the florist to buy her a bunch of yellow and red roses which he would give to her later. That should earn him some brownie points.

The next day was dreary. Mist was clinging to the coast and a heavy drizzle drifted across Lymford. Milly was still quiet the night before, and although she appreciated the roses, she admitted that she wasn't feeling very sociable. Jake probed further but she was reticent to say anymore, hinting that it was 'the time of the month,' although he knew that didn't normally affect her in this way. In the end Jake went home to his houseboat around 11pm, promising to call her in the morning.

At 7.30am he was wide awake. It was now quite light at this time, but he lay there with the duvet around him not wanting to get up yet. He ran his hand through his hair, sighed and finally decided to get up and make a coffee. When he got home last night, he drank half a bottle of Merlot and watched three episodes of Colin from Accounts. It was the third time he'd seen them but loved it. He'd only got five hours sleep worrying about Milly. With the water boiling he decided to have a quick shower and then he would sit down in front of the laptop. Time to find Amey Lorimer.

At 10am Jake was driving out of Lymford, going through the New Forest, and on his way to meeting Greg. The services were pretty quiet and he was relieved to find Greg tucking into a McDonalds breakfast. Jake put his hand up as he approached and Greg half raised his, but didn't crack a smile, looking quite serious. He reckoned that Greg didn't smile a lot.

'How's it going?' Jake asked as he sat down opposite.

'I'm okay, feeling a bit nervous if I'm honest.'

'I get that,' Jake said reassuringly, 'it's actually a bit of a commitment to get me on board with this. You don't know what's going to turn up.' Greg nodded, and wiped a bit of egg away from his mouth as he finished his sausage and egg McMuffin. 'Right, let's crack on. First of all, I've traced Amey Lorimer to an address in Salisbury as you say. I've called her, and after a bit of persuasion I've arranged to go and see her tomorrow. Have to say, I get the impression she's a bit of a formidable character.'

'I think she is,' Greg agreed, 'I wouldn't want to get on the wrong side of her. I actually liked her, but she made me nervous, my mother was not a fan. We actually met once face to face before Pat Tweddle took over.' Jake was realising that Greg was a pretty nervy character all round.

'What was he like?' Jake asked.

'Completely dismissive, if I'm honest. It was like he wasn't interested.'

'Have to say it sounds a bit odd.' Greg just nodded, as if his head was too heavy for his neck.

'So, tell me more about this Menorca connection and what the investigation did find out?'

Greg pushed the detritus of his breakfast to one side and clasped his hands.

'Well, we know that Layton went backwards and forwards to the island a few times. I asked him about it once, but he would clam up. He'd changed. As I said before none of us had a lot to do with him in those last few months, but I think he would stay for a few days each time. Don't know where exactly but I did find some receipts from a hotel. Think it was Castell something, Barcelona Hotel?' Jake felt a slight sinking feeling.

'Would it be Es Castell do you think?' Hotel Barcelo Hamilton?' he asked.

'Yes, it could be. Do you know it?'

'I've an apartment, left to me by my parents in Es Castell.' Greg raised his eyebrows at Jake who felt another blast of trepidation run through him.

Greg continued.

'Let's be honest, I knew it wasn't an honest job. By this time Layton couldn't lay straight in his own bed he was so bent.'

Jake laughed and was suddenly drawn to Greg's eyes. They were sad despite being a light blue colour. Jake was starting to feel sorry for him. He clearly had money, but Greg was not happy.

'The trouble is,' he continued, 'we don't know much more than that. We don't have a mobile phone for him, he didn't do social media, it was 2012 and I suppose it hadn't caught on in the same way as it is now, and he didn't keep diaries.'

'What about friends?' Jake asked.

'Not many. He had a girlfriend for a few years but when Layton went off the rails she dumped him.'

'Can I have her name.'

'Sure, it's Jane Colton. She lives in London now, but again I don't know where and I haven't really heard anything from her since they split up.'

'Male friends?'

'Honestly, couldn't tell you. He seemed to lose contact with his school friends and he wasn't that popular with people in the business. He was arrogant, knew it all, he would often call everybody else "plebs." Obviously, that's not going to endear you to others.'

'What about you?' Jake asked. This seemed to take Greg by surprise, he frowned at Jake.

'I had nothing to do with Layton's dealings. As I said before, the family may not have been whiter than white, what with the Brendon's business, but I'm sure this has nothing to do with it. That was all about bribing a few councillors so we could set up shop where we wanted. Murder is a completely different level.'

Jake shifted in his seat, and he felt he was repeating himself. 'So, this is what prevented you asking too many questions? You didn't want to draw too much attention to the family as a whole?'

'Yes,' Greg looked down at the table as he said this and pushed a tiny piece of bread around in a circle. 'I know it sounds kind of cowardly, but we were also bloody scared.'

'I don't want to sound harsh, but it almost seems you sacrificed your brother's death to save your own reputation?'

Greg's eyes flashed up at Jake with a look of anger which, after a few moments, took on a look of acceptance and resignation. 'Errr .... maybe we did. Maybe we did.' Greg looked as though he was almost in tears as he said this. Jake saw this as a look of guilt, and possibly a betrayal of his brother.

They went on to talk about the investigation but there wasn't much to add there. Greg was on the wrong side of it so he knew that was going to be down to what Amey Lorimer could tell him. After an hour they both left with Jake promising to keep Greg up to date. He got back into the Audi, just as the rain started to fall like a monsoon and headed back to Lymford.

CHAPTER TEN

Jake got back to Lymford just after noon. He was driving down Spencer Street, which crossed with the High Street, where he was going to park. Normally, he would walk from the houseboat to the office, a ten-minute stroll, but the rain was relentless. Out of the corner of his eye he saw Milly coming out of the doctor's surgery, she was zipping up her coat and getting her umbrella out before stepping out of the shelter of the porch. Jake stopped and turned the car around, drawing level with her just as she started to walk down the street, presumably on her way home. He drew level with her and wound the passenger window down.

'Hey, do you want a lift?' he called out, the rain almost deafening on the roof of the car. Milly looked shocked to see Jake and seemed to lose her composure.

'No, it's okay, I'm almost home.'

'Are you sure? Shall I see you later?'

'I was going to give you a bell. I'm going to have a quiet one tonight if you don't mind.' The look on Milly's face was a bit distant, he knew something wasn't quite right but felt a bit lost for words.

'Are you not on the radio today?'

'No, Ryan's standing in for me,' there was a moment's hesitation, 'look I better get going otherwise I'll drown.' Jake frowned, debating with himself whether to say anything else, he decided to leave it for now apart from saying he would call her later. He turned around again and drove on to the car park, while Milly turned right up the hill towards her apartment. Now he was starting to worry about her.

He unlocked the door to his office and climbed up the stairs. There was a sense of dread as he switched the lights on and turned on the Dolce Gusto. He popped a cappuccino pod in the machine and his Chelsea mug underneath. While it gurgled away he checked his phone, he'd heard the buzz of a text as he came up the stairs. It was Luke asking if he wanted a swift beer at 6pm, Jake decided he definitely did, now that Milly had given him the cold shoulder. The coffee had finished its mechanical whirring's, so he added some milk and a teaspoon of sugar and sat back down with his feet on the table. He knew he should get on with the case, but he couldn't help thinking about her. Was he still in the doghouse? Had he done something else wrong? Was there a health issue that she hadn't told him about? He thought she looked pale, not her usual self. He'd learnt early on in their relationship that she can close up, much like himself at times. He would let her know that he knew something wasn't right, so he sent her a text.

The rest of the day was spent on the internet, studying again the information Greg had sent him, and jotting down his own notes. Menorca might be an important element to this one, which he may be able to get some help with, as well as how the original investigation went. He will find out more tomorrow when he meets Amey. He found there was another, more gruesome murder at around about the same time. This was at a holiday centre over at Hayling Island. The more he read into that one the more it intrigued him. He noticed that Amey Lorimer seemed to have led that one as well and, as far as he could tell, that was also unsolved. He started to think that either she was involved, or far more likely, she was a particularly useless detective. Further searching didn't reveal who the victim was apart from a woman. He briefly pondered whether there was a connection, but they were completely different types of murder, so it was unlikely. However, he would ask about it to both Amey and Greg.

Jake looked at his watch and realised it was 5.50pm. He decided he'd made some progress and had a good basis to take things forward. He was conscious that he still had Natalie's investigation, the wandering husband to deal with. He would try and wrap that one up as already he'd discovered that he wasn't going to

Bournemouth on a Tuesday evening, but to a little house in Ringwood. He had pictures of the husband kissing a woman several years younger than him on the doorstep before going inside. He then came out again about three hours later. Such a cliche Jake thought. He would follow him one more time and then present it to Natalie. Jake hadn't received a text back from Milly which raised his anxiety a bit. He shut the office up and made his way to the Seafarer's to meet Luke.

'Moretti for me,' Jake shouted as he closed the door. Luke was already at the bar, chatting to the barman. Jake knew they were seeing each other but were trying to keep it quiet. Like many small towns Lymford liked gossip, and Luke was trying to keep out of the spotlight. His last relationship was with a well-known Olympic sportsman, so everybody knew about it and liked to comment on it.

'On its way. How's our resident sleuth getting on?' He called back to him.

'Oh man. It's been a bit of a day. I think I need some advice.' Jake laughed as he raised the pint to his mouth. He took two large mouthfuls and instantly felt better.

'You know sometimes Jake I think I was only put on this earth to be your counsellor!'

'Well perhaps you shouldn't be so fucking good at it then. I haven't thanked you for getting me out of trouble last time.'

'I had your back mate.' Luke lowered his

voice, but beware, Jenna is just around the corner, you can see her in the mirror.' Jake looked up just as she caught his eye.

'Fuck, she's just seen me. Let's grab a seat quickly, with just two chairs.' They walked over to the window and sat down.

'Ahhh, how's the two best looking men in Lymford then?' Jenna staggered over to them.

'I'm sure they're fine if you know where they are?' Luke said, without looking at her. 'It's only six, how come you're drunk already?'

Jenna ignored this comment.

'Come on you two, don't be modest.' Jake was feeling irritated and decided he couldn't be bothered with small talk.

'I think you should go and sit back down Jenna with your friends, we have important issues to discuss, and you'll just get me into trouble.'

Jenna looked indignant and put her hand out on the table to steady herself.

'Well, I tried getting you into trouble, but you would have none of it.' This came out almost incoherently.

Jake nodded and said, 'that's right.'

'See you later,' Luke added, hoping that would send her away. She looked at them both, screwed her face up and tottered back to her seat, holding on to two pillars as she went.

Jake took another two mouthfuls of Moretti and leant back in his chair.

'So, I need to run this past you. Milly has been really quiet recently and I saw her coming out of the doctors earlier on. She was a bit off when she saw me, so I know there's something wrong. What I don't know is whether it's me, or is it something else? Truth is I'm a little scared to ask her directly. I have texted her but not had a response. What do you think I should do next?'

Luke leant back in his chair and frowned at Jake. 'Well, you know what you've got to do, don't you? Ask her directly, in a very nice way, and if she doesn't say anything then be patient. At least she'll know you know, and in a way, it puts the ball back in her court. Not a lot more you can do. But for god's sake don't get bloody stroppy.'

Jake pondered for a bit, took another sip of beer, then nodded. 'Do you know, a year ago that's what I would have done, thrown my toys out of the pram for not telling me anything. Probably would have acted like a complete prick.'

Luke leant forward, 'look I haven't told you this but there is something. I only know because I was in the same doctors a couple of weeks ago and she was in there. She was upset and we went for a coffee.' Jake looked at Luke wide-eyed, mouth half open. Luke carried on, 'she actually didn't say anything because she said she needed to tell you. Whatever it is, she's dealing with it in her own way, for now.'

Jake stammered, you …. you don't think she's going to dump me, do you?'

'Do you know the trouble with us men is we always think it's about us! Look, I don't know but I very much doubt it. Remember I was in the doctors when I saw her. Give it a few days and I'm sure you'll know.' Jake shook his head a little but felt just the slightest bit relieved. He finished his pint and shook his glass to indicate if Luke wanted another. Luke nodded.

Jake frowned again as he stood up to go to the bar. 'Okay. I get that but you know she wanted us to go and see Isabella rather than go to Menorca next week. It seems that she may want to speak to her about something.'

Luke nodded, and a sarcastic smile appeared. 'So, she's going to want to speak to Isabella about dumping you, is she?'

Jake walked to the bar knowing that Luke was right. He felt frustration, annoyance, perhaps a bit of anger, but he was going to have to keep a lid on it and stay cool.

CHAPTER ELEVEN

Jake was on his way to see Amey. He was now focussed on the mysterious death of Layton Jones and thoughts of Milly would have to be on hold for now. He would need to be very careful with Amey, scope it out a little as to how she saw it rather than make it seem in any way he was doubting her skills as a Detective Sergeant back in 2012. He wanted to get her onside although he suspected she may be a tough nut to crack. He had some questions mapped out in his head, but he also didn't want it to come across as some sort of interrogation. He had a few butterflies as he drove down the A36 and saw the spire of Salisbury Cathedral come into view. She lived in an area called Harnham and the satnav was directing him round the ring road and up to a confusing junction that seemed to be taking him back out again. He came onto an elevated residential road, and then turned left before going right again, parallel to the road off the junction. There was a large transmitter at the back of the houses and Amey lived almost in front of it.

The house was probably built around the 1950's. There was a smart garden in front with very neat borders and an abundance of daffodils now in bloom. Jake parked in the road and got out. It crossed his mind that it was a very standard looking house, a door to the left, a big window to the right, and then a small frosted window the other side of the door. As he looked at the door, making sure he had the right number, the door opened and this rather rotund looking woman was staring at him. He was reminded of 'Vera' from the ITV series. He smiled and walked down the drive.

'So, you're Jake, are you?'

'Yes, I am, pleased to meet you.' He resisted the urge to call her Vera.

'You better come in and tell me what this is all about, and then I'll decide whether I want to tell you anything.' Jake knew he was going to have to be on his most charming behaviour.

'Thank you for seeing me. It's a lovely house you have here?'

'Don't give me that bullshit lad, it's dated and needs redecorating right through.'

'It's a lovely location though. The view over Salisbury.'

'Yep, it is that. Only been here a couple of months, just deciding what to do with the place. Lived further down the road before coming here.'

'Lovely, lovely.' Jake mumbled, unsure what to say next.

'Go and sit down in the living room and I'll bring tea through.' Jake did as he was told. He sat down on the sofa, suspecting that the solitary comfy chair was where Amey usually sat. After a couple of minutes Amey reappeared with a tray. It all seemed far too twee for a retired DCI who didn't mince her words.

'I know what you're thinking,' she said, looking up at him with the teapot in her hand. 'Underneath it all I'm a big softy, despite what you've been told.'

'To be honest I haven't been told anything, apart from your name.' Amey handed him a cup and saucer and told him to help himself to milk and sugar.

'Come on lad, what do you want to know?'

Jake could feel his hand shake slightly with the cup and saucer, so he put it down and took a deep breath.

'As I said on the phone, it's the murder of Layton Jones in 2012. His brother, Greg, came to me a couple of weeks ago and asked me to look into it. I understand it was never solved and he feels the need to have some answers.'

Amey grunted and shifted in her seat. She visibly stiffened.

'That family were shysters. Wouldn't trust them.'

Jake jumped in, 'I know, he told me how the family were into a little bit of bribery trying to get Brendon's outlets opened up.'

'Well, councillors are always up for a bit of bribery, they're all shysters as well.'

'Greg recognises that, to be fair to him. I think that's why the family were a bit reluctant to....' Jake knew he had to be careful with his words, 'appear too needy when the investigation seemed to stall a bit.'

Amey looked at Jake and crossed her legs. He suddenly thought of Sharon Stone in the movie 'Basic Instinct.' He had to stifle a giggle as the comparison was absurd. Amey sighed.

'It was 2012, the Olympics were about to start, and every fucker was being used to cover that. I only got six weeks into the investigation before it was handed on and there was nothing I could do about it.'

'So, can you tell me how far you did get?'

Amey looked as though Jake really was opening up an old wound. She seemed to soften.

'It's my biggest regret that I wasn't able to solve both those murders.'

'You mean the one in Hayling Island as well?' Amey looked at Jake and said. 'I need something stronger. That's the beauty of retirement, if I want a drink at 11am in the morning then I bloody well will have one.' She got up and poured herself a whisky into a glass that just seemed to be waiting for her. 'I won't offer you one as you're driving.' Jake smiled. Amey sat back down with a heavy thump.

'There was so little to go on. We found out who Layton was, tracked down his movements as best we could. He'd spent time in Menorca but couldn't get anything on that. Why was he there and who would want to kill him?' She downed the whisky in one gulp and got up to pour herself another. 'I wasn't able to get anywhere, but he was clearly into something pretty bad, but we couldn't find out what.' She swilled her glass and looked deep into it. She looked up at Jake. He thought the whisky was taking effect now and this may work in my favour. She carried on.

'I was going through my own problems at the time, I thought I was doing my job well, but maybe I wasn't. It was early days, but you start to think, he was fucking low life and what do I care? Then the conscience of the job, and getting a result takes over again.' Amey seemed to be rambling a little. 'Then we had the other one, down in that bloody Hayling Island, which I had to pass on to DCI Patrick Tweddle, or DCI Pathetic Twat as we called him.' Jake couldn't help but notice the venom. No love lost there.

Amey wasn't finished.

'I think there was a connection, but I was overruled. It was a bit of a hunch as it was a true Jack the Ripper type scenario. But...there was a phone, dropped at the scene, that identified a WhatsApp group that met in Winchester, and we know that Layton used to go to Winchester quite frequently. There was nothing else on the phone, and we couldn't trace the others in the group. The numbers were no longer valid and the names were clearly false, but the woman who was killed used to meet them at The Green Room, on a Friday, on a fairly regular basis.'

'How many were in this group?' Jake asked.

'Four. They were named as Bob, Lucy, Bill and Phil.'

'And Lucy was the one killed?'

'Correct, young man. Well, I think so, but I don't think it was ever proved beyond doubt.'

'Would you not think they would have deleted the messages pretty regularly?'

'Maybe,' Amey took another sip, 'but apart from the place in Winchester they really didn't give much away. The language was clearly coded. Pathetic Twat then blanked me because I was "interfering with his investigation," so I never knew much more about that one.' Amey hesitated again, 'and then it was off my desk, and my team.'

'What did you do?'

'I went on sick leave, lad. HR advised me to. I was off for a month. When I came back it was all handed on, and they were clearly getting nowhere. Tweddle was heading up both investigations.'

Jake felt a little sorry for her. He wondered whether to ask her why she went on leave but decided to leave that for now.

'What about Layton?' he asked.

'So, he died from a cyanide injection. He was pretty riddled with drugs though which were self-induced. He had no identification at all. His clothes were old so we couldn't match them to any recent purchases. We don't know how he got there. Quite honestly we weren't getting anywhere until the family filed a missing person's report, then we finally had a name, but little evidence of what he'd been up to apart from travelling to Menorca.'

'What about the woman who found the body?' Jake asked, trying to remember whether Greg had told him her name.

'Karen Carpenter,' Amey replied, 'nice woman, was out training for the London Marathon. She lived in Lymford.'

'Ahhh, where I'm living.' Jake added, raising his eyebrows.

'Look lad, I'm not sure what else I can tell you. But...' Amey seemed to be pondering, now with an empty glass. 'Let me think about things, me old memory cells aren't as great as they used to be. Give me your email address.'

Amey got up and grabbed a pen and a piece of paper and wrote it down. She refilled her glass again. 'That's it for now,' she said. Jake wasn't sure whether she meant the whisky, or it was time for him to go. 'Here, I'll find out that Karen's address as well, although she may have moved now.'

Jake took the hint. 'Well thank you for your time. It was much appreciated.' They both moved off to the front door.

Suddenly Amey let out a gasp, as if she

was in pain. 'Jesus Christ I nearly forgot. The strangest thing, first on the scene was an alleged copper called Joe Attwood. He was fake, not a member of the force, and he disappeared after we turned up.'

'What did he do?' Jake asked.

'Nothing much. Looked after Karen, did all the right things, and then he was gone. I reckon he was part of it, maybe there to survey the scene and report back.'

'Why do you say that?'

'It doesn't add up why he would be there otherwise. It's a kick some people get. Pretend to be in the force, or a firefighter. He was asked to keep an eye on the scene. Harmless in its own way but still part of it. These days it would be on that bloody tik-tok thing.'

'And you've no idea who he was either?'

'Not a fucking clue lad.'

CHAPTER TWELVE

Jake pulled back out onto the A36, on his way back through the New Forest. It was now lunchtime, so he decided to treat himself to a Big Mac Meal, the golden arches loomed ahead of him. He got out and went inside rather than using the drive thru. After a ten minute wait he sat down and took another ten minutes to finish it off. He mulled his meeting with Amey over in his mind. There wasn't a lot to go on, he would contact Karen Carpenter, but Menorca definitely needed more investigating. When did Layton go there? What flights? Did he hire cars? Where did he stay? He wondered whether Cesar could help him. Cesar basically saved his life last year and was in the Menorcan Police. This could be his advantage. So, another trip to Menorca was going to be needed, but he had a trip to Italy first, which he was looking forward to. Hopefully, it would be a chance to get closer to Milly again and really find out what was troubling her.

Getting back in the office he turned the radio on. Her show was due on in a minute, he was keen to know how she sounded. The news bulletin finished, and it was over to her. A quick bright and breezy hello and it was into

Coldplay. Jake walked over to his laptop and for the umpteenth time looked at news reports from twelve years ago of Layton's murder, seeing if there was something else for him to look at. There was no mention of the fake PC. It seemed the only person who could talk about him was Karen Carpenter. So, he tracked her down without the help of Amey. She was living only about a mile away, He called her number and arranged to see her later that afternoon.

Karen lived in a nice four bed detached house overlooking Lymford. She opened the door and the woman who was training for the marathon twelve years ago was clearly still looking after herself. She wore Lycra bottoms and a running top, announcing that she would be running ten miles after her meeting with Jake. Tall, attractive with long dark hair tied in a ponytail, she appeared to be about his age. Karen smiled and led him through to the kitchen where she had coffee on the go. She offered Jake to sit down at the breakfast bar. He looked around but couldn't see any pictures, or evidence of a partner or children. Karen caught his gaze and confirmed she was single as she poured coffee into two mugs.

'I was married for five years, but it wasn't a good one.'

'I'm sorry to hear that, but must admit that's none of my business,' he stated quite emphatically.

'True, and you're here to talk about my bit of excitement twelve years ago,' she said, sitting down opposite Jake.

'Yep. As I said on the phone, the brother has asked me to look into the murder, as it has never been solved.'

Karen nodded without saying anything.

'I'm more interested in this PC who turned out not to be a PC. What was he like? What did he do? Probably most importantly, what did he look like?' Karen put down her cup.

'Well, he was very nice. I totally believed him and still find it tough to think he wasn't real. It isn't easy to describe him, it was getting dark, his jacket was buttoned right up and he kept his helmet on. He was certainly young, early twenties I'd say, a bit younger than me then. Nice looking lad, said he was only two months in uniform, blue eyes and I think his hair was fair, but you couldn't see much of it.'

'Did he say anything, or do anything, which you thought was odd?'

'Not really. He seemed a bit mesmerised by the body. Stared at it for quite a while. Oh, he gave me his jacket because I was getting cold.'

'Did you give it back?'

'No, he disappeared before I could. I gave it to DS Boyle.' Jake noticed a glint in her eye when she said his name.

He frowned. 'But that would have DNA

on it. Were the police not able to trace him from that?' Karen shrugged. Jake tapped his pen against his teeth. Amey didn't have much to say about DS Matthew Boyle. He'd need to ask her. 'Did the police stay in contact with you?' Jake asked.

'Not a lot. I went to the inquest. DS Boyle updated me a couple of times and then it all went a bit quiet. It was he who told me they had to wind it down a bit because resources were being switched to help with the Olympics.'

'And after that, later in the year?'

'Again, nothing really. I was getting married the following year, so I started to forget about it. Other things on my mind. It's never actually gone away and occasionally I've searched the internet for updates, but....' Karen shrugged again. 'Nothing.'

'Is there anything else you can tell me to help?' Jake was almost pleading.

'I would love to, but I'm not sure there is. But, if you've any questions in the future I'll be happy to help.'

'Thanks.' Jake said as he got up. 'Just one thing. Did you know about the other murder over at Hayling Island at the same time.'

'A little, I remember people talking about it, but that's all. I never watched TV and rarely read newspapers.'

'Did it cross your mind that they may be linked?'

Karen shook her head. 'No, not really.'

'Ok. Well thanks again.'

'Good luck,' Karen called out as she shut the door behind Jake.

CHAPTER THIRTEEN

He decided to call it a day and went straight round to Milly's. Jake texted her to say that he would cook Delia Smith's meatballs and tagliatelle, which he knew was one of her favourites. They were going to give Isabella a call and finalise arrangements for going to Italy. It was Thursday today, and they were going on Sunday. Jake decided to put Layton's case to one side for now. He dropped Greg a text to let him know that he would be AWOL for a week. He got a thumbs up emoji reply. However, he decided he would ring Amey in the morning and ask about the jacket.

He busied himself and asked Alexa to play some Imagine Dragons. Demons was the first song, so he asked Alexa to turn the volume up. He browned the meatballs and made the sauce, throwing in onions, paprika, garlic and tomatoes. After a few minutes he put it all in the oven for an hour. Milly called him.

'Hello lovely,' she said, sounding brighter than he expected.

'Ciao, baby.' Jake replied.

'Just to say I'm leaving the studios now. Be back as soon as. So glad you're making the meatballs. I've got wine there.'

'I know, I've already opened one bottle and am letting another one breathe.'

'Cool. Look forward to that.'

'More than seeing me?' Jake couldn't help himself.

'Food always comes before you Jake, but to please you I'll say nothing in this world is better than seeing you,' she paused, 'apart from seeing Chelsea beat Spurs.'

'Well, I'll second that. One thing before you go, and I don't want to sound soppy. I do love you; you know?'

Milly felt guilty. She felt guilty that she didn't say anything back following Jake's last comment, and she felt guilty that she hadn't shared her problems with him, giving him the cold shoulder in recent days. She really hoped he would understand.

They had a nice dinner and Jake called Isabella once they'd both finished eating. Two bottles of wine were almost finished, and they both admitted to feeling a bit drunk. Jake decided once the call was done, he would ask Milly again what was wrong. Isabella was excited about seeing them and said how she couldn't wait to show them her new part of Italy. It was on the Tuscany/Umbria border, about an hour and a half south of Florence. Milly had booked an Airbnb for two nights in the city, but Isabella stressed this would not be long enough. All being well they would be back to see her again and stay longer next time. Jake said goodbye and settled back on the sofa next to Milly. She'd been a bit more talkative this evening but still not her usual spark. He cleared his throat.

'So, I want to know what's wrong? Don't tell me there isn't anything because I haven't just come out of my cave for the first time and believe it or not, I can be sensitive to these things.' Jake leaned into Milly and looked at her, she continued to look straight ahead ignoring his gaze. She let out a burst of air from her lungs and put her wine down on the table.

'Look. I don't think we should move in together just yet.' She drew the words out as she said them.

'And can I ask why?' Jake replied, very calmly.

'It's not that I won't want to, at some point, I'm sure.'

'Yes, but why?'

'I just think, at the moment, both of us still enjoy a little bit of independence. You know, a place where we can be on our own for an evening from time to time. We both like that don't we.'

Jake just nodded.

'Do you not think there's an element of truth in that?' Milly looked at him this time, 'you love to go back to the houseboat and do your own thing, be on your own for a bit.'

Jake was going to disagree but realised Milly had a point. He also recognised there was a small but tangible sense of relief when she said this. But it was surely just a case of adjustment.

'But, what about you?' he said, 'is that what you like doing?' Milly swerved the question.

'I know you have to get out, but I reckon it would be a good idea to rent somewhere, for a while, and give ourselves a bit longer. There are some great new apartments near the station that overlook the river. One of those would be lovely and I've been speaking to someone who's buying a couple of them to rent out. It's got two bedrooms, a nice living room with a view, and a stone's throw from the High Street.'

'Oh, I see,' Jake said, turning away and getting up. 'You've thought this through.' He walked out into the kitchen, feeling confused and agitated. Occasionally he still had counselling sessions, he had a lot to talk about following the events of last year. He wanted to contextualise what Milly was saying without getting angry. He opened the fridge and looked in. He wasn't looking for anything and didn't know why he did it. He closed it again and leant against the worktop. He heard Milly shout and ask him what he was doing. He wandered back into the living room.

'I'm a little hurt, to be honest. I'm a little hurt that you've been thinking this for a while, and not said anything until now. I was going to ask you the other night whether we wanted to officially move in together, but you didn't seem to be in the right mood.' He noticed Milly bite her lip. He felt confused, deep down he had a nagging feeling this wasn't the real reason for her recent mood. He debated again whether to say this, but instead he wandered over to where his hoodie was draped over the chair.

'Look, I'm going to go. I think it's probably best.' He picked the hoodie up and rummaged for his keys. He knew the walk would do him good, he could feel almost a sense of despondency, which was closing in on a sense of hurt, but he wanted to keep it to himself.

'If I don't see you beforehand, I'll pick you up at 6am on Sunday.' Milly got up and kissed him on the cheek, 'I can't wait. Seriously. We will talk properly when we're there.'

The air was pretty cool, even for March when Jake got out onto the main street. His head was fuzzy, but he passed an off licence that was still open, so went in and bought a bottle of rum to take home with him.

CHAPTER FOURTEEN

Jake groaned as he came to the next morning. His stomach flipped over as he spotted the half empty bottle of rum on the side. He'd been drinking it neat after he got home, he couldn't normally stand it neat. It always had to be at least two thirds Coke.

He'd gone to bed naked; clothes were literally thrown around the houseboat. He remembered toppling over as he took his jeans off. Jake checked his phone, no messages or calls while he was unconscious. It was 10.25am, which made him groan even more. He switched the heating back on and went for a shower, hoping this would wake him up a bit but he knew he was going to feel rough for the rest of the day. At some point he would still need to phone Amey and ask her about the jacket that Joe Attwood gave Karen.

Milly was passing the level crossing at Brockenhurst just as Jake was getting conscious. She'd debated whether to call him this morning but decided to leave it. It was Friday and she really needed to be focussed on her work. She'd been invited to a meeting where they were discussing a new music festival that was taking place in the summer. She was going to be a co-host, so they were going through the lineup, who would introduce who. She needed to up her game as she'd been distracted for a while and needed to get back on track.

As she drove through the forest she thought again about last night. She'd never intended to say what she did to Jake. She even surprised herself. She needed to distract him so that she didn't tell him the real truth. Why she'd been such a crabby bitch recently. She wasn't quite ready, she had another appointment later today, then she felt a real need to talk to Isabella as well. She wasn't sure why, but then she would come clean to Jake. It could be the end of their relationship. She hoped not, but it could be.

It was 11.30am by the time he rang Amey.

'Hi,' he said, trying to sound as bright as he could muster. 'Is it ok if I asked you a couple more questions?'

'Oh, it's Jake is it? I haven't added your name on my phone. Didn't really think I'd hear from you again. Maybe I underestimated your dedication.' Jake couldn't tell whether this was a compliment, or sarcasm. Maybe a bit of both.

'Like a dog with a bone,' he laughed, hoping that would soften her mood.

'Fire away then lad.'

'I wanted to ask you about DS Matthew Boyle and the jacket that Karen Carpenter gave him, which Joe Attwood handed to her when he turned up at the scene. Surely that would have DNA on it?'

'Umm,' there was a pause. 'That's something I kicked myself over. Matthew Boyle was an idiot. In those days I tried to trust him, gave him some rope, but he was useless. He told me that he gave the jacket to the labs, there was some hair fibre on it, but they couldn't match it to anyone. Anyway, to cut a long story short, Boyle left about two years later due to sheer incompetence. Then it was a little quiet with me and I decided to get it checked out again. It appears that there was no record of the jacket, or it being tested.'

'What did you do?'

'I marched down to where he was working, as an assistant store manager in Sainsbury's. He said he lost the jacket, or it was stolen, before he had a chance to get it tested.'

'Did you believe him?'

'The bloke was stupid enough, but if I'm honest, probably not. But what could I do? I figured if he was mixed up in it in some way then he wouldn't be working in a supermarket, and he would have left the force sooner.'

'So, why did he leave?'

'Too many blunders, he just didn't have the skills to investigate. Quite frankly he wasn't that bright. The Chief Super had a word with him one day and the next thing I knew he'd resigned.'

'Is he still working for Sainsbury's?'

'As far as I know, over in Winchester.'

'I may pay him a visit then.' Jake thought it curious that Winchester cropped up again. 'OK, thanks for your help anyway. Do you mind if I perhaps call you in the future?'

'Now then lad, I'm happy to help, I may come across as a grumpy old bird but I'm not precious about my unsolved crimes, and still love a bit of detective work.'

Jake put his phone down on the bed and wrote a note to track down Matthew Boyle when he was back from Italy. Maybe he'd visit The Green Room at the same time.

Jake and Milly didn't see each other until Sunday, so when he picked her up at 6am the atmosphere was a little frosty. As they drove up the M3 to Heathrow, Milly asked him more about the investigation in an attempt to warm the air between them. Jake for his part decided he wanted to enjoy the next few days and decided to make light of the living arrangements. He admitted the apartment Milly talked about would be nice and he would go and see it when they got back. As they sat down for breakfast in the airport, following a stressful journey through security, Milly grabbed his hand and smiled at him. Jake realised it was the first time he'd seen her smile for a while.

Jake smiled back and spoke. 'We'll have a

good time. Let's enjoy it.' Milly agreed.

They arrived in Florence with the sun shining and a temperature of twenty-one degrees. There was a tram that took them to the centre of Florence, and they had quite a long walk to their Airbnb. They stopped and admired the Duomo and noted a restaurant they would come back to for lunch. They found the code to get into their apartment complex which took them into more of a courtyard, which led to six flights of stone steps to their apartment at the top, where another code was needed to get in. They were pleasantly surprised; it was comfortable and would do nicely for a couple of days. They dumped their bags and after ten minutes went back out to get something to eat. There were early signs of the tourist season starting to pick up. It was mid-March and, being the weekend, crowds were flocking around the main tourist sites. They promised themselves a walk down to the Ponte Vecchio bridge later in the afternoon.

They sat outside at the restaurant and ordered wine and pasta. Isabella called and told them about the wine windows. You literally go up to a window in a wall along the street, tap on the window or ring a bell, and someone will peer their head out and take an order. You then drank it in the street. Isabella said it was quirky and touristy, but why not. Her main advice was just to walk around the city and soak it up. Milly consulted her Florence guidebook for the first time and suggested they do a treasure hunt, and a food and wine tour. They raised their glasses of Chianti to that. Two days would not be enough in Florence. Jake even idly thought it would be a great destination for a proposal, but he closed that thought down, for now.

The next day was another bright and sunny one and they spent most of it walking, eating and drinking. The food and wine tour was great fun, and they literally walked from restaurant to bar to restaurant, trying different wines, nibbles of food, ending with a bigger meal that left them stuffed and almost unable to move. It was a long walk back to their apartment. They were lucky as the season was early and they got on the tour at the last minute. They staggered back to their apartment after five hours of indulgence and as happy as they had been for weeks. However, Milly knew there was a big conversation to come, and she was very nervous.

CHAPTER FIFTEEN

They had a confusing bus ride back to the airport. Thanks to a helpful local they discovered that they needed to download the bus app to pay for their ticket. A British woman they were speaking to, who had lived in Florence for ten years, told them that many tourists get on without realising it, hoping they can pay on the bus and then get stung by the inspectors for not having tickets. 'It's a racket,' she told them.

They picked up their hire cars back at Florence airport. It took an hour, Jake was already aware that not much happens very quickly in Italy, and there's a lot of bureaucracy. A seemingly pointless duplication of paperwork. They were on the road by 11am heading south to Sansepolcro. By 12.30pm they were passing through the town and heading to Isabella's new home just outside.

They went slightly uphill and turned left into her villa. She came dashing out just as Jake had remembered when he went to her home in Naples eight months ago. She couldn't grab hold of them quick enough.

'I'm so excited to see you both,' she grabbed Jake and Milly and pulled them together in a three-way hug.

'Great to see you sis,' Jake said, feeling a wave of emotion that he couldn't quite pinpoint, but was pleased it was there.

'Oh, this looks lovely,' Milly said, glancing up at the villa. It had a typical Tuscan look about it, with yellow walls and a red tiled roof. Isabella guided them round to the back of the house and as they reached the seating area they both stood there in awe. There was a small bank that led down to a good-sized swimming pool, from there the ground slipped away so you were overlooking a valley. There were large hills beyond that were covered in trees. The whole area of the garden was framed by tall, thin cypress trees, typical of a Tuscan scene.

'Jesus Isabella, this is fucking incredible.' Jake exclaimed.

'It is special isn't it. I'm having renovations done inside. It used to be rented out to large groups, but the owners decided to sell this one. They have others further up the hill. You should see the views from those!'

Milly seemed far away as she spoke, 'I think this is the therapy I need right now.' Jake and Isabella looked at each other. Isabella frowned while Jake raised his eyebrows.

'Okay then. I'll show you to your room, then come down when you're ready and we'll have wine out here. It still gets a bit nippy in the evening but it's lovely watching the sun go down. Isabella pointed to their right where another low tree covered hill seemed to undulate in a way that seemed as if it was protecting the villa. 'Obviously, as we're in Tuscany, it will be Chianti.' Both Jake and Milly smiled, but in the back of Jake's mind he just had this feeling there was an elephant in the room, and he hoped the door would soon open and its arse would be kicked out.

'I feel like all I've done is drink alcohol in the last week,' Jake said, after two large glasses of wine each. He stood up and went to admire the view. Dusk was now falling, and so lights were coming on across the valley. The pool shimmered in its blue light, looking inviting although it would be cold at this time of the year. Isabella wobbled slightly into the kitchen and Jake went back and sat down next to Milly. Isabella shouted back to say that it wasn't anything special, spaghetti carbonara and a caprese salad. They both shouted back their appreciation. The three of them had nibbled on olives and small bruschetta to help soak up the wine.

'Feeling better?' Jake asked Milly who had seemed back to her normal self. She rolled the glass between both her hands, looked at him and sighed. 'I think this is as good a time to tell you as any,' she replied.

'At last,' Jake said, 'you're worrying me to

death.'

'I'm sorry,' Milly took a deep breath but looked down at the table. 'But do you mind if Isabella hears it as well? It's the reason I wanted to come here, a bit of moral support.' Jake looked confused but agreed. Milly quickly got up and went to find Isabella. They both came back out with Isabella looking worried.

Milly looked Jake in the eyes.

'I had a miscarriage, about three weeks ago now.' Isabella gasped slightly but nothing from Jake, so she carried on, 'I didn't know I was pregnant, and it hit me hard. I didn't want to tell anyone; I was going to keep it to myself.' There was a pause and she looked down at the table and took another sip of wine. Jake was clearly computing this in his head, while Isabella reached out and grabbed her hand.

Milly felt the tension rise. Jake got up and started pacing up and down the veranda. He couldn't quite work out his emotions. They were all swimming around in his head, and also his stomach, and he couldn't make out which was the strongest. He could feel Milly staring at him now and he needed to say something. He sat back down opposite her. He knew this wasn't about him and it was about her, and his feelings were not important right at this moment.

'And how do you feel now?' Jake stuttered. 'You've obviously had time to come to terms with it?'

Milly frowned, 'I wouldn't say I've come to terms with it, but obviously it's shocked me into thinking about children.'

'And do you? Think about children I mean.' Jake was biting his lip. Milly took another deep breath.

'This will probably sound awful, but I'm a bloody selfish woman in my mid-thirties and I don't think I do.'

Jake just slowly nodded.

'How do you feel?' Milly asked, 'it would have been your child as well?'

'Don't worry about me,' he reassured her.

'But I do Jake. I have been. I realise this could be a game changer.'

He hesitated. 'This is obviously a conversation that we've never had, and I wondered whether we would soon be having it.' Jake was pausing, assembling his emotions a bit more. 'I'm trying to work out whether what you've told me has changed my thoughts, the ones I had about children before today.'

'Which were?' Milly asked tentatively.

'I'm a selfish bastard as well, who's not getting any younger, but I'm so enjoying my life as it is. I came to the conclusion a while ago that it's not a necessity for me to have children to have a fulfilled life, and there's plenty of people who do want children in this world. I mean look at me and Isabella's biological parents. We're lucky to be here.' Jake could see Milly's eyes water and small tears gathered on her eyelids. She half smiled and he picked up a tissue from the table and handed it to her. 'But you had a little life inside you for a short while. Are you getting over that?'

Milly looked down at her hands. 'When it happened, I didn't know how to deal with it. And I know I should have told you earlier, but I just needed to try and come to terms with it myself first.'

'And now?'

'I'm...getting there,' she said. It was a shock, and I know I'm not over it. But it's made me think about things. And I think …. I think I'm feeling a little relieved.' She looked up at him. 'Is that terrible of me? Is that bad? How do you feel, now that I've told you.'

'I told you, honestly I'm fine, I'm fine. This isn't about me; this is about you. I'm so sorry.' Jake smiled, but he knew he would need a bit of time to get his head straight. He came round and gave Milly a hug. Isabella dabbed her eyes with a napkin that she'd already put out on the table.

'I'm so sorry as well,' she said, darting her eyes between both of them, having kept quiet. She felt she was intruding but knew that Milly wanted her there. After a minute of silence between the three of them she spoke,

'I haven't had children and am pretty sure I won't. In a way it's a little un-Italian not to, but I don't think it defines your happiness. Far from it.'

Jake spoke. 'Life has options. It's up to us what options we take, and I think the normal family unit isn't a rule anymore. Whatever makes you happy should be your aim.' Another pause which Isabella broke, as she stood up. 'Right then, who's for food? We also have tiramisu. I promise you it's the best in Tuscany!'

CHAPTER SIXTEEN

They got back from Tuscany five days later. Isabella had been the perfect host giving them the inside story on Italian life and the jaw dropping reflections on political life. She once worked in the mayor's office in Naples.

Milly was back on her show and, from listening to her, Jake could tell there was something of her old bounce back. She was severely winding up the news reporter on air for not knowing the capital of Canada was Ottawa, and not Toronto. They had a daily quiz between Milly, the news reporter and the travel reporter, five questions each day and it rolled over to the end of the week. The loser bought cakes. This week the news reporter was Elias and so Milly was being even more sarcastic than normal.

Jake was reflecting. He was surprised by his own reaction to Milly's miscarriage. Deep down he didn't feel ready for children, and very much doubted he ever would be. However, this was in contrast to the emphatic response he'd given Milly where he was more certain he didn't want children. On the other hand, they were able to move on and have a good time with Isabella. Jake discovered more about her life and the trauma she had been going through for a few years. The gambling and mixing in wrong circles could have killed her, in more ways than one. She seemed happy now and had met a new man, Lorenzo, a restaurant owner in Sansepolcro who definitely met with Jake's approval. He came away thinking he had another home in Italy, and all was okay with Milly again, although he never quite understood why she wanted to tell Isabella at the same time as him. He decided it was the female perspective she needed.

It was now getting towards Easter, the clocks changed, and it felt like the country was drying out a bit after a long winter. Jake had spoken to Matthew Boyle on the phone and arranged to go and see him in Winchester. Amey had traced the number she used to have for his personal mobile, but it was no longer used. Jake eventually got through to him by phoning the store directly. He looked up The Green Room and decided to pay them a visit at the same time. Maybe there will be staff around who may know something about the people who apparently met there. He looked down at his phone as it started to ring. It was Amey.

'You've got me thinking lad. Since your visit I keep on coming back to both those cases. Maybe a few years on and not under any pressure to get a result can add a bit of perspective. I suppose once a detective always a detective, and now that I'm retired with not much more to do than prune me roses and watch Bargain Hunt, well, perhaps I can be of use to you, combine resources a bit more. What do you think lad?' Jake hadn't yet said a word and was tempted to say, 'I think you have the wrong number.'

'Umm, yes, maybe.'

'I don't want to get paid for it. I'll do it for fun.'

Jake was trying to think on his feet why this might not be a good idea. The obvious one being that she might take over, he would have to make it clear this was his case, his rules. But she could carry on here while he went over to Menorca.

'Why not,' he finally replied, 'let's give it a go. Can you come down to Lymford? We could kick off here, in my office. How about tomorrow?'

'Good lad! I've got a dreadful town twinning meeting first thing but can be there about noon? Let me know your address.'

'I'll ping it across to you. Noon would be good. Just one thing though, perhaps you don't need to call me lad. Jake is fine!'

'Not sure I can promise that lad.' Then Amey was gone. Jake wondered what he might be letting himself in for.

He decided to leave everything to do with the investigation until he saw Amey. He gave Greg a quick call with an update. Jake could tell he was surprised to hear that he might be including Amey in the investigation, but he admitted that he struggled to find a reason to really object. He asked him about Pat Tweddle and Jake said that he wanted to go over that with Amey, see if he could find out a bit more about him, and where he was now.

He arranged to meet Matthew in Winchester the day after tomorrow, which was a Friday. He thought it better not to take Amey with him, although she may insist. He would then go along to The Green Room for lunch, suss things out there. He looked at his watch, it was 2.30pm. He decided to go for a run, then get ready to catch the train to London. He and Milly were watching Chelsea play Brighton in a crucial match this evening. If Chelsea lost, they almost certainly wouldn't get into Europe for next season.

CHAPTER SEVENTEEN

Amey rang the doorbell to Jake's office spot on noon. He ran down the stairs and let her in. She bustled round his office after taking her coat off. His new sofa had arrived, and he felt his office was almost complete. She had a large backpack which he found out was stuffed with documents relating to Layton's murder, and the Hayling Island case, some of it her own, some of it that she had found on the web. Jake got her a cup of tea, coffee for himself and they both sat down at either end of the sofa. She pulled out a notepad and pencil and rested them on her lap. Jake immediately felt just a little intimidated. He also remembered that Steve Crumpler was a great help in his case last year and two heads should always be better than one. Maybe, in the future he should get a partner. Amey leaned forward and dipped her chocolate Hobnob in the tea, she then tried to stuff most of the biscuit in her mouth. Elegance was not one of Amey's strong points.

'Now then,' she started. 'I'd like to go back to Hayling Island. I still think there's a connection with Layton.'

'What makes you say that?' Jake asked.

'Well, they were close together, both unusual, certainly unusual for Hampshire, and both gave very few clues as to the perpetrator.'

'But one was a very clean murder, the other one was really violent. That's not normal for a serial killer, is it?'

'No, it's not lad. But it may be if it's some form of ritual type killings.'

'Really?' Jake leaned forward and took a sip of coffee, which was still too hot and almost burnt his mouth. 'Shit,' he exclaimed. Amey looked at him.

'Oh, don't make a fuss lad. You youngsters feel pain when a fly lands on your face.' Jake smiled; he'd had a similar discussion with Isabella when he scraped his knee getting out of her pool. Jake quickly composed himself.

'Well,' he started, 'I've been thinking about Layton. Why are we so sure he was murdered? Could he not have got up in the tree and administered the lethal dose on himself? By all accounts he would have been in a pretty bad way, maybe enough was enough?'

'Aha,' Amey countered, 'a theory that we had for a while, but the dose was injected in his back. Wouldn't he just put it straight in his leg, or arm? Much simpler.' Jake nodded. 'Then there's the fake PC. Why would he be there if it was a suicide?'

'Yeah but why would they put him up the tree, why take that risk of being caught hoisting him up there? It makes no sense.'

'I agree, which makes me come back to the ritual. They wanted to do it in a certain way. The ritual is worth the risk. The murderers could easily have been seen coming out of the holiday home in Hayling Island, or people hearing the screams of the woman being killed. Killing doesn't make sense anyway, think about it, you'll always be at risk of being caught. There's been plenty of cases where being public with the murder is part of the thrill for the killer.'

'But this isn't one man on his own, is it?'

'Nope, I'll give you that. This is at least two people agreeing to do it this way.'

Jake put his feet on the table, Amey looked at him and then his feet. Jake took his feet off the table. He got up instead and wandered across to the window.

'You know the mind of murderers better than me. I just don't get why you would go to such elaborate lengths to do it…. I mean get a body up a tree after already killing them.'

Amey just made a small grunt.

'Finding this fake PC would be a bonus. You know I saw Karen Carpenter, but she couldn't really shed much light on him,' he hesitated, 'I'm going to see Matthew Boyle tomorrow, then I thought I'd go to The Green Room.

'Want me to come with you?'

'Would you mind if I say no.'

'I get it. I think the poor lad was always a

little scared of me.' Amey laughed. Jake realised this was the first time he'd seen her do that.

They both decided to go and have lunch at the Four Feathers, at the top of the High Street in Lymford. Amey told him a bit more about how she got into detecting, and the annoyance she felt being taken off. She accepted that she wasn't in a good place at the time, and DCI Pathetic Twat had lived up to his name, but there was always something not quite right about it. Jake said that he would go to Menorca next week, he explained about Cesar and how he may be able to shed some light on what Layton was doing out there, although it may be a forlorn hope. Jake noted a slight look of concern on her face, but she quickly added that she would go and see Jane Colton, Layton's old girlfriend. Matthew Boyle interviewed her twelve years ago and she wasn't convinced that she couldn't give them more information than was forthcoming at the time.

Matthew Boyle was just finishing his supermarket shift when Jake arrived, they decided to just sit down in the restaurant there rather than go anywhere else. Matthew, or Matt, as he insisted, wasn't what he expected. Tall, quite muscular, with close cropped dark hair, however he seemed quite nervous and a bit agitated. Jake explained what he was doing and his old colleague, Amey Lorimer, was now helping him. Matt smiled at that:

'She never really liked me. Mind you I've changed since then. I don't think the whole police thing and then becoming a detective was for me. I didn't really have the patience.' They sat down after Matt cleared the table himself of the previous occupants' sausage, egg and beans dinner, half of which was left on the plate.

'I can see that she wouldn't suffer fools easily,' Jake joked.

'No, and I was a bit of a fool back then to be honest.'

Jake sat back in his chair. 'I mainly wanted to ask you about the jacket, and what happened to it.'

'Ah yes. I really don't know what happened to it. Karen Carpenter gave it to me. The vanishing PC, he did a good job of disappearing into the shadows without a trace.'

'But DNA probably would have identified him, so that jacket was a mistake. Did he somehow get it back from you?'

'He might have. The fact is I left it in the back of the car, went to get it the next day to take it down to the lab, when we knew that PC Joe Attwood didn't exist, and it was gone. The thing is I'd left the car unlocked outside Southampton Police Station, thought I was only going to be a minute, got waylaid, then forgot. I was going on a date with a young WPC, so I never came back till the next day. As you can imagine DCI Lorimer tore my guts to shreds.'

'And, I suppose as it turned out it was the one crucial bit of evidence you had.'

Matt nodded.

'Karen remembered he wore gloves so we couldn't check for anything else he may have touched.'

'That was a bit odd, wasn't it?'

Maybe, but it was February and pretty cold.'

'What about his car, the one he arrived in?'

'Well, again, we didn't take much notice of it at the time, apart from it being a silver Golf. Obviously, it was gone by the time I took Karen to her car.'

'Is there anything you look back on now and think, what about that? You know, something that might have been overlooked?' Jake asked.

'Well, there is. We found a phone number on a piece of paper when scouring the area for clues. It was crumpled and damp so I couldn't be sure how long it had been there, but it couldn't have been for more than a couple of days. One of the DC's called it and someone called James answered. It was a mobile, he said that he was in London and had no idea why his number would be found in the middle of the New Forest. He said he was a builder and maybe it was someone who'd recommended him, and it had fallen out of their pocket. We tried the number again once we knew the body was Layton Jones, and it no longer existed.'

'So, you think that is significant? Did Amey know about it?'

'Oh yeah, on the first call she got them to check where the signal went to, the triangulation points or whatever it is. It was traced to right here in Winchester, pretty central.'

Jake raised his eyebrows.

'So what happened then?'

'Nothing really. Amey decided it wasn't significant and then that was the point where the Hayling murder happened, and we were both taken off the case. I suppose you have to consider how many James might there be in Winchester? And we didn't know that the number hadn't been dropped before the murder. This James might have been on a job in Winchester, and he just meant that he lived in London.'

'What were your thoughts about being taken off the case?' Jake asked.

'To be honest, it seemed a bit fishy, but the boss wasn't right, and so that was the reason to give it to a new team.'

'But you wanted to stay on the case, presumably?'

'Yes, I suppose so.' Matt was hesitant.

Jake mulled this over for a few moments, wondering why, as a detective, you would answer in this way.

'Did you think there was a connection between the murders?' He asked.

'I think Amey had a point, but DCI Pathetic Twat told her to butt out, and then we all moved on to "lighter" duties.'

Amey hadn't really talked about this. 'And these lighter duties were more mundane stuff?'

'Yep, it was then pretty quiet for us, and the boss…well she took some time off.'

Jake nodded. He would ask Amey a bit more about this. 'Look, thanks Matt for your time anyway. Can I call you again if it may help?'

'Yes, of course,' he replied as they both walked to the store entrance. 'And give my regards to the old girl. I actually quite liked her, even though she was a tough old bird.'

Jake smiled and nodded. 'I get that feeling.'

Matt called him back. 'Quite honestly, I think you're on a hiding to nothing with this one. I would question whether it will be worth your time and effort.'

Jake just raised his eyebrows and smiled.

CHAPTER EIGHTEEN

He pushed the door open and walked inside. Jake immediately liked the look of The Green Room. It was busy, but not loud, and had an air of respectability about it. Cool jazz was playing in the background, but it was in the background and not bombarding your ears, so you could easily ignore it. Chat was easy and you wouldn't have to lean in to hear the person next to you. A tall dark-haired woman came up to him wearing a crisp white shirt and dark trousers. She had the appearance of Middle Eastern or North African descent, and a smile that didn't seem forced.

'Have you booked?' She asked.

'No. I've come in on the off chance. Just me.' Jake attempted a pleading facial expression.'

'I can squeeze you in, here by the window.'

'Oh, great,' he replied, thinking about how he was going to phrase his next remark. 'This may sound like a strange question,' he pulled the chair out and took his coat off, 'I don't suppose anyone working here now was here twelve years ago?'

She looked a little startled, clearly thinking "what's this guy?" Well, you're looking at one. I started in 2010, been here ever since. I'm now a co-manager,' she replied, frowning a little.

'Oh great,' Jake responded. 'Let me introduce myself, my name is Jake Stone and I'm a private investigator.' This still sounded odd to him when he heard himself saying it. The woman's frown deepened. 'I just wanted to talk to someone who used to work here and may remember some people that, I believe, used to come here on a fairly regular basis.' The frown softened a little.

'Interesting,' she replied, 'look I'm a bit busy at the moment, but if you want to come back, or wait for an hour then we will have calmed down a bit and I'll be happy to have a chat,' she paused, 'my name's Sofia by the way.'

'Is it ok if I stay? I can have some lunch and do some work.' Jake asked.

'Of course.' Sofia turned around and picked up a menu off the bar. She handed it to Jake who had a quick scan and chose a cappuccino and eggs Benedict.

'Super,' Sofia said and walked off down the room. She stopped and had a quick word with one of the other staff, who glanced briefly at Jake. Jake could see him pull a face which showed intrigue, as far as he could tell. Not for the first time in this job, it made him feel a bit self-conscious.

He looked around him, surveying the place and the people. There was an elderly couple close to him, probably in their seventies, smartly dressed, who were talking about the theatre. Seemed like they were off to see an Agatha Christie play later. There was a couple close to the door, probably in their twenties, much more casually dressed in jeans and jumpers, they were on cocktails and clearly having a good time. Then there was a mother, with a pushchair, probably in her thirties. She looked a little harassed and was preparing to leave. The rest of the room was obscured to Jake by the bar which was long but disappeared out of view from his corner position. He took in the surroundings and liked what he saw. He pulled his iPad out of his backpack and logged on. The Wi-Fi code was up on the wall, then he realised he wasn't sure what to do, what was he going to look up right now? He looked out of the window instead, there was a pedestrian crossing outside and a man was gesticulating at a driver who didn't stop at the red light. The driver put his hand up to apologise. Jake ran his hand through his hair and decided to write notes from his meeting with Matt earlier. Ten minutes later, the man with the intrigued look came across with his coffee and eggs. Jake suddenly remembered his first meeting with Isabella, down the road at The Ivy, when they both had eggs Benedict. That was nine months ago, but it seemed like a lifetime. This city was proving to be a bit of a magnet for him, perhaps he'd do well here if ever he felt like expanding his business, which was highly unlikely.

Two coffees later, The Green Room was emptying out and Sofia finally sat down opposite Jake with a coffee of her own. 'Now then, how can I help?'

'Well,' Jake started, shifting in his seat, he realised his bottom and his left leg had gone to sleep. 'I've been asked to look into a murder from 2012. A bloke was killed in the New Forest, and no one has ever been caught for it. Soon after there was another on Hayling Island, and no one was ever caught for that one either. To be honest there's not a lot to go on, and Hampshire Constabulary have more or less closed them down as unsolved. The brother of the first victim has asked me to investigate and see what I might come up with.' Sofia's frown was back, but he wasn't sure if this was a good sign or not. He carried on. 'Anyway, the brother seems to think he may have come here quite regularly, and a WhatsApp group was discovered on a phone at the second murder, which also indicated meetings here. This would have been around 2011 and 2012. It's a long time ago but they used to meet on a Friday. There would have been four of them, three men and a woman.' Sofia's expression changed, as if she was casting her mind back and trying to remember something.

'Was WhatsApp even around then? Hang on a minute,' she said, 'on a Friday you say?' She leaned forward rubbing her eyes. 'It may be completely irrelevant, but I do remember a group that came in about once a week, four of them, always wanted to sit here, where it's a bit quieter. I remember them because we nicknamed them "The Secret Friday Club." They were always serious, stayed about an hour and never gave a tip. We used to groan when they came in as none of us really wanted to serve them. It became a bit of a competition to see if any of us could make them smile when they paid.' Jake could feel a sense of excitement enter his chest; this could be a breakthrough.

'Did anyone win?' Jake asked. Sofia shook her head, 'I don't think so,' she was thoughtful again. 'I can't really remember what they looked like though, not young, not old. I'd say the woman wasn't exactly a looker, dark hair, shoulder length.'

Jake interrupted. 'Could one of them be quite short, with dark hair? I know that's a bit generic.'

Sofia shook her head again, 'I really don't know, and I don't have a clue what their names might have been.'

'When did you stop seeing them?' Jake asked.

'Oh,' Sofia turned her head to the bar, 'it's hard to say, I know it was before we had any good weather because we joked once we should save them a seat outside, as their miserable faces would drive the customers away from the inside. So, it must have been the winter before the

Olympics.'

'That's brilliant,' Jake said enthusiastically. 'Is there anyone else here now who would remember them?'

'Maybe Sue will, she'd probably just started behind the bar then, the others have left since.'

'Is Sue here today?'

'No,' Sofia said, looking disappointed. 'I can ask her tomorrow when she's in?'

'That would be brilliant,' Jake replied. He shuffled around in his pocket and pulled out a business card, 'Ooh, old school,' Sofia joked.

'Sometimes paper is better than technology!' Jake replied. 'If Sue is able to shed any light then give me a call, or text, or email. Or if you remember anything let me know.'

'Yep sure,' she replied. They both stood up and Jake noticed the bar staff were trying to look nonchalantly in their direction, waiting to pounce on Sofia. Perhaps they thought she was in some kind of bother. Jake smiled inwardly; he never got that sort of reaction working for the civil service.

He stepped out onto the pavement, as a cold wind whipped down the road, reminding him that proper spring wasn't here yet. He heard Sofia call his name just as he was about to walk off.

'One thing I do remember is that a young lad used to join them, I think on their last few visits. He didn't stay long, but it just seemed a bit odd, like he was getting instructions.'

Jake thanked Sofia and couldn't prevent a little smile from crossing his face.

CHAPTER NINETEEN

Jake drove back to Lymford with a feeling that he had some news on the case that hadn't been discovered previously. He rang Amey with an update.

'So,' he could hear Amey musing, 'what are you thinking our mysterious PC is this lad that went into the bar in Winchester? Like he was some kind of errand boy.'

'Got to be a chance, hasn't there?' Jake said, 'maybe a complete red herring but worth considering I'd say.'

'Not going to deny that lad. What about descriptions? Any good?'

'Not great, if I'm honest,' Jake replied, 'except I have a hunch that maybe the woman could, and I emphasise could, be the second victim in Hayling, and one of the blokes could be Layton.'

'A slight leap of faith isn't it lad?'

'Just considering the possibilities.'

'So, you're saying that there is a connection now?' Amey said. Jake felt pleased with his thought process, although he could tell she was sceptical. He imagined you would be with the experience that she had.

'I'm just saying maybe there is a connection, and it's something we should work on.'

'OK,' Amey said, and then went quiet. 'I'm going to have to check in with the old head office and see what they want to do. If there's a new lead, then we really need to tell them. Leave it with me and I'll get in touch.'

'Will they want to take over?'

'Not necessarily, it may be just keeping them in the loop, then they come in with arrests. I left on good terms and am still in touch with the Chief Super.'

Jake could see the advantage in teaming up with Amey, and he wasn't too arrogant to realise he could learn a lot from her.

'Look Jake,' he was pretty sure that was the first time she actually used his name, 'you skive off to Menorca and I'll carry on here.'

Jake summoned up a little bit of courage, 'I've got a question though, which I hope you don't take offence at.'

'Go on.'

'Surely, it was obvious that the two murders could have had a strong link. Why were you taken off so quickly?'

Jake could hear Amey take a large intake of breath and it was almost as if she was mumbling.

'Sometimes lad, you have to do what you're told. Sometimes you know it's not right. Sometimes you know you'll be beating your head against a brick wall. I was surrounded by brick walls, and I never understood why they were built. As I said before, I needed to take some time off myself, get my head together. I wanted to continue but I was advised differently.'

'Is this why you're keen to get involved now?'

Jake heard another intake of breath.

'Maybe lad, maybe.'

Jake waited a moment and then they said their goodbyes.

It was 5pm and Milly was just finishing her show. She pulled her cans off her ears and breathed a huge sigh of relief. It was Friday and that was her live work done for the week. She had to record a dance show to go out the following Saturday, but she could do that at home. That was always fun as she had free rein to choose the music she wanted, however she felt that the management teams who now owned The Crunch had other ideas, and they would dictate music policy soon. Across the desk she asked Elias how many people he was planning to shag this weekend, but he was adamant that he was now in a monogamous relationship and had been for two months. Milly was relieved that he appeared to be settling into a more normal life. She still felt a duty to look out for him, although she would never admit it. He was the one who got her maternal feelings in gear although he was nowhere near young enough to be her son.

She had a chat with 'Producer Mike,' as he was always known, and grabbed her coat and bag from the cloakroom. There were builders around the foyer finalising the touches to the station rebrand. The Crunch was here and Coast FM was becoming a distant memory. She still wondered how long she would be here. She felt a little uncertain about the future, Jake was her anchor at the moment. She called his number.

'Can you do me a favour and go and get some garlic bread from the Co-op, or somewhere?'

'Hello Jake, how was your day?' He replied sarcastically.

'I'm sure it was great. You can tell me later.' She didn't rise to the bait.

'Well, actually it's been very interesting if you were going to ask.' Milly could tell he was dying to update her. She thought her job was interesting but had to admit that his work could sometimes beat hers. At least he was his own boss.

She hadn't told Jake, but she was having her first therapy session since the miscarriage. Why she hadn't told him she wasn't sure. She got into her car and set the satnav and drove out of the car park. She tried to think about what her feelings were, she was relieved that Jake had taken it so well. She still had guilt even though he now knew everything. She also knew that her and Jake needed to go back to the issue of where he was going to live. Before she'd told him about what happened, she'd suggested the apartment by the river. She still felt this would be the best idea for now, although a few weeks ago she wanted them to move in together. Why had she changed? She didn't want it to change their relationship, that was for sure. She would talk to her therapist about this specific point.

Jake walked to the Co-op and got the garlic bread. He also got two bottles of wine and a large bar of Dairy Milk. He was tempted to pop into the Seafarers, but resisted it. Instead, he went home and picked up some clean clothes. He looked around the houseboat, he would be sorry to leave it, but he probably spent only three nights a week here now. Milly's place had a lot more room, but he was conscious that they hadn't talked again about where he was going to go. He was off to Menorca in a couple of days, and he wasn't sure how long he'd be there. He really needed to discuss it with her this evening. He'd decided he wanted them to live together but they both had to be sure.

CHAPTER TWENTY

It was a week before Easter and the schools had broken up. The plane to Menorca was still only three quarters full and Jake managed to get a seat with nobody sitting next to him. He'd booked a window seat and watched everyone coming towards him as they filed into the plane, they either walked past or bustled around him. That was always a minor triumph and meant he could spread out a bit. There was a man sitting in the aisle seat of his row who leaned across and said, 'that's a bonus for us,' and nodded at the seat.

It was too early in the year for the real sunseekers, but it should be pleasant. A lot of the restaurants wouldn't be open yet so Jake would be living off what he cooked. Takeaways were not that prevalent. He'd emailed Cesar three days ago who said he'd be pleased to see him again and invited him to his house for a meal the following day. Jake said that he may have a little job for him, or at least wanted his thoughts about something.

He picked up his hire car and drove away from the airport. It was a strange feeling being back. The first time since Dave was killed and Jake had ended up in hospital. He realised it was a bit of a boil that he needed to lance. Menorca had always been a happy place for him, and he didn't want that to change. He'd had a very long conversation with Isabella in Italy about it as she felt like that about Naples. She had no intention of ever going back but for her there was a long history, whereas for him it was a moment in time that shouldn't spoil all the happy memories he had of the place. He saw the signpost to Alaior, where Dave had his villa, and felt relieved he didn't need to go in that direction. Instead, he turned left at the roundabout and headed to Es Castell, with a food stop at the Binipreu shopping centre. That was familiar and comforting.

Once he turned into the garage, underneath his apartment, he felt a sense of contentment. That was a relief. He unlocked the door and dumped his bag on the downstairs bed. He went upstairs to the kitchen and living room and had a good look around. He hadn't really seen it since the day he left to go to Dave's house the previous year. He'd gone to hospital and from there had gone to the airport for the flight home. Milly had picked up his stuff from the apartment. He opened a cupboard and found an unopened packet of biscuits which he had bought last year, they were still within date, so he opened them and stuffed two down his throat while he walked out onto the balcony. The chairs were still stored away so he would get them later. The mid-afternoon sun was shining through, and the hire car had said it was 22 degrees. Jake decided it was warm enough for shorts, although all the locals he could see were still wrapped up. He unloaded the shopping and went downstairs to unpack, ready for catching up with Cesar later.

Milly was relieved. She and Jake had spoken about moving in together and she'd reassured him that at some point she wanted them to. They were together for the long haul, and he seemed to take it well. She'd explained that she was having a few therapy sessions, following the news of the miscarriage, where she was told that it was perfectly natural to feel the need for a bit of space and that everyone can react differently to that sort of news. She just felt having Jake there all the time would make her feel a bit claustrophobic at the moment, and it would be better for them to take their time, look for a new place together later on, and for him to rent the apartment by the river for now. He hadn't objected and could see the benefits. It was closer to Milly's own place than his houseboat, and it would be much easier for her to stay there as well. The houseboat had always been too small for her to keep any of her own clothes there, or to even stay more than one night.

She was on her way to the studios to record another interview. This time it was retro with the lead singer of a very well-known 80's band, but next week it was going to be Imagine

Dragons, one of Jake's favourite modern bands. They already had tickets for later in the year when they were playing live in Rome. They played there last year, and friends told her they were awesome. It was an outside gig at the Circus Maximus. She was hoping she may be able to scrounge upgrades to VIP. Jake would literally be over the moon. Her phone rang. It was him.

'How's Menorca?' She seemed to shout, as most people do when they speak hands free in the car.

'Sunny, warm, just nice. Be nicer if you were here too though.' Jake said.

'I know, but some of us have other work to do. I'll get there for a proper holiday soon.' Milly replied, as she pulled onto the M27.

'Anyway, just thought I'd let you know I've arrived, all is well, and hope you're feeling okay?'

'Yep, I'm good. Give my love to Cesar and tell him I'm looking forward to his garlic mussels soon.' Milly was well aware that Jake wasn't a lover of seafood, but the local area had an abundance of fish and seafood on offer in the restaurants. Cesar was apparently quite an accomplished chef.

They said goodbye and Milly turned the radio when they'd finished talking, tuned to The Crunch, and Elias was reading the news in almost flawless English. She smiled and realised she was happier than she had been for a few weeks.

Jake rang Cesar and confirmed he'd be with him about 7pm. It was only a short walk to his house, towards the harbour in Cala Fonts. He'd got two bottles of red wine and he'd brought over a large bar of Dairy Milk for Cesar's wife, Maria. This was a special request. Jake got the chairs out of the spare room and opened one up on the balcony. He sat down with a can of Red Bull and looked across the water, which stretched between Mahon harbour and the open sea. There was an island in the middle and beyond that was a large house, on top of a hill. He knew that it had been the setting in the 1970's for a very poor film called "Spanish Fly". It starred Terry Thomas and Leslie Phillips, and Terry Thomas lived there producing wine with the added ingredient of flies. Jake had seen it a few months ago on an obscure film channel. It would never pass the moral decency test now with scantily clad girls and unbelievably bad acting, but it was fun to see how Es Castell and Cala Fonts looked fifty years ago. He believed it was some sort of yoga retreat now, charging thousands of euros for a holistic week in the sun.

Cesar opened the door and gave Jake a big bear hug. Jake winced a little.

'How is the shoulder?' He asked, this being where Jake was shot last year when Dave Constantinou was killed.

'Still a bit sore but not too bad.' Cesar smiled and then frowned.

'That was something eh?' He said, leading Jake through the small hallway and into the kitchen. He introduced Maria to him. A slim, dark-haired woman, which was tied back in a ponytail, but with an unmistakable Spanish look about her. She greeted him like an old friend.

'Maria is cooking tonight. I usually do most of it,' Cesar joked, 'but I remembered that you prefer meat to fish, so it's pork in a mustard sauce with lots of local cheese to follow.' Jake smiled and remarked how great that sounded, and Cesar poured out three glasses of wine. The two of them then moved onto the terrace. It was cooler now, but Jake was still in shorts, but also wearing a grey hoodie. Cesar had thick jeans, a shirt and jumper. He remarked that it's the time of year that it's nice to be sat outside again but is generally a bit too cold not to have thick layers in the evening. They sat down with a view of other apartments opposite. No sea view here, but it was pleasant with plants dotted around and a wooden railing that looked as if it had been recently treated. They both took a sip of wine and Jake let out the predictable response of 'Ahhh.'

'How long are you staying?' Cesar asked him, 'you know it's *Semana Santa* here this week? Holy Week. We've parades on Good Friday. It's quite a special time.' Jake said that he'd read about it on the plane over. Cesar invited him to join the family to watch it and eat with them, especially as he would be on his own. Jake was thankful and said he would definitely be here until Easter was finished, so would be honoured to join them. Cesar's father was a neighbour of Jake's and would have joined them this evening, but he had a rehearsal for the local parade.

'So, tell me,' Cesar changed the subject. 'How's the lovely Milly and why is she not here?' Jake put his glass on the table.

'Work. But she hopes to come out soon. Depends on how long I'm here but it could be she can get here in a couple of weeks, for the weekend, if I stay that long.' Jake then found himself unexpectedly confiding in Cesar about their recent troubles but stressing that things were getting better. He also explained about them not living together just yet. He found the Spaniard very easy to talk to, his English was very good.

'How do you feel about that?' Cesar asked him. Jake looked at Cesar, musing the question over in his head.

'If I'm honest, I'm a bit disappointed, but I get it. There's a part of me that thinks it would be nice to move into a bigger apartment of my own for a while. But she's definitely a keeper.' Cesar frowned, 'sorry, it's a phrase to mean that I think we have a long term future, not someone to drop.' Jake laughed and added, 'it's probably a bloody American saying.'

'So, you're happy?' Cesar asked, still frowning a little.

'Oh yes, we'll buy a place together at some point. I'm sure of it.'

'You British are obsessed about buying property,' Cesar joked, 'most of us around here rent.' Jake nodded, aware that in Europe renting is very common, but generally with tougher laws than in the UK, which protects the tenants.

'So, tell me more about this investigation?' Jake explained what he knew so far and the coincidence being the connection to Es Castell. 'It keeps drawing you back,' Cesar said, 'one day you'll have to come and live here.'

'I can see a day when I start spending the winter here.' Jake said, realising that wasn't a bad idea.

'It's very quiet in the winter,' Cesar said, 'I never know whether I love it, or hate it. The weather's not so good but obviously there's not many tourists. There's a freedom that you don't get in the summer, and it feels like you've got your island back. But then hardly any restaurants are open. Cala Fonts, down by the harbour, is dead and the locals aren't making much money. People work hard during the summer to make as much money as possible, so they can get through the winter.' Jake remembered his adopted dad, Isaac Stone, telling him this when he was much younger. They came in October one year, on a family holiday, not long after they'd bought the apartment, and realised that everything was starting to close down. His parents liked coming in late May and September, when it was warm, but not too hot. It was a little quieter, but most things were open. Jake leant back in his chair, the wine starting to relax him. There were a few moments of silence between them, then Cesar jolted him back into the here and now.

'So, what do you want from me?'

'To be honest,' Jake turned his head to face Cesar again, 'I'm not sure where to start. We know Layton Jones came here several times in 2011 and 2012, he stayed at the Hamilton, and he was clearly meeting people. Where and why is a mystery at the moment. So, I suppose it's more a case of knowing if there was something strange, or odd in the police records from then. It's not much to go on. I'd like to go to the Hamilton and find out a bit more. I assume they still have records of who stayed back then, but I'm not sure they'd be willing to talk to an English private investigator.

Cesar nodded, 'so that's where I come in?' Jake looked guiltily at him again.

'Well……yes, if you could help at all?'

'You'll have to start putting me on the payroll.' Cesar said this rather seriously. Jake just nodded at him. 'I'm on duty for the next couple of days, we're not that busy now so I'll have a look at the police records and see if anything springs out. Best I keep it a bit quiet though. Then, maybe when I'm off duty after that we'll go down to the hotel. You won't be surprised to know I know most of the staff.' He laughed, 'some of them are relatives of mine and Maria's, and the manager is a cousin. Tony, he recently came back from ten years in Madrid and Gibraltar. His English is very good as well, having gone to university in Manchester. I'm told he has a bit of a northern English accent.' Jake laughed, 'well Tony sounds like quite an English name as well. Seriously though Cesar, I really appreciate it, and I don't want to get you into any trouble.'

'Don't be crazy. Always like a bit of intrigue. Thought I might be looking at going down the detective route. It sounds interesting. Always been happy being a regular policeman but now I feel I want a bit more. If I'm honest nothing much happens here in Es Castell. It's up the road in Mahon you get the excitement.'

'Or Alaior,' Jake added, referencing where he got shot, and Dave was killed last year.

'Or Alaior,' Cesar agreed.

CHAPTER TWENTY ONE

Amey was driving up the M3 on her way to see Jane Colton. She lived in Sunningdale, a rich village that straddled the borders of Surrey and Berkshire. Clearly Jane had done well for herself as her address was The Furrows, and it was off the London Road in the village. She had instructions to press the buzzer when she got to the wrought iron gates and Jane would get the gates opened. Amey did this, and a voice at the other end asked her to drive up to the front door. This involved a hundred metre sweep to a mock Georgian style house, which appeared square and symmetrical. Amey wasn't impressed. Generally, she didn't like the nouveau riche, which inevitably Jane would be. Often, they had no manners, no respect, and a perceived entitlement that they weren't entitled to. She got out of her car and walked up to the large dark blue door. It had two knockers, one that was fake and the other that knocked. Amey scoffed to herself and muttered, 'all knockers, no knickers.' She had no doubt that Jane had fake boobs, Botox and an orange tan.

The door opened and this rather demure, short woman in jeans and a Levi Strauss t-shirt said hello. Amey wondered at first if she was the cleaner. She held out her hand, which Amey shook, and introduced herself as Jane, Jane Shepherd now. Amey scrutinised her a bit further, no apparent work done, and her blonde hair looked as though she'd just come out of the shower. Her smile was a struggle, her mouth moved but her eyes stayed slightly dead. She turned around and Amey followed her into the kitchen, as instructed. Jane offered her tea or coffee, Amey opted for tea. She noticed there were several empty bottles of champagne on the side. Obviously, they were not a Prosecco family and champagne was the drink of choice in this house. Amey couldn't help tutting and this came out rather louder than she intended. She sat at the large breakfast table and looked at a family photo. There was Jane, a man with greying hair in a suit, and two boys, aged about seven or eight. Jane put two cups on the table and sat next to Amey. They adjusted themselves so they were at forty-five-degree angles to each other, ready for a conversation that neither really wanted to have.

Jane followed Amey's gaze towards the photo. 'My husband, Julian, works in the city as a stockbroker.' Of course, Amey thought to herself.

'He catches the train to work every day, plays golf on a Saturday and we go for Sunday lunch at the same pub week after week. I shop, and I meet the girls for lunch twice a week, and have a lover on the side on Thursday afternoons.

A waiter at the pub we go to. He's young, very virile, and satisfies me in ways that Julian never will. Regrettably he goes back to Egypt next month.' Amey was astonished that she'd come straight out with this personal information. This was clearly a woman who had money but hated her life. Amey felt a little bit sorry for her, she herself had not had the most exciting life for the last few years. She put a spoonful of sugar in her tea. 'Very stereotypical, isn't it,' Jane said as she looked down at the sugar bowl. It was a statement rather than a question.

'And what about the boys?' Amey asked.

'They've gone off to boarding school. They're ten now, so Julian wanted them to go to Marlborough College. Not that far away I know, but there's a perfectly good school just up the road.' Jane sounded quite bitter.

'Okay,' Amey said, with certainty that she wanted to move on. 'As I said on the phone, I'm here about Layton Jones, I wanted to know what you could tell us about him and what he might have got mixed up in before he died. As you know, it was never solved. I've left the police and am now working with a PI to try and solve it.'

Jane nodded. 'Well, I remember speaking to a Detective Sergeant at the time.'

'Matthew Boyle?' Amey interjected.

'Yes. We literally had a five-minute conversation and I never heard from anyone again.'

Amey huffed. 'What did you tell him?'

'That me and Layton had become distant, and I hadn't seen him for several months.'

'Were you able to help? Give them any clues why he would have been murdered?'

'Not really. I remember the DS got a call soon after he met me and he kind of ended the conversation there.'

Amey scowled. 'So, he never asked you about people Layton might have known, people he talked about before you two split up?'

Jane shook her head. 'No, that was it. I never heard anymore. I called Greg, his brother a couple of times, but he didn't seem to know what was going on himself. After a while I met Julian and forgot all about Layton.' Jane now looked wistful. 'Have to admit, I missed him. At least he had more life in him than boring, fucking Julian.'

Amey finished her tea. 'Look, what I need to know is what was going on with him before you split up.'

Jane got up and walked over to a chest of drawers. She opened a bottom drawer and pulled out a book which she opened. She walked back with a photo in her hand. She passed it to Amey. It was a picture of two smiling people at what appeared to be a music festival.'

'Glastonbury,' Jane said. '2011. Just before he changed. We were happy that weekend.' Jane hesitated. 'There was one thing that I didn't like about him. He was a bit of a nationalist.

He would often moan about immigration, and just after Glastonbury he went on a march in London. You know, close the borders, prevent blacks and Asians from coming in. It was after that, he changed even more.'

'In what way?' Amey asked.

'He became more racist. Went to meetings which I knew were far right causes. Then one day, I think in September that year, he announced he was going to Menorca for the weekend. When I asked what for, and why couldn't I come, he said he had business with Tommy in the red house.'

Amey shifted in her seat. 'Tommy who?' She asked.

'I don't know, he never said anymore, and to be honest we drifted apart. By November we weren't seeing each other.'

Amey knew all about this, it was the sort of radicalisation that you didn't hear much about. The white English mobs who screw with the heads of people who are somewhat prejudiced towards ethnic minorities but persuade them that the country will go to hell and back if they're not controlled, contained, or even driven across the channel. Amey liked to keep an open mind.

'Was he a violent man?' Amey asked, very matter of factly.

Jane looked thoughtful before replying. 'No. I never saw any evidence of that. But he became angrier. He would shout at the TV whenever he saw asylum seekers on the news, or human rights campaigners. He never used to do that before going to these meetings.'

'Did he mention any other names associated with these rallies or meetings, or contacts that you were aware of?' Amey asked.

'I don't think so. Not that I can remember.

'Was there a name that he gave to any of the groups?'

'Oh yes, he mentioned the Albion Defence Group once. He was a bit drunk and seemed to regret letting it slip. He told me to forget he'd said it straight afterwards.'

Amey was scribbling away with her notes. She wrote down a number on a piece of paper and handed it to Jane. She'd heard enough for today.

'Look, if there's anything else you remember then please give me a call. Me and my accomplice, Jake Stone, are determined to get to the bottom of Layton's murder.'

Jane nodded and thanked Amey for coming, she seemed brighter than when she'd opened the door earlier. Amey turned the car around, turned left outside the gates of Jane's house and headed for home. Thoughts swirling around her head like paper in a tornado.

CHAPTER TWENTY TWO

It was a sunny twenty-three degrees in Menorca, and a drizzly ten degrees in Salisbury when Amey called Jake the next morning.

'How's it going lad?' Amey was very chirpy.

'Nicely thank you,' replied Jake, just swallowing a piece of croissant which just had jam on it. He'd forgotten to get any butter when he arrived so needed to remedy that today.

'Well, getting straight to it.' Amey was clearly not one for wasting too much time on pleasantries. 'Been to see the ex-girlfriend, and she says Layton joined, or at least mentioned the Albion Defence Group. Never heard of them myself but I got on to the old internet when I got back home…and I have to say they're a nasty bunch, or rather they were a nasty bunch.' Jake was listening intently; he was sitting on the balcony of his apartment with a coffee in his hand. Amey carried on, 'she said that Layton went to Menorca to meet Tommy at the red house. She didn't know whether it was called The Red House, or that it was a house painted red. Anyway, I found out that Tommy is Tommy Phillips, look it up, he was the leader of this group and they're as right wing as you can get. It was all about driving ethnic minorities out of Britain, or more specifically England. They make the National Front, or English Defence League look tame.'

Jake managed to speak. 'So, is he still running the show?'

'Nope, he died in 2017 and it seems the organisation died with him.'

'Just as bloody well,' said Jake, shaking his head. 'So, what was it, this Tommy lived in Menorca?'

'Looks like it. She didn't know any more than that and I couldn't find anything that confirmed he did, although the internet said he lived abroad.' Amey was hesitating. 'I'm not going to lie to you lad, I've hardly slept a wink thinking about it. If he was part of this group, and they were planning something, what led him to be killed? We need to find out whether the woman at the Hayling murder was part of it as well. But the biggest thing for me is why were the investigations scaled down so quickly. I know we had the Olympics and that caused problems, but does that explain it?'

Jake felt that Amey was actually talking to herself, which amused and annoyed him at the same time. This was his investigation after all. He looked up and his gaze drifted across the water to the other side, where a red house sat on top of the hill.

'Well, I may have an idea about the red house,' he said, his own mind ticking over, 'I might be looking at the red house you're talking about right now.

Jake went on to explain that he and Cesar were going to the hotel that Layton apparently stayed in, and he would find out a bit more about the house, who owned it, and what was going on there back in 2012. Maybe that would be a bit of a break. He was worried for a moment that Amey was going to be making all the running, he was feeling a bit of pressure to keep up.

'I don't suppose it's the only red house in Menorca.' Amey suddenly sounded a bit negative, was she just trying to get some sort of upper hand? They agreed to speak again in a couple of days, after Jake had been to the hotel. He sat back and pondered this new working relationship. He had to accept that she used to be a DCI and had many years of experience, he had been a private investigator for just fifteen months, after years as a dogsbody in the civil service. He decided he could learn from her, and embrace it, but he also didn't want to feel like the understudy, the DS and the DCI.

Jake had another day before Cesar was free for them to go to the hotel. He felt a little hamstrung, he'd found out the red house was called Sant Phillippe, and had quite a history. Built in a colonial style it commanded a view over the waterway from Mahon to the open sea, and for a fair distance inland. It was relatively remote so Jake could see that it might be an ideal base for a slightly clandestine operation. It felt ironic though that an organisation that claimed to be so patriotic was based eight hundred miles away from the country it claimed to represent, and love. He couldn't get any access to owners or occupiers of the house. It dawned on him again that contacts were so vital in his line of work, Cesar could be really important for him. Again.

By lunchtime he was hungry but decided to go for a run before eating. He went downstairs and changed into shorts and a t-shirt and opted to go along the road to the outskirts of Mahon and back. This took just under an hour and was torture, he'd neglected the running for most of the winter. It occurred to him how dedicated Karen Carpenter must have been back in 2012 to keep running through the wind and rain, through the forest, and then come across a dead body. There was something of a steely determination about her. He wondered whether she had something else to hide. There was something nagging at him, like a cold draught which you can't find the source of.

Amey was muttering to herself as she watered the plants scattered around her house. Normally, she'd be watching Bargain Hunt now, and then the BBC News, followed by the local news. She still kept a keen interest in local news, mainly for anything that the police were caught up in, but that could be frustrating as she always wanted to know the full story about what was going on, especially with a murder investigation. She often couldn't resist contacting some of her old colleagues who were still around, tapping them up for the juicy bits. What was really going on, what the press couldn't report on.

She was deciding what to do next. She felt the need to focus a bit on the Hayling murder. She didn't have much on that. She went to the scene at the time, and remembered she felt queasy once she'd seen the body. Matthew Boyle had to say hello again to his breakfast in front of a crowd of onlookers, much to her amusement. She'd told him to grow some balls at the time, it probably was a bit harsh, but she was still annoyed with him for losing the jacket that Joe Attwood was wearing…and just being Matthew, who she considered a waste of space, and wondered how he ever got into the force in the first place. She'd retrieved the phone and took it back to the station with her. That had revealed the WhatsApp group, something she hadn't really known much about until then, and revealed a connection to Winchester. By the time she was taken off the case, and went on sick leave, no one knew who the woman was. She was Jane Doe, and it appeared to be her phone. But Amey had known better.

Jake met Cesar outside the Barcelo Hamilton Hotel, which was located right on the waterfront in Es Castell. Mahon was a few kilometres upstream while the open sea was a couple of kilometres downstream. Ferries would frequently pass by the hotel, mainly on their way to Barcelona, or Valencia. They could loom quite large against the backdrop of the lush slopes on the other side. From the hotel there was a slope that took you down to the waterside and the restaurants that lined the front round to the harbour at Cala Fonts, quiet now but come the summer it would be packed with tourists looking for an evening meal.

'Isn't the island lovely at this time of the year?' Cesar had suddenly appeared behind Jake as he gazed across at the houses opposite.

'I was just thinking that,' he replied, turning around. 'I've never been here at this time of the year. So much greener.'

'Ah yes, we had a lot of rain in February and the flowers have come out well. The light is at its best now as well. Soon things will be a little browner and a little hazier.' Cesar smiled. 'OK, let's go inside and see Tony, he knows we're coming.' Tony was in the lobby and gave Cesar a hug. He held out his hand to Jake and ushered them over to some comfortable seats by the window. He had a notepad on the table so Jake could see he was prepared. He couldn't help but notice that Tony had an incredibly ordinary look about him, no particularly distinguishing features, dark hair, dark eyes, quite pale for a Spaniard, maybe a little overweight, but with an accent that was clearly not English, but some words that sounded as though he'd come straight out of Lancashire. Tony indicated to a colleague for some coffee to be brought over, after checking with Jake what he would like.

'Now then, you were asking about Layton Jones?' Tony said, flicking his eyes between the other two. 'I found him booked in here three times, between October 2011 and February 2012, which is a bit odd. Obviously, that's a quiet time of the year but it's just after we were renovated.'

Jake spoke. 'Is there anyone working here now who was here then?'

'Yes, there is, and I'd say you wouldn't normally remember anyone that far back. However, Juan, our bar manager does.' Jake raised his eyebrows in anticipation.

'Layton Jones would sit at the bar most evenings. He only stayed four or five days each time. He drank a lot and Juan thinks he was involved in some business over here. He was always out during the day, but interestingly,' Tony smiled, 'when he was drunk one evening he told Juan that he was scared. This was on his last visit.'

'Did he say what of?' Jake asked.

'No, but he found out that he used to go to Sant Philippe, across the water.'

'The red house?' Jake questioned; his suspicions confirmed.

'That's the one,' Tony replied.

Cesar shifted in his seat; it was his turn. 'So, we know that it was occupied by a nasty English chap called Tommy Phillips at the time. 'A bit ironic that a chap called Phillips bought Sant Philippe. He got into trouble a few times for disturbing the peace, but most of all he and a few friends were suspected of setting fire to a building in Mahon that was used by refugees from Africa.' Both Jake and Tony now stared at him, 'but we couldn't prove it. The only evidence we had was they were drinking in a nearby bar and were seen leaving in that direction. Thirty minutes later it was in flames.'

Tony nodded, 'I remember hearing about that.'

Jake was thoughtful. 'Is Juan here now?'

'He will be later.' Tony replied. 'You're welcome to come back.'

'When did Tommy Phillips leave?' Jake asked Cesar.

'Not sure, we know that one day the place was empty, probably around 2013, and the company that owns it now bought it and started to turn it into a retreat.'

Jake sat back and picked up his coffee. He told them both about the Albion Defence Group, which neither Cesar nor Tony had heard of. Things were starting to piece together a little bit. Not why he was killed, but at least what he was doing just before it.

Later Jake was sitting back on his balcony, finishing off a packet of biscuits he found tucked at the back of a cupboard in his kitchen. If Layton was part of the ADG and suppose the ADG killed him, why would they do it? On the other hand, was he killed because he was in the ADG? And that's why the woman in Hayling was killed as well. But it's very unusual for a woman to join an organisation like that, or so he thought. Probably, the truth was that neither of those theories were correct. He didn't know what this was turning into.

CHAPTER TWENTY THREE

Milly put the phone down feeling a little excited. She'd managed to get time off to go to Menorca after Easter. She wanted to check with Jake that he would still be there, which he said he would. She would come out the day after Easter Monday and they decided to fly back home together the following weekend. She wanted to talk to him again about doing the podcast, about what happened the previous year. She'd mentioned it to Isabella when they were in Italy, however she was still to be won over. It would be raking up old ground again, but in a strange way it did end with a good news story, Jake and Isabella were reunited, which was a good thing, but Milly understood the sensitivity of it. Isabella had said she would think about it. Jake was halfway there. A nice holiday together and she would aim to charm him round. She'd already pitched the idea to the new bosses of the radio station, and they were keen. It was definitely something they wanted to expand into more as a way of diversifying.

She wasn't sure what she was going to be doing this weekend now. It was Easter, Jake was in Menorca, and she only had two shows to do. Hers were never recorded and as they were afternoon shows it meant she had Saturday and Sunday free. She decided on some retail therapy and a couple of nights out with old friends.

Amey put the phone down on Jake and could tell that he was still pretty confused by what had happened in 2012. She took stock and went over everything again in her head. Layton was now linked to the Albion Defence Group, and sooner or later so would Hayling Island and the woman that may have been called Lucy from the WhatsApp group. Four of them used to meet at The Green Room. She wondered about speaking to Pat Tweddle but that was a wound that needed to remain closed and not aggravated. She needed to track down Joe Attwood. She also wanted to go back and get hold of the police files on both the murders. She'd found out that her old Super at Southampton was ill, it seemed that he had a stroke a while ago and so she felt it insensitive to approach him, but she was always on good terms with the archivist, and he was still in charge of the storage of the records. She would charm him, although Amey's version of charm was a little blunt. Jake was quite tenacious, and she was starting to admire him for that, but she really wanted to get some sort of control, leave certain elements of this investigation to her and she would feed him what he needed to know.

Jake's ear was a little red and his phone needed charging. His speakerphone didn't seem to be working so the phone had been clamped to his head for nearly an hour. He was pleased that Milly was coming to see him, although he felt the need to get back to Lymford soon. He would enjoy a few days with her and put the case to one side until they got back. He would call Greg later and give him an update, to find out if he knew anything about Tommy Phillips and the Albion Defence Group. As much as he loved his job it could be a little all-consuming at times and he'd had to turn down work recently. It even ran through his head that he should get a partner. He went on to his website which his friend, Pierre, tended to look after for him. The front page had been jazzed up in different fonts and effects while still retaining a level of maturity. After all, a Private Investigator's online presence is not supposed to look like a website for Selfridges at Christmas. Even Jake agreed that there was a very nice picture of him with a mouth closed smile, looking casual but professional. Pierre had said it had the look of someone who would take you seriously, and 'be there for you' in your hour of need. Especially the females. Luke had been there at the time and said some men may also be attracted to that picture, so he would attract a full spectrum of clients. Jake told him he was ridiculous, but Luke and Pierre insisted that an appealing PI to the eye could always be a benefit. Jake's preference would be for him to look a little more grizzled, and world weary, he felt that would look a little more authentic. More Cormoran Strike.

He checked his emails and there was one from a person in Bournemouth wanting to track down a timeshare salesman from the eighties. It sounded like he might just want to do the salesman harm. Jake replied to say he was too busy just at the moment but try him again in a few months if he still wanted help. He got up from the comfy sofa and wandered out to the balcony. He looked across to the red house and wondered what went on there twelve years ago.

Mid-afternoon he took a long walk round to the hotel so he could have a word with Juan. He didn't see Tony but asked for Juan at the reception desk. After a few minutes a tall silver haired chap appeared, probably about fifty-five years of age. In truth Juan couldn't add much more to what Cesar and Tony had said that morning, he affirmed that Layton was tense on his last visit and would knock back large quantities of rum. One thing he did remember was that he was joined by a woman on that occasion. They sat down away from the bar and appeared very serious. Juan couldn't remember her too well except she was quite tall with long dark hair. He'd added that she was 'not a vision of beauty.' Jake wrote this down to remember to tell Amey. His notes were getting a bit messy now. He tried to always put everything into a word document on his laptop once he'd got some new information when he was on any case. He'd started a new folder for this case and called it 'Death in the Forest.' He hadn't yet put anything into the folder, so he knew this was a job he really needed to get on and do for the next couple of days. This should help to organise his thoughts, but maybe the woman seen by Juan was the Hayling victim.

The next morning was a little cool and drizzly, but according to his weather app it would clear, and the Easter weekend promised to be sunny. Good Friday was the following day so there was no excuse. He didn't get up until 9am and climbed the stairs to the living area. There was a bottle of Tempranillo by the kitchen sink, empty and ready for recycling. However, his head was clear, and he made a cup of tea and took some bread out of the freezer. He turned the TV on and as his apartment block had a satellite dish, he was able to watch Sky News. The UK was preparing for an Easter snowstorm, the government was in another crisis with Ministers resigning and another conflict was erupting in the Middle East. Meanwhile, Sky was excited to announce they would shortly have the winner of the *Celebrity Drive a Farm Vehicle* competition live in the studio. Apparently, it was an influencer called Reggie Royal who liked to tell people how to apply male cosmetics. Jake sat down, with tea and toast, and turned on Spotify instead. He fancied a bit of Nineties Ibiza Chill, so finished his breakfast, opened up his laptop and purple book of notes, with Morcheeba playing in the background soothing his soul.

Amey was still a bit of a legend at her old station in Southampton, a lot of her old colleagues had now left but she had a reputation that lived on. No-nonsense, abrupt, and a very good clear up rate. She'd always known that had she still been around she would have solved the two murders her way. Everyone at the station knew there was a story that shouldn't be raised. Don't ask too much, keep under the radar, and move on. DCI Pat Tweddle took over as a figurehead for the investigation, but it was clear that no great effort was going to be made to solve them. Because the murders were so different it took a while for the penny to drop with most of the officers that there may be a connection between the two. But that's as far as it went. Amey had left by this time and there was nobody who was going to confirm or deny it. Hampshire CID moved past it. The only person who never forgot them was George. George was the chief archivist and Amey was on her way to see him.

CHAPTER TWENTY FOUR

Sleet was falling as Amey pulled into the car park. She'd called George and he was delighted to hear from her. He told her to come in on Good Friday, things would be a bit quieter, and they would use the visit as a social call. He got her signed in and they walked down the stairs to, what he called, his vault. This was a quiet, slightly murky world where George reigned supreme. At sixty-nine he wasn't yet ready to retire. He was a bald man, he'd said that he literally lost his hair overnight through a rare skin disease forty years ago, and it never grew back. His face was pinched, and he didn't carry an ounce of spare fat on him. He regularly played football until he was fifty and had recently taken up walking football. His reading glasses seemed to permanently be lodged at the end of his nose.

'It's a good ten years since I've been down here George.' Amey said, dodging around boxes that were waiting to be catalogued on the computer.

'Strange times, those.' He said this as if it brought back bad memories. Amey suddenly felt a shudder. It wasn't a good time for her, and she wondered if she was doing the right thing, getting involved now. She wasn't entirely sure of her motivation but felt she was needed. 'You know I was asked to catalogue these together after you left,' George turned to look at her as he said this. 'Why would that be, do you think?'

'Umm,' Amey replied, without saying any more.

'Here they are, I've pulled them out for you.' George pointed to a rickety table with a nice plush office chair. 'Comfy enough for an occasional nap,' he smiled as he pulled it out from under the table for her.

'Thank you George, it's much appreciated. Any chance of a cup of tea?' George nodded and shuffled off to his little kitchen at the end of the store.

Amey opened the first box, written on the side was 'Brockenhurst 022012 - Layton Jones.' She took her coat off and settled herself down, feeling a little nervous about what she might find. There were various photos of the body and the area, statements from Karen Carpenter, statements from his family, and her own notes that she'd made at the time. It was notable there was little from DCI Patrick Tweddle. This was not a surprise to her. She studied them but nothing seemed to leap out at her that she didn't already know, which in some ways was of comfort. While George was bumbling away, she took photos with her camera, knowing this was highly illegal. She then opened up 'Hayling

Island 032012.' This was far more gruesome. The photos revealed the woman who was nailed to the bedroom wall by her hands, just as Jesus was nailed to the cross, with her stomach cut open, blood was splattered everywhere. Amey remembered when she had walked in and seen it for the first time, thinking it was some sort of religious murder. She could never understand why she was killed in that way; it would have been such a risk. However, there wasn't much in the box. Statements from the cleaners who found her, Janice and Agu. There were various photos of the scene and notes from DCI Pathetic Twat that confirmed little progress had been made and resources were pulled back. This was July 2012, there seemed to be nothing after this date. Amey thought back and could remember she had already been encouraged to go on sick leave by this time, so Tweddle had full reign to do what he wanted. She took more shots of the evidence but there was little that was worthwhile and new to her. Nevertheless, she was satisfied with her visit and considered it worthwhile.

After thirty minutes she decided there was nothing more to be had here. She thanked George and agreed to meet up for a spot of lunch one day. As she got outside the sleet had turned to proper snow, so she decided to get back to Salisbury as quickly as possible. 'So much for spring,' she muttered to herself as she drove out to the A36 heading home.

It was 6pm when Jake got back to his apartment after spending the day with Cesar and his family. They'd gone to Mahon to see the parades and costumes typical of the brother and sisterhoods known as '*Cofradías.*' They wear long tunics with contrasting-coloured sashes and tall pointed hats with attached full face masks. At first glance you may think it's a meeting of the Ku Klux Klan, but Jake found it a fascinating spectacle. Popular in many Catholic countries in the Mediterranean, he'd heard about it once before when his parents went on holiday to Sevill, but had never seen it himself. Many of the local populace would now be going to church so he decided to make his excuses. Jake actually had a cynicism towards all religions but knew the traditions could be interesting. He carried on updating his notes on his laptop for a while and then gave Milly a call. She told him it was minus one degree and snowing hard. Even in Lymford, right on the coast there was already two inches of snow, while further north in Hampshire it was six inches deep. Thankfully it should become mild by Sunday and be washed away before her flight to Menorca on Tuesday.

Amey was looking out over a snow-covered scene. She'd got home eventually but it had taken twice as long as normal. Snow was drifting across the road at Pepperbox Hill, just outside Salisbury and she'd just heard it had been shut. The iconic pointed cathedral was barely visible through the flakes and life below her was quiet. Salisbury would normally be buzzing on Good Friday with tourists, services at the cathedral and various events that would be kicking off to celebrate the first Easter, and perhaps more importantly for many people, the longer days and Spring arriving. A time to celebrate the end of Winter. She turned away and decided to email Jake the photos she'd taken at the police station. She'd attended a *silver surfers* course a year ago and now felt she was more of a dab hand at things technology-wise, so she uploaded them to her own laptop so she could take a better look at the evidence again, and attached

them all to an email for Jake. Tomorrow, she should be going to a friend's house in Weymouth but doubted that would happen.

CHAPTER TWENTY FIVE

The next few days were quiet as far as any investigation was concerned. Amey had made it to Weymouth on Sunday, once most of the snow had gone. Jake had got bored in the Menorcan sunshine and was counting the days until Milly arrived. He'd spent some time on Saturday going through the information that Amey had sent him. He'd scrutinised the photos and was shocked by the scene from Hayling Island. There was a picture of some of the police who had cordoned off the holiday home. He wondered whether any of them might be Joe Attwood. Probably, only Karen Carpenter could give much of a description. He made a note to send it to her, just on the off chance. There was a picture of both Matt and Amey together, both with quite shocked looks on their faces. Amey looked much the same while Matt was visibly different, longer hair and he was visibly larger than when he'd recently seen him. Having said that he looked that much younger.

On Tuesday morning he arrived at the airport ready for Milly's flight in. It was due at 11.40am, it was only five minutes late when he checked the board. As he waited by the arrivals area, which was basically the foyer for the airport and took you straight into the car rental bays, he felt his stomach flip over. He was excited to see her. After half an hour of waiting she came through the doors with a big wide smile. He was going to try and be cool but in the end he almost ran the twenty feet to get to her. He picked her up and swung her around, surprising even himself.

'Jesus Jake,' Milly exclaimed, once their lips had finally parted. 'Have you been on a course for romance since you've been here?'

'What can I say, I'm pleased to see you,' he replied.

'I can tell,' she said, looking down. 'Anyway, it's nice to see the sun as well. Wait till I show you some of the photos from last weekend. Lymford had six inches of snow, then it was all gone by Sunday morning.'

'I can do better than six inches,' Jake grinned, and Milly punched him in the arm. 'Anyway, let's go. I'm looking forward to showing you Menorca without me being in hospital this time. Cesar invited us round for dinner tomorrow, so I've got good old traditional steak and chips for us this evening.'

'Do we have wine and beer?' Milly asked.

'Errr...what do you think? We're getting hammered this evening.'

'Excellent,' Milly replied.

Their day basically consisted of food, wine, sex and a walk down to Cala Fonts. The next day Jake dragged himself out of bed at 10.30am leaving Milly to carry on sleeping. He went up the stairs to put coffee on and stuffed a pain au chocolat in his mouth, coughing as flakes got stuck in his throat. His head was pretty clear, and he promised himself he would leave the investigation alone today. Nevertheless, he'd printed off a lot of the information on the Hayling case that Amey had sent through which he couldn't help picking up. He sat down on the balcony to have a look through while he drank the coffee, and ate another pain au chocolat, just more slowly this time. From what he could see, after the first month there was little progress. It was as if the investigation of both murders was almost shut down around April/May 2012. Amey, and Pat Tweddle indicated this was because of manpower being moved to the Olympics, and the security requirements around it. But this was two murders, close together, in an area that's not used to them? The WhatsApp messages were by far the biggest lead, but little seemed to have been done to track down who the victim was. He could see no evidence to try and trace Bob, Lucy, Phil or Bill at The Green Room in Winchester. Both he and Amey were now certain that one of them was Layton, and was Lucy the holiday home victim? If so, who were these other two? He wrote a few notes down, mainly for when he got back to England at the weekend. Jake knew there was a strong smell of a cover up, but why? He glanced up again at the red house across the water.

Milly came up the stairs half an hour later and went straight for a cup of tea. Jake could hear her humming away to herself as she pottered around the tiny kitchen. There was a door that led straight from it onto the balcony, as she came through she kissed Jake on the top of his head, then slumped into a chair next to him.

'You're really enjoying yourself, aren't you?' She said as she idly picked up the papers on the table. She grimaced at the sight of the body. 'This looks religious,' she remarked, looking at the way it was pinned to the wall.

'Umm, I know, which isn't like Layton's death.' Jake sighed. Milly started staring at the picture of the uniformed officers who were at the scene in Hayling Island. They all were in full uniform, and they were at a distance, but one didn't have his helmet on and appeared to be adjusting the strap on it.

'That one looks like Morgan Ellis,' Milly seemed amused.

'Who?' Jake said, distractedly.

'You know, Morgan Ellis.'

'What, the actor Morgan Ellis?' Jake looked quizzically at her and grabbed the picture off Milly. He studied it for a few seconds. 'It can't be. They say everyone has a doppelganger.' He screwed his face up as if it would help him to see better. 'I see what you mean. Younger but some sort of similarity.'

'You know he comes from Winchester?' Milly said as she picked her phone up and started a search for *Morgan Ellis actor*. Jake frowned at her as he started to ponder the possibility. 'I didn't know that.' He paused and looked at the picture again, 'No, it can't be,' he said, frowning and picking up his own phone. Milly scrolled through pictures trying to find one that was older.

'I always fancied him. He was a regular on that daytime soap called *Acre Avenue,* it was about life in a street in Bristol, and he played a junior cleric at the local church. It only lasted two years.'

Milly then found photos of him from that time.

'Look, there is a similarity,' she passed her phone over to Jake who glanced between the photo and the phone. 'It's got to be a coincidence surely?' He was trying to convince himself one way or the other.

'I interviewed him last year on my show,' Milly was intrigued, 'he was lovely. It was just before he went off to Hollywood to start filming *'Death in the Afternoon,'* which comes out next month I think.'

'Is that the one with Lily James and Chris Hemsworth? There's already quite a bit of hype about it.' Jake responded, his mind flipping over.

Milly tapped her finger on the table.

'That's the one. And do you know what it's about?' She looked at Jake with her mouth half open and eyes wide. He shook his head, switching his attention from the pictures to Milly. 'It's about a group of people meeting up in a bar, in Seattle, and planning murders that take place in the afternoon. But....' and now her eyes widened further, 'they're contract killers, and under orders to vary the types of death to try and negate the idea they were the work of the same man. Morgan told me that it was an idea he put to the film company three years ago.'

'Fuck.' This was all Jake could say for a minute. His eyes were out on stalks at the thought of what this could mean. He scrolled through his own phone this time. Morgan had changed his appearance since his *Acre Avenue* days, his hair was longer, he naturally looked older and carried a permanent, closely cropped beard. His career soared after the soap. He starred in a couple of mystery dramas that were popular on the BBC, took on a few film roles, could be seen on an advert for John Lewis and Wikipedia told him that Morgan divided his time between Los Angeles and the Hampshire countryside, where his wife and daughter lived. Jake came across an article from The Guardian which headlined - *'Is this the nicest British actor?'* The article went on to say how approachable Morgan was, the things that he did for charity, and his love for his family, and the support he gave his local football club. He'd helped Winchester City financially when they looked like they were about to go out of business. Morgan was now on the British A-list of celebrities, or pretty close to it.

'I just can't believe that Morgan Ellis could be Joe Attwood. It's mind boggling.' Jake stared at the sky, but he wasn't focussed on it. He turned back to Milly, 'I must find out what he was doing in 2012 then,' Jake looked defiantly at Milly, who leaned over and put her hand on Jake's arm before speaking. 'You know it might be that Morgan was actually in the police in 2012, you know before he became an actor.' Jake looked at her with a certain amount of incredulity, before shaking his head. 'Well, that will be easy to find out.'

'Granted, but do you have to do it now? Could you not wait till we get back home? It would be easier. That's only three days' time.' Jake was torn but decided to get his priorities right and put Milly first. But this was a game changer, and he knew it was going to be hard to focus on anything else.

'You're right. What I'll do is give Amey a call and let her know. She can get on with it while we're away.' He smiled and leant over and gave Milly a kiss, knowing that he would secretly snatch some time when he could to look into the famous Morgan Ellis.

CHAPTER TWENTY SIX

Amey had told Jake that she'd heard of Morgan Ellis, but he wasn't high on her list of known celebrities. Having said that, no one was really high on her list of known celebrities. She hated celebrity culture. She was a big fan of BBC4 and its historical programmes. Detective series just made her angry, although she did have a secret guilty pleasure for *Midsomer Murders*, mainly because it was so preposterous and not trying to stick to any realism.

Jake had asked her to do some checking on Morgan which she said she was happy to do. The thought that he was there in Hayling Island meant that he was, almost certainly, PC Joe Attwood from the New Forest and an almost incredible discovery. Even if it wasn't Morgan they might have a face to a name. Amey uttered caution and said she was highly sceptical but agreed it's one worth considering. She realised this had deflated Jake's enthusiasm, but that was alright. First of all, she went on to her iPad and looked at his images which she could enhance. She noticed that the modern-day Morgan had a scar on his forehead, the 2012 copper didn't, but the eyes, mouth and jawline looked the same, or at least very similar. After half an hour she shuffled into the kitchen and got out a couple of paracetamols, she had a headache coming on and the whisky she drank last night was taking its toll. She glanced across at the bottle of Glenmorangie which was empty. She was trying to limit herself to three smallish glasses per night, but this strategy wasn't proving very successful at the moment. She was getting a bit worried about her dependence on alcohol so vowed to go alcohol free two nights a week. Easy to say with a hangover.

As she finished a glass of water, and stood leaning over the sink, she wondered about Karen Carpenter, could she identify Joe Attwood as Morgan Ellis? If this did prove to be a lead, then she knew they would need to inform the police. She would need to make some calls but until they were one hundred percent convinced Morgan Ellis was involved, they'd better keep it to themselves. She walked through to her window that looked across Salisbury and tried to get some perspective. She thought about who could be starting to get a bit twitchy with her and Jake raking up the past, and what might that mean for them. She felt a little boxed in. What was for the best?

Amey shuffled back to her living room and went to the large oak dining table where she kept the papers relating to the case. She was looking for Karen Carpenter's address and phone number. At the same time, she thought she'd put it to Matthew Boyle, whether he thought Morgan could be Joe, but like her she didn't think he'd taken much notice of him at the murder scene in the forest. She found Karen's number and gave her a call, no answer and no answerphone. She followed this with a call to Matt, but he didn't pick up. He was probably working, so she left a message.

Jake was distracted and Milly knew it. They spent the next three days touring the island, going to Mahon and Ciutadella, and had a long walk around the coast in the southeast corner of the island. It was nice but Jake couldn't stop thinking about Morgan Ellis. It would be mind blowing if he was Joe, and the repercussions would be huge. The day before they were due to fly back they'd settled themselves in a bar at Cala Fonts, having a couple of cocktails, and deciding where to eat. Milly smiled at Jake as she sipped on her Espresso Martini.

'Bet you're looking forward to tomorrow?'

'Why do you say that?' Jake looked quizzically at her.

'Well, these last few days have been lovely, but don't think I haven't been aware of your illicit meetings with your laptop.'

Jake made a weak attempt to defend himself at first, but Milly was too smart for that.

Jake looked wide-eyed at her. 'It's such a big thing though isn't it. Potentially? I mean Morgan Ellis, conspiracy to murder, the clean cut, whiter than white actor who everybody loves.' Milly nodded in agreement.

'You know. I love you Jake, I can say that with confidence now, and I think you love me. But I'm okay with you devoting yourself to work when you've a case like this. I mean I don't fear that you'll start an affair with Amey, although I've never met her.' Jake let out a small scream and laughed. 'What I mean is, it's cool, I get it, it's nice to see you wrapped up in your job after what you've been through.' Jake could feel his eyes water. He just leaned over and said, 'I'm so lucky to have met you.' She gave him a playful slap on the arm…and agreed with him.

CHAPTER TWENTY SEVEN

It was Sunday when Amey and Jake arranged to meet up. They booked a table at a pub near Ringwood, which was halfway for both of them. As Amey got out of her car the wind whistled through the car park, throwing up a piece of cardboard that came flying towards her. She dodged it and managed to get her hand out of the way just as her car door was blown shut. She swore none too quietly and received stares from a family parking next to her. She apologised and muttered to herself.

Jake was already sitting down when she walked in. She took her khaki-coloured mac off and unwound a dark blue scarf from around her neck and placed them on the back of her chair. 'Feel like I've been thrown into the middle of a tornado. Look at my hair.' Jake chuckled as she did look a bit of a mess.

'It's fine,' he said, reassuringly. They both ordered roast lamb and then got down to business pulling out their notebooks.

'So, what have we got so far?' Jake started, as he sipped on a lime and soda. 'Layton is killed by a lethal cyanide injection and falls out of a tree near Brockenhurst. Karen Carpenter discovers it and Joe Attwood; aka Morgan Ellis is first on scene.'

'Maybe,' Amey counters, 'he may be Morgan Ellis.'

'Okay, let's say that for now.' Jake pauses, 'you and Matt Boyle arrive, and Joe disappears. And we've established that Morgan Ellis wasn't employed by Hampshire Constabulary at the time.'

'With the jacket.' Amey interrupts. Jake realises he will need to mention every detail.

'With the jacket,' he repeats, 'and no one knows who he is. Your investigations get curtailed somewhat.' Amey nods. 'Matt loses the jacket, but a piece of paper is found on the ground with a phone number on it. Your team calls it and a builder called James answers it, says he's in London, but the call was traced to Winchester.' Jake started flicking through his notes looking for anything else Matt had told him.

'Not my finest hour that, but I think we can discount it. Personally, I think that's a bit of a red herring,'

'Do you think so?' Jake questioned. He could see that Amey seemed a little uncomfortable.

'We've no idea that piece of paper with the number on it wasn't there long before the body appeared.' Jake was surprised she was so dismissive. As if reading his mind Amey came back. 'Trust me, I was a detective for a long time. Some things you can smell without needing the evidence, and this James's phone number is one that's not got legs to help us.'

Jake conceded that she had far more experience than him, and she was probably right, but he wasn't going to forget about it. Something nibbled away at him since Matt had told him.

'But do we think other forces were at play here?' Jake questioned, not wanting to use the words, *cover up*, just yet.

'It smells a bit. I grant you that,' she said, but not elaborating further.

'Going back a bit,' Jake said, 'the New Forest murder. I can't get over how strange it was. Why go to all the trouble to string a body up on a branch? And then a fake PC waiting for it to be discovered. It's madness.'

Amey just nodded in agreement.

The pub was now rammed, and dinners were coming out thick and fast. Jake couldn't help but admire the size of a Yorkshire pudding that went past him on its way to a table in the corner. For a moment he forgot why he was here. 'I love food,' he said out loud, although it wasn't clear whether he was actually talking to anyone in particular.

'Yes, yes, don't we all lad.' Amey was quite dismissive. Jake turned back to her.

'So, you then get called to Hayling Island, nasty murder, lots of blood, discovered by a couple of the cleaners,'

'We haven't talked to them yet,' Amey stuck her hand up as she said this.

'Good point. Anyway, then you find the phone with the WhatsApp messages. We have a Bob, Lucy, Phil and Bill talking about meetings at The Green Room in Winchester, and we think that Lucy is the second murder, and Layton may be Bill or Phil?' Jake looked to Amey for reassurance.

'Yep.' She stopped short of elaborating again.

'Surely the 'Winchester' alarm bells were ringing by then? I mean you knew Layton was going there.' Jake stopped himself. 'Oh no, you didn't know until his family reported him missing, what two months later, and you were off the case by then?' Jake felt guilty as he could see the recollection of this still hurt Amey. She seemed to steel herself and flicked over a page in her own notes.

'That is correct, and I don't know what really happened after that. But Matt was kept on for a while after I'd gone. He should know a bit more.'

'I'll go see him again,' Jake said, just as their dinners arrived. Silence then took over for a couple of minutes. He took in a mouthful of roast potato and started talking again for which Amey reprimanded him and told him to not talk with his mouth full. Jake felt suitably told off. Once he'd swallowed, he looked up again, this time waving his knife, Amey frowned at him. Jake stopped chewing as something came back to him which was vital. He didn't want to look obvious but casually picked up his notes. He could feel Amey staring at him and it was as if he had been caught lying about nicking a bar of chocolate from the shop. But it wasn't he who was lying. He found what he was looking for, and his notes stated that Greg had known Amey, she'd spoken to the family a couple of times before she went on sick leave. She was still around when Layton's body was identified. Jake didn't know what to do. Should he tell her now, or should he hold on to that information. Store it up, but for now pretend she's right and she hadn't met Greg previously. Why would she say that? He found it hard to believe that Greg would say they had met when they hadn't. What was the point? Jake was losing his appetite. He decided to carry on as normal, some tiny seed of doubt lodged in his mind.

'But according to Greg, Layton's brother, they knew he was going to Menorca and Winchester, and the family told DCI Pathetic Twat this once they'd identified the body. But nothing much more seems to have happened.'

'Seems like it,' Amey said, rather resignedly. 'It seems like we as a force blamed lack of resources, the Olympics coming up etc., but actually there was a lack of will. Two unsolved murders.'

'OK, so what do we know now?' Jake said as if he was moving on to a new chapter. He let Amey take over this time, as she pushed her almost empty plate to one side, he needed to have his wits about him and really listen to what she was saying. The dynamic had shifted, and he wondered whether he was really on his own.

'So, Jane Colton, ex-girlfriend of Layton, says that he got into far-right extremism, joined this organisation called the Albion Defence Group, and would go off to Menorca. We know where he stayed and he'd visit their leader, Tommy Phillips, in this big house that you can see from your apartment balcony. Him and Jane became distant before he died. We discover that Layton used to meet with three other people, on a Friday, at The Green Room.'

Jake put his hand up.

'That reminds me, Sofia was going to get back to me as one of her employees may remember more. Sue was her name. She wasn't working when I went there, and apart from Sofia she's the only one still employed. Is DCI Pathetic Twat still around?'

'No, lad. Well, he is, but went off to Canada. Vancouver I think, years ago. Got a fishing lodge somewhere, away from it all.'

'Is he worth talking to? Will he say

anything?' Amey sat back in her chair and eyeballed Jake.

'I'd say no. I think he was a patsy, just doing what he was told. He did what he was told because he was another bloody useless detective.'

'So, we're going for the "cover up" scenario, are we?' Jake leaned forward and almost whispered this. He regained his composure and said this almost in an attempt to get her reaction. He felt his avenues were opening up further for him to explore. Amey herself, was a new one.

'It could be,' she replied.

One of the staff appeared and they were asked whether they were happy with their dinners, it seemed more than a little insincere, but they both said they were, and Jake decided on tiramisu for dessert and Amey went for banoffee pie. His appetite was quickly back. Once their plates were cleared away Jake got out the photo from Hayling Island, and the potential ID of Morgan Ellis. He'd had the photo blown up and printed out and was now more convinced it could be him. He held it up to Amey.

'So, what do we do about this one?' he asked, genuinely unsure what they should do.

'Well, it's our big one, isn't it? Potentially our entrance into the secret garden, the clue that unlocks the Escape Room.' Jake looked at Amey with amusement. It hadn't struck him before that she would know what an Escape Room is. 'If I was in the force still I'd be knocking on his door this afternoon. But we're private investigators. Well, you are, I'm the hired help.' Jake noted the hint of sarcasm. 'But we've both done our research in the last couple of days and know there's another Winchester connection. He was raised there and still lives just outside it.'

'It's too much of a coincidence, isn't it?' Jake seemed pretty clear now. 'And I was told that a young man joined this secret Friday club occasionally. He wasn't well known then, so maybe it was a job on the side for him. What's the consequences if he was just a kind of spy for them, reporting on the scenes and nothing more than that?'

'Not sure the answer is that simple, lad.'

Jake frowned, but nodded, having a pretty good idea what she was about to say. 'If he opened his mouth he might find himself, or his family, being visited by persons unknown in the middle of the night, and that could be the end of his acting career.'

'No more *Death in the Afternoon.* You know what Milly said that movie is about don't you?'

'Yes lad. And why do you youngsters never call them films anymore? Not sure I like the way we've Americanised that word.' Jake was often accused of acting older than he was, mostly by Milly, but even he would struggle to call movies films these days.

Desserts arrived and they had a few quiet minutes again, during which Jake insisted on paying for the food. He would add it to Greg's bill.

Amey was due to get back for a meeting of the Salisbury Garden Club, and Jake wanted to catch Chelsea on TV at 4.30pm, so they decided to round up.

'Right,' Jake said, wanting to take charge. 'I'll go and see Karen Carpenter again with this picture. Contact Matt Boyle to find out what happened after you left, and I will also contact Sofia again to see if this Sue remembered anything. What about you?' he could tell he was saying this as if she needed to pull her socks up. He waited for a reaction.

'Well, young man, I shall ignore your tone first, then I shall dig a bit more into the Albion Defence Group. We know Tommy Phillips has died but who else was in it at the time? I also want to find a way of getting behind the scenes as to who was pulling Pathetic Twat's strings, without having to go to him.'

They both stood up and put coats on. The wind was still racing through the car park when they emerged outside, but the cloud was breaking up and glimmers of blue sky were appearing. Jake opened his car door and remembered. 'The cleaners, we need to speak to the cleaners.'

Amey nodded, but they didn't decide who would. They agreed to speak in a couple of days. Jake drove off, knowing he needed to be sure he'd got it right that Greg had known Amey, if so, she was lying and where did that leave him, and what should he do?

CHAPTER TWENTY EIGHT

Jake arrived at 10.30am. He was viewing the apartment by the river that Milly had seen for him. He'd warmed to the idea, and he'd take it on a six-month tenancy if he liked it. Milly walked through the gate to the complex a couple of minutes later and gave him a kiss on the cheek.

'I've got the key so we can go straight in and have a mooch around. Is that okay?'

'It is on the top floor, isn't it?' Jake asked. 'I don't like the thought of anyone living above me. The sounds you might hear, especially if it's not carpeted.'

'Yeah, yeah. There's only eight of them altogether. Mostly taken up by yachtie types so far, I believe.'

There were only two floors, and Jake was relieved to see that he actually had his own access from the outside. He could go up his own stairs to get to his own door. There were two bedrooms so he could use the spare for a lot of stuff that he still had in storage. He started to realise how cramped the houseboat was for him and he'd probably outstayed his time there. The living room combined into a kitchen but was quite spacious and had a superb view over the river, then on to the Solent and Isle of Wight. The railway line was just below, and he could see the ferry port, so there was a lot to see through what was quite a large picture window. There were blinds and curtains in all rooms but apart from that it was empty and ready to move in. Milly was excited by it and Jake could tell she would be strongly encouraging him to take it. He admitted to her it was really nice and he liked it, but just wanted a couple of days to be sure. Milly nodded and assured him she would apply no pressure, but he would be a fool not to take it. He knew he would go with it, and wondered ultimately whether she would move in with him here. It did give him a better option.

Jake was back in his office at 3pm, listening to Milly on the radio. He didn't listen very often, and it was still a slightly surreal experience to hear her voice, which he thought always sounded just a little bit different. Nevertheless, a voice he knew so well but talking to thousands of people. In the age of the internet and apps she sometimes had listeners from across the world, often expats who wanted a slice of the south coast to connect with. Listening to her now, he felt proud that she was his partner. He smiled to himself and looked down as he saw 'Amey' flash up on his phone.

'Now then lad, I've been thinking about Karen Carpenter.' Amey was straight in there as normal. They had never really talked about their personal lives to each other, which he found strange bearing in mind they were both nosy, curious investigators. He decided to cross that ground next time they met up. Amey carried on, 'did she not recognise Joe as Morgan Ellis when you went to see her? I can't get an answer when I call her.'

Jake bit his lip as he'd already said he would contact Karen. He decided to let it go and thought about what she said for a moment. 'Well, obviously she never said so, but I remember she said that she didn't watch TV or read the papers.'

'What does she do for a living?' Amey asked, he could hear the disbelief in her voice.

'Marketing,' Jake replied. 'I think it was for an Italian coffee company.'

'She's in Marketing and she's not in touch with the media? Think about it, not sure I buy that.'

'It's a good point,' Jake conceded, 'are you thinking she's not as clean as we thought she might be? That she's involved?'

'Might be worth talking to her again,' Amey suggested, 'now we're pretty sure who Joe is.'

'Maybe I should stake her out for a bit, some surveillance, see where she goes and what she does.'

'It's what you dicks do, isn't it?' Jake thought she was sounding offensive. His patience was starting to wear a bit thin with her now.

'Ahh, I thought you'd been nice to me so far. About time the police detective had a go at the private detective.' Jake tried to sound jovial as he said it.

'No offence lad, but we are the professionals. Done enough surveillance myself in the old days, especially before mobile phones. The times I remember looking for a phone box that I could use to ring into the station. Don't know you're born these days.' At thirty-five years old, Jake had often heard the argument about mobiles and the internet making life easier for the millennials, but the downside was aspects of social media and the pressures that could bring. He mostly kept away from it, and when he did it was for professional reasons, rather than personal. Milly, on the other hand, was much more in tune with Tik-Tok and X, but he'd told her many times that he wasn't interested in whether Dua Lipa had just arrived in Paris or Helsinki, and especially not what Rihanna thought of Ariana Grande's appearance at the Berlin music awards in a silver dress with a long train. However, he was interested in what Morgan Ellis was currently up to.

Jake finally responded. 'Yeah, yeah, heard

it all before. Karen lives locally so I'll go and see her first before deciding whether she needs to be put under the microscope a bit better.'

'Good lad,' Amey responded. 'I'm going to have another word with George, the archivist at Southampton. He's got a good memory, see what he can tell me off the record.'

Jake put his phone back down on the desk and ran his hand through his hair. Wandering to the window it occurred to him this was his new favourite spot to think. Standing, looking out over Lymford High Street. In the end he decided to go back to the houseboat, change into shorts and t-shirt and go for a run. He picked up his laptop, coat, keys and phone and headed down the stairs and out.

The next day he drove over to Karen's house again, but decided he wasn't going to make contact, he would just see if there was any movement from the house. He had a flask of coffee, a pasty, a bar of Galaxy, prawn cocktail crisps and a can of Carabao. He parked the other side of the road but just down a bit from her house. Surveillance was not his favourite job, unless he knew there would definitely be something going on. After ten minutes he sensed that this would be a waste of time, he only saw one person actually on the street and she was a jogger. He knew that his low boredom threshold would get the better of him, so he switched on the radio and listened to a phone-in about the Post Office IT scandal. He wanted to put music on, but it never seemed right under surveillance conditions. An hour passed and all was quiet, he contemplated just knocking on the door and seeing if she was there. He weighed this up in his mind. If Karen was there, it may alert her to be on her guard if he didn't have a real motive to call. He would need to get his story straight first.

He opened the pasty, fresh from Tesco, and chewed that down, pouring himself a second mug of coffee from the flask. Just as he swallowed the last bit of pastry, which again nearly stuck in his throat, Karen's front door opened. For a moment no one came out, and then she appeared putting on a long black coat, shutting the door behind her. She put her keys in her bag and turned left, walking down the road towards Jake, but on the opposite side. He checked her in his wing mirror as she carried on down the road so did a three-point turn in the road to follow her. He decided to park up and follow on foot. If she recognised him then Lymford was a small town so he could make up any excuse why he was there. He kept at a distance of around fifty metres. She stopped and took her phone out of her bag. Jake stopped himself and pretended to check his own phone but without losing sight of her. She didn't turn around, but started running. She was approaching the station, so Jake was convinced that she was getting on a train. He would have no option but to get on as well.

Lymford Station was no more than a square Georgian brick building, with one entrance, two ticket machines, toilets, a vending machine and one platform. It was the end of the line with one track. The train was waiting, and he knew Karen would see him if she looked around. There were three carriages and she made straight for the first one. She pressed the button and went inside. Jake looked up at the departure board. It was leaving in one minute so there was no time for a ticket, and it occurred to him he would have no idea where she was going, so where would he get one to? He got into the second carriage, at the front of it he tried to peep through to see where Karen was sitting. The first few seats were empty. He had no option but to go in and hope she was facing away from the direction he was coming from. If she wasn't, and she saw him, then it was game over and he would just put his hand up and acknowledge her. No more undercover secrecy. He went through and looked ahead, he was pretty sure he could see the back of her head, sat next to a grey-haired man, about five rows up. He put his head down and was able to sit right behind them. Unseen. The train started to whirr and pull out of the station. A conductor went through the carriage but walked straight past Jake. He would have to decide where he was going so he could buy a ticket from him. He could choose any station between here and London Waterloo, but the further he chose the more expensive it would be. What the hell, he'd charge it to Greg Jones anyway.

Jake was enjoying himself now, he felt like he was a spy and a detective all rolled into one. He smiled inwardly to himself thinking it wasn't really John Le Carre stuff, but it was fun. Karen and the bloke she was sitting next to started talking, so Jake quickly got out his notepad from his jacket and scribbled down what he could hear. After a few minutes the conductor started coming down the carriage checking tickets. He got to Karen, who clearly had already bought her ticket. Fortunately, he was reading out to everyone where their ticket was taking them to, and he heard Basingstoke mentioned when he read Karen's. The danger now was if he was to ask for the same, she may recognise his voice. He decided quite literally to play dumb, and scribbled in his notepad, "return to Basingstoke please." The conductor got to him, a bald chap with glasses who Jake had seen before. He remembered that he was telling him a few months ago how his back ached and he'd taken up yoga. It helped massively and recommended the class to him, should he ever need it. He nodded at Jake who held up the piece of paper, and put his other hand round his neck, as if to indicate he couldn't talk. He mouthed 'sore throat.' The conductor frowned but seemed to understand immediately. Jake held out his card to the machine and got his tickets, the conductor wished him a speedy recovery and hoped he would feel better soon. Jake settled back into his seat and listened.

CHAPTER TWENTY NINE

George met Amey at a Costa Coffee on the outskirts of Southampton. She wasn't a fan of the coffee chain, but it was convenient. She ordered a tea while George had a Chai Latte, which produced a bit more scorn from her who had never heard of it before. She accused him of trying to be trendy, and he was too old for that. They settled at a table by the window. There were few customers at 2.30 in the afternoon.

Amey took a sip of her tea and winced, before looking at George. 'So, you know what I'm looking into, but I'd like to know the talk, especially after I went on my,' and she coughed, 'sick leave.'

George looked a bit nervous, 'Come on man, you were known as Ian Fleming around the station. Eyes and ears everywhere, storing up mental notes for when they might be useful.' George looked as though he was about to object, but then he smiled, and spoke in a whisper.

'It became a bit like the mafia if I'm honest. Believe me it was best to keep your mouth shut as you didn't know who was who, and what was what. People you thought you could trust you just didn't know. It was pretty toxic at the time.'

Amey took another sip and grimaced again. 'Matt Boyle, tell me about him?'

'I'm not sure. Your team was basically split up, some of them moved stations. Matt stayed on but was moved to other investigations. He clearly wasn't happy with what happened once you were moved off the cases, and he didn't get on with Tweddle,' Amey interrupted, 'let's just call him Pathetic Twat eh?' George nodded, 'he would often tell Matt to shut up. I remember he came down to see me once and basically offloaded. He was saying there was a conspiracy going on, he didn't like it and had to decide whether to make a stand or just go along with it.'

'And, in the end he went along with it?' Amey asked.

'I think he must have felt he had no choice. Eventually he left. He was very distracted, and you certainly got the feeling he didn't want to be there anymore.'

'Not such a bad lad then.' Amey was talking to herself. She looked up at George again who was picking his nail. 'Was there anyone else who seemed unhappy?'

'Look, there were new people in who didn't question the murders. They quickly drowned anybody else out. PT clearly had some power which was going to his head. He seemed to change from an average, fairly quiet DCI into somebody that seemed to be almost in charge around the place. He used to insult the uniform staff, was constantly talking to the Chief Super, but at the end of the day seemed to do very little.'

'How long did he last?'

'About another year, that's when he went off to Canada.'

Amey sat back in her chair. 'So, what of the Chief Super, what do we reckon?'

'Your guess is as good as mine. He wasn't someone I saw very regularly but I think he was keeping a bit of a low profile.'

'So, it all stinks a bit doesn't it George?' He nodded again. 'What about since then, has there been any talk about the murders since? Anyone say about looking into them again?'

'Only once that I remember. About four years ago a new DCI came in and we had a long chat down in my basement. She didn't like the idea that they'd been put on the shelf and forgotten about. She was really concerned about the families and how they must be feeling. I believe that she did go over the cases herself, but I could tell she was very wary next time I spoke to her. I reckon she was warned to concentrate on current cases and not to worry about them.'

'I suppose they could have gone to the cold case unit?'

'Could have,' George agreed, 'but they didn't.'

They chatted about the world in general

for a while and Amey asked him to give her a call if he thought of anything that might be useful. She also asked that he keep her and Jake's investigations quiet, which he promised to do. He was used to it.

It was late afternoon by the time Jake had returned from his train trip to Basingstoke. He was pretty sure he managed to avoid being seen by Karen Carpenter. He discovered that she worked in Basingstoke, and some of the conversation he heard involved trouble she was having with some of her Italian bosses. In reality he would have been lucky to have heard anything that would have helped his investigation, but suddenly she mentioned Jake's visit to her house, to the companion on the train. At this point he wanted to shrink into his seat, it would look even more suspicious if she suddenly realised he was there. The companion had quite a commanding voice and Jake heard him ask Karen if she'd spent all the money. She replied that it had gone a long time ago, but she didn't like lying, or at least not being entirely truthful. Jake underlined this in his notepad with the question "Paid off?" scribbled down. As they approached Basingstoke, he discovered that her companion was her brother who she hadn't seen for a while. Another piece of the puzzle which troubled him, and indicated there were probably no easy answers to this case.

Jake walked over to his white board that he'd now set up in his office and underlined the words, *'cover up'*. Now there seemed no doubt, which might make things very difficult. He felt there was no option but to try and speak to Morgan Ellis. He searched him again on the internet and established that he appeared to be in the country at the moment. *'Death in the Afternoon'* was due to be premiered in cinemas next month, and this would be here rather than in America, so the chances were he would now be in Winchester. Jake had his email, phone number and links to his social media accounts. He contemplated what to do. He also needed to tell Greg that the costs were rising and he didn't see a straightforward solution to what happened. He called Greg who didn't seem to mind. There was still money in the family, even though Brendon's had collapsed. He promised to pay now if Jake wanted to send him an interim bill.

It had become unseasonably warm. It was April 20th, and the temperature was twenty-five degrees according to the weather app on his phone. Jake arrived at Milly's with a proposal. He quickly had to backtrack and say it wasn't that type of proposal, for which Milly confirmed that she never thought for a minute it would be.

'How about an overnight stop at my uncle and aunts? Up at Micheldever?'

'That would be nice,' Milly replied. 'Haven't

seen Geoff and Fiona for ages.' She was busy cutting up mushrooms for a Bolognese, as well as trying to listen to a podcast that she had helped Elias put together. It was about life in Sweden during the Winter. Jake made a sarcastic remark about how riveting that sounded. A mushroom was launched across the kitchen and hit him on the forehead. 'Well, let's do yours then?' This was about the tenth time she'd asked him, and he knew that she would wear him down eventually.

'I'll make a deal with you. When I finish this investigation, we'll talk properly about it. It's not just me, it's how Isabella would feel. I'd also like to know that Geoff and Fiona were comfortable with it. They are still my real family as far as I'm concerned.'

'I know I get that; we can ask them when we see them.' Milly responded.

'Something else as well. I know I said about a podcast about Brendon's, and what happened to them.' Milly nodded, scratching her nose with the knife. 'Gross man! Anyway, you better not do that until my investigation is over with. I don't want to upset Greg at this stage.'

'It's on the agenda for Elias, but he's only going to do some basic research at the moment. I had thought of that.'

'Okay. Good,' Jake responded. He switched thoughts again, 'you know something?' Jake said hesitantly.

'I'm pretty bright. I know a lot of things,'

Milly added sarcastically. Jake ignored her.

'Morgan Ellis lives nearby. Just down the road from Micheldever.' She turned around looking at him.

'And you're thinking you could go and pay him a visit?'

'Well, you know him. Maybe you could pretend that you wanted to get him on the show again?'

'Oh yeah, so you tag along, and I say, "by the way, this is my boyfriend. He's a private investigator and would also like to talk to you."

Jake screwed up his face. Milly was now waving the knife at him which had been cutting up mushrooms. 'That's a no then?' There was a moment's silence and Jake conceded that was a ridiculous idea.

'From what you've told me though, you're going to have to try and talk to him.' Milly said as she turned the podcast off and got the spaghetti out of the cupboard.

'I know. We're not going to get anywhere without it now. Think I'll just have to go straight for it. Call and ask to speak to him. He'll probably knock me back.'

'Well,' said Milly, 'would it be better for Amey to do that? Maybe she's got a bit more clout, she doesn't have to say she's no longer in the force at first. Morgan seemed like a very decent bloke to me, so he might agree to meet her out of respect for her position?'

Jake pondered this for a moment, but quickly decided that his new cautionary approach to her meant that he wanted to keep her at arm's length. If he was able to talk to Morgan Ellis, then this could be an important step forward.

CHAPTER THIRTY

Morgan Ellis was exhausted. He'd only been back in England for the last couple of days and he'd done Breakfast TV, several online and newspaper articles, the Graham Norton Show and now back home in Winchester the local media were after him as well.

Death in the Afternoon was due to be premiered in two weeks and he really wanted to chill for a couple of days. This latest film worried him. The story seemed like a great idea at the time but now in reality it felt a little foolish. The memories of 2012 were almost buried, why did he not leave them there, rather than bringing them back for the sake of a good story, and a chance to enhance his career.

He sat back on the sofa with a strong coffee and let out a long sigh. His daughter, Isabel, was at school. Now six years old, he and his wife Anna had decided to make the UK their base, and so Isabel was at a private school close by. Morgan had met Anna on the set of *Acre Avenue* ten years ago. It was his first real break, and he was suddenly getting a lot of attention, including a lot of female attention, and he took advantage of this. Anna was cool towards him, but she had a slightly exotic look about her even though she was born and brought up in Newcastle. She was two years older than him with long dark hair and dark eyes. She had an almost perfect bone structure to her face with a warm smile, and everyone loved her. She rebuffed his invites to dinner three times before he managed to persuade her to join him in Pizza Express after a rehearsal. He dug into his deepest reserves of charm and humility while they shared a Margherita pizza and two beers. After two hours she agreed to spend the day with him in Brighton at the weekend. This went well but it was another three months before she slept with him. In that time, he kept his powder keg dry so as not to jeopardise his chances. They'd now been happily married for seven years having made Winchester their base, being his hometown and, as Anna agreed, in a nice part of the country. She gave up acting to set up her own business as a furniture restorer, which she found much more rewarding than slaving herself to the entertainment industry. Morgan loved his job but didn't have too much love for Los Angeles. If *Death in the Afternoon* gave him more options to work in Britain, then he would be a very happy man. He smiled to himself and could feel he was about to drift off into an afternoon nap. The house was quiet, and he had the whole evening for family time. They would have a takeaway and all three of them enjoy an evening of mindless television, probably of Isabel's choice.

Jake knew where Morgan lived and pointed out the entrance to Milly while they spent two nights with Geoff and Fiona. It was concealed quite well from the road. There was a shared drive, with one house to the right, Morgan's was straight ahead but a large wooden gate obscured any real view of the house itself. His uncle and aunt were able to provide some background information, as Morgan's parents lived in Micheldever, and they knew them before he became famous.

'His dad, Melville, does a brilliant Elvis Presley impression when he's had a few to drink.' Fiona said, as they cleared the dinner away and brought out the liqueurs. Milly was having fun, Geoff and Fiona seemed to know a lot of people and always had tales to tell. Fiona waved a bottle of Grand Marnier in one hand, and a bottle of Brandy in the other, inviting everyone to choose their tipple of choice. They all opted for Brandy. 'He's only recently retired, must be sixty, he was quite a big noise in the drinks industry,' Fiona was sliding down the side to being tipsy and Jake noticed the slight slurring of her words.

'Did you ever meet Morgan?' He asked, taking his first sip. Milly looked across at him. She was well aware that as much as Jake loved his relatives, he was also here to gain information.

'Oh yes. Lovely lad. Haven't seen much

of him in recent years,' George interjected. 'He struggled for a while, as an actor, but you'd see him help out at jumble sales and such like. I paid him once to do some gardening for me when I had my ankle operation. He was so grateful.'

'When would that be?' Jake asked.

'Oh, must have been summer 2011. I remember because I was laid up for six weeks.' Geoff replied.

'Was he quite well known in the area then?' Jake questioned further.

'No. I wouldn't say so. It was before *Acre Avenue.* I think he'd barely had a speaking part. He'd been living in London but came back to Winchester because he couldn't afford the city anymore.'

Fiona cleared her throat. 'What are you up to Jake? Why are you so interested in him?' Milly tried to conceal a smile by putting her hand to her mouth, then mischievously said the same thing. Jake flashed a quick scowl at her and weighed up whether he should tell them. He swore them to secrecy and gave them some details about the investigation, and the suspicions of Morgan's involvement. They were both open-mouthed.

'I just can't believe he could get mixed up in something like that.' Fiona said, getting up to get the brandy bottle again. She refilled everyone's glasses. Geoff was thinking.

'You say all this happened around the

spring of 2012?' Jake nodded. 'I know he moved back to London just before the Olympics, this was before *Acre Avenue* had started. I remember because Mel was telling me. I know this because I asked him whether Morgan wanted to help me in the garden again, but he'd just moved the previous week. Remember Fi, we had that party to celebrate the opening ceremony. It had been a terrible summer until then. Your mum and dad came Jake.'

'So, he had the money to do that? Move back to London?' Jake said.

Fiona stepped in. 'Yes, but he probably had an advance as he may have known about *Acre Avenue* by then. A contract may have been signed; doesn't mean he could afford to move back to London because he'd got blood money. No, no, no, I'm not having it.' Fiona waved her glass around defiantly in defence of young Morgan.

'Who else did he know around here?' Jake asked.

'I'm not really sure to be honest,' Geoff said, 'he was a popular lad, and he attended a theatre arts group. You probably don't know but the city's quite laid back when it comes to famous people, so there's been no song and dance about him. It's relatively recent that he's become well known, and now locals are proud that Morgan comes from the place. Whereas, here in Micheldever, a full six miles away, we were proud of him the first time we saw him in an advert for Dairy Milk.'

Fiona laughed, 'oh yes, he was only about twenty years old, his first time on TV, and he sang that awful catchphrase - what was it now?'

"Dairy Milk, it loves to love you and you love to love it," Geoff mimicked, trying to recreate it.

'Oh my god,' shouted Milly in disbelief, 'that was him? It was truly awful. I switched to Yorkie for a while because of it. Wish I'd realised that when I interviewed him, I would have had a bar put on the desk.'

Jake had remained quite thoughtful.

'Right, one last question. Do you know who ran the theatre group? I wonder if it's worth me thinking about talking to them.'

'Hang on,' Fiona said, 'we had a flyer through the door from them the other day, they're doing a show soon.' She got up and rummaged through a drawer, 'here we are, they're performing a musical medley, and it says choreographed by Louise Jenkins, I think she was the one who told him that he should give acting school a go.'

'Oh yes, I remember him telling me that he was a shit dancer, but Louise said his acting and singing were good.' Geoff added.

Jake made a mental note to remember the name. He decided it was time to push thoughts of the case away for the evening, so he switched to talking about his new apartment, which prompted Fiona to ask why they weren't moving in together. They reassured them that their relationship was strong, and this may be only temporary. Geoff and Fiona had seen his houseboat once, in the winter, so were pleased he was moving out of it, although Jake reiterated he would be sorry to leave it.

CHAPTER THIRTY ONE

Morgan decided to switch off his phone so he could fully envelope himself in peace and allow himself to drift off to sleep. It was an hour later that he awoke with a shake of his shoulder. Isabel wanted to play badminton out in the garden which he reluctantly agreed to. He asked her to give him five minutes. He glanced across to their kitchen area and could see Anna scrolling through her iPad. They'd recently had the house refurbished to some degree. It was built by an architect about fifteen years ago and was a little unusual but in need of some updating when they bought it. There were levels to the house rather than floors. Once through the main gate there was a front garden area with various bushes and trees which they'd strung lights across it for effect. As you went through the front door there was a wooden corridor with concealed doors on the left, these led to bedrooms and a storage area, you then entered a square living area which was mainly a playroom for Isabel. At the back was another level which was accessed by eight wooden steps. You then had a dining area directly in front and the kitchen off to the left, all open plan. To the right was the main comfortable, carpeted living area. This had a huge U-shaped sofa, storage cupboards at the back, and an eighty-inch TV stuck to the wall. This was where Morgan was resting, feeling extremely content and thinking he would stretch his five minutes to Isabel for as long as possible.

Anna put the radio on in the kitchen and started humming to Taylor Swift. He looked across and smiled. He knew that he should put his phone on but resisted it. His agent would no doubt be telling him he'd booked him somewhere else to appear. Real fame was taking some adjustment, but he knew he couldn't moan about it. He loved acting, and he'd wanted to act with the best, so the talk shows, radio broadcasts, and personal appearances went hand in hand with it. He'd always known that but was also desperate to keep his feet on the ground. That's why he was happy living just outside his hometown. There were still people around who knew him as little old Morgan Ellis, where he went to school, college and got involved in the arts. He knew the pubs well, although it never really had a club scene, he would often go to the Theatre Royal and his parents still lived up the road. There was only one cloud in his life, and that was 2012. Because of it he'd not been in The Green Room for twelve years.

Jake lay in bed looking up at the ceiling.

He could feel a tickle in his throat and hoped it wasn't the first sign of a cold. It usually was for him; a tickle became a sore throat that became a full-blown cold. Two years ago, he would have wondered if it was Covid, but these days few people tested, and why would you anymore? He decided he felt fine so got up and went to the bathroom. He ran the shower and shut the door quietly. Milly was still sound asleep. She hadn't got to bed until 2am. Her and Fiona were deep in drunken conversation when he and Geoff had gone to bed at midnight. Unfortunately, Milly wasn't quiet at 2am and insisted on biting Jake's ear and kissing his cheek. He told her to go to sleep. She'd then reached for his groin area, but he still resisted her advances. He was too tired and said he wouldn't want to take advantage of an inebriated woman. Once he was out of the shower, he was tempted to tell her he was ready now. It took a strong will for him to dress quietly and walk downstairs. Fiona was already in the kitchen.

'How are you feeling?' Jake enquired, with a smile.

'I'm not too bad. Milly got me on the rum, she's a very bad influence!'

'Oh, I don't know auntie, I think you've had many years of practice.' Fiona whacked him gently with a wooden spoon she'd just taken out of the drawer.

'Cheeky boy. I'm a respectable lady I am!'

Jake scoffed. 'The new apartment was her idea.' Fiona looked at Jake above the top of her reading glasses.

'I like her,' she said, as if she'd been asked for her opinion. 'No, sorry that sounds judgemental. I mean we had a good chat last night. She's a strong woman, knows her own mind, and I think she's good for you. I know I've said that before but it's worth saying again.'

Jake wandered to the coffee pot and took a mug down from the cupboard. He poured the coffee in, added milk, and one sugar. 'I agree. She steadies me.' Jake hesitated as he sat back down on a stool by the breakfast bar. Fiona was getting bacon out of the fridge. 'Did she tell you about the miscarriage?' Fiona sighed as she reached for the frying pan that was hanging on the wall.

'Yes, she did. She got quite emotional. I think she's been trying to hold it back in front of you.' Jake nodded.

'I know she's been putting on a stiff upper lip. I wish she wouldn't,' he said.

'It's her way of dealing with it,' Fiona said, looking at Jake, 'I get it, something similar happened to me many years ago. I believe her though when she says she's not ready for kids.'

Jake looked surprised and took a sip of his coffee. 'We're in our mid-thirties, I'm not sure we ever will be. Does that sound bad? Are we selfish?' Fiona walked over and put her arm around Jake's shoulders.

'No, love. Were we selfish in not having children?' Jake suddenly wanted the kitchen floor to open up and swallow him. He stuttered, 'I…. I don't mean….I mean do you think me and Milly are selfish? No….no sorry that doesn't sound any better. I'm only judging us, not anyone else.'

'There's plenty of children in the world, we're not short of them. You live your life in the way that makes you happy.' Fiona ruffled Jake's hair and walked back to the frying pan which was waiting for the bacon.

Jake felt very sheepish and drew circles with his forefinger on the kitchen top. 'Tell me to mind my own business, did you and Geoff want children?'

'We couldn't,' Fiona said while continuing to bustle round the kitchen, 'not after the miscarriage I had.'

'Oh, I'm so sorry, I never knew.'

'And why would you Jake my love? It's not a subject to really talk about these days. We've had a good life so far, plenty more of it left yet.'

'I bloody hope so,' Jake said, but couldn't help feeling a bit melancholy. 'Tell me, when did you miscarry? If it's not too personal to ask?'

Fiona looked down at the worktop and smiled. 'About three weeks after you were adopted. I remember thinking then I hoped my baby would turn out like you. You were so sweet.'

Jake smiled at her. 'Do you remember the

last time we were having an early morning conversation, just you and me?' Fiona waved her tongs in the air and laughed. Jake had this sudden feeling of love for his aunt that was very comforting.

'Oh yes. You'd just found out that Dave was your real father and Isabella your sister. Then you got shot in Menorca. You've certainly been living an interesting life recently.'

'That reminds me. Isabella wants us all to go to Italy in the summer. A family holiday!'

'Ooh, that sounds fun. I've been saying to Geoff I would have expected her to invite us by now. We haven't seen her since last September.'

'To be fair, I think she wanted to get the house, and herself, sorted out first. She now seems ready.'

'That would be lovely anyway.' Fiona let the bacon sizzle in the pan as she broke some eggs into a bowl, while Jake went to grab some plates from the cupboard.

'Changing the subject totally. I've been thinking back about Morgan Ellis. When he was helping Geoff in the garden that time, he came in here and I made him a cup of tea. Loved tea I remember, rather than coffee. He told me how he'd met someone who could be the answer to his money issues. I assumed he meant an acting job, but maybe it's what you're investigating now?'

Jake just nodded and said 'Umm. I fear it might be. Fear for him, not me.'

CHAPTER THIRTY TWO

Jake debated what to do. Does he speak to Amey first, or does he call Morgan and arrange a meeting? If he agreed to see him then Jake would have to get it right. He can't go straight in and accuse Morgan of anything. He will need to nurture the conversation so that he can prise information from him, but in a friendly manner. However, this is where he could do with Amey's detective skills, the gentle interrogation techniques that get the information needed. He decided to wait until he was back in the office as he really needed to be in the right environment to make the call, but he was pretty sure he would do this without her. It would be the most important call he's made so far with the investigation, and he wanted to get it right. It would be a real test for him, not least because Morgan was a high-profile person.

Amey had been on the trail of the cleaners in Hayling Island, Janice and Agu. Agu had gone back to Nigeria ten years ago and she couldn't find any more information on him. Janice was retired and living in a bungalow on the island. Amey spoke to her on the phone, but she wasn't able to provide any more information than was already known, in fact her memory seemed very sketchy and Amey wondered whether she may be suffering from a touch of Alzheimer's. Amey crossed them off her list and put her phone down on the table. She picked up her glass of red wine, despite it only just being past noon, and thought what to do next. What was her next move? She was satisfied with this outcome, nothing to worry about there.

Milly drove them home just after 1pm. Jake's throat was now very scratchy, and he was hoping that any cold he may have coming could be fought off with lots of paracetamol and water. He asked Milly to slow down as they drove past Morgan's house and saw a black Lexus pull up in front of the main gate. A smart, dark-haired woman got out before they went past and out of view of the driveway. Jake announced that he thought it must be Morgan's wife. The rest of the drive was quiet, and three quarters of an hour later they were back at Milly's. Jake felt worse. He could feel an ache come on and really felt he wanted to sleep, so he slumped on the sofa and started to feel sorry for himself. Milly offered to make him some soup, from a can, which he accepted, and then came the first sniff, which made him groan.

'I've never known you ill Jake, apart from the shooting, I hope you're not going to be a pain.' Milly said, lacking much sympathy.

'I'll be alright,' he said, shifting on the sofa. He thought that he'd like the idea of Milly looking after him again, but he doubted that her bedside manner for a cold would be the same as when he had a bullet removed from his shoulder last year. 'Man Flu can be dangerous though you know,'

'If you're that bad go to bed and I'll bring you the soup there.' Milly said, thinking that she preferred him in another room if he was going to moan on her sofa for the rest of the day.

Jake replied, 'I will do soon, once I've had some soup. Have you got Heinz Tomato?'

'Yes,' came the reply, although it sounded more than a little terse. Jake smiled slightly to himself as he heard Milly open a cupboard in the kitchen.'

He had a restless night, and when he looked across at his phone it was 6.30am. It was light and Milly was not in the bed. He pulled back the duvet as he was sweating and swung his legs onto the floor. He felt awful. He ran his hands through his hair and rubbed his face to try and bring some life back into it. He felt grey and coughed for the first time. He slowly got up and padded his way into the living room. Milly was asleep on the sofa with a spare duvet over her. He found some more tablets, got some water, and went back to the bedroom. Today would be a rest day, he was pretty sure of that. He climbed back into bed and before long he drifted back to sleep.

The next thing he knew Milly was shaking him. He groaned, moaned and turned over.

'I'm off to the station,' she said. 'I've left more water by the bed, there's more soup in the kitchen, and the tissues are just over here.' She pointed to her dressing table by the window, where the curtains were open.

'Thank you,' came the muffled reply from Jake who was talking into his pillow. 'Can you draw the curtains please? It's very bright in here.' Milly went over and did as he asked and came back and sat on the edge of the bed. She felt his forehead and pulled her hand away just before he coughed and sneezed. 'Better bring the tissues over here,' he said.

'And the magic word is…?' Milly responded.

'I'm sorry. Please.' Jake replied.

'Look, you're a bit hot, but I'm pretty sure you'll live. I gotta go now but I'll ring you before I go on air. Is there anything else you need?'

'Some Lemsip maybe?' Jake replied with a sniff, 'and hurry back.' Milly raised her eyes to the ceiling. 'I saw that,' he said, turning over again and folding the end of the pillow under his head. 'Love you Milly,'

'Yes, yes, I love you too Jake, but I don't love Man Flu, just bear that in mind.'

'You're cold and heartless,' Jake replied, again muffled as his mouth was mostly buried in the pillow. Milly kissed him on his cheek and said she'd see him later.

His phone was on silent, but as he drifted in and out of sleep, he heard it vibrate on the side table a couple of times. He knew one would be Milly and she would have left a message. At 3pm he decided to get up and go to the toilet. He picked his phone up and took it off charge. He had three missed calls, one was Milly, another was Greg, and the last number he didn't know. Looking at his texts Milly had just asked how he was, so he replied that he felt like *shit.* Greg had left a text to say he was just *phoning for an update,* so he replied saying he would give him a call tomorrow. The last number had left a voicemail message. He dialled into it. A nervous sounding woman calling herself Sue left a message:

'I understand that you're investigating a couple of unsolved murders and came to The Green Room recently. I may have some information about the so-called Secret Friday Club that Sofia mentioned. Call me on this number if you're interested in what I may know.'

Jake remembered that he was going to chase this up as Sofia had said that someone called Sue was working there at the time. He decided he would give her a call straight away, despite a pounding headache. She picked up almost immediately.

'Hello, it's Jake Stone,' he said, trying to

sound much brighter than he felt.

'Oh hi,' Sue replied. 'Thank you for calling back. Sofia said that you'd been here and enquiring about the SFC, as we called it?'

'That's right,' he replied, 'I know it's a long time ago, but I wonder what you remember about them?'

'Hang on a minute, I'll just go somewhere a bit more private.' Jake could hear the hubbub of the bar and then a door closing, then silence. 'Right, that's better. Well, there were four of them most of the time. They came in for a few weeks, same time, same day.'

'Did you know their names?' Jake asked, sniffing as he did so.

'Not that I can really remember. I'm sure the one who seemed to be the leader, or did the most talking, may have been called Rob, or Bob…. something like that.'

'Layton doesn't ring a bell?' Jake asked.

'I can't say for sure…but I don't think so. He used to wear a baseball cap, jumper and jeans, same thing every time. They were pleasant enough, but I didn't trust them. You always got the feeling they were up to something. There was a woman, very pointed features, very straight, you couldn't warm to her, never gave a tip and never said please, or thank you.' Jake was now sure this was the Hayling woman, Lucy, and maybe one of the others was very likely to be Layton. So, who were the other two? As if Sue could read Jake's mind, she said, 'the other two were always quiet. One was very smart looking, about forty I'd say, he seemed a little out of place. Nice haircut, slightly greying. I quite fancied him to be honest. On the other hand, the fourth one was a bit of a brute. He was stocky, a bit shorter than the others. Looked as if he could have been a football hooligan.'

Jake was writing this down but realised he could do with a face-to-face conversation with Sue, when his head was clearer.

'Listen, can I meet up with you in a couple of days? Come to the bar?' He asked.

'Um, yes alright,' Sue said. 'My shift finishes at 3pm on Thursday, we could talk more then.' Jake was thinking he could take some photos with him, and he remembered what Sofia had said, that occasionally a young man would join them. Today was Monday so they agreed to meet in three days' time.

CHAPTER THIRTY THREE

Jake went straight back to bed, but his mind was in overdrive. He really needed to go and see Morgan. He hadn't heard from Amey for a few days, he wondered what she was up to. He just couldn't put together a solution in his head. Why were Layton, and the woman known as Lucy killed? Where is James? Who is James? Who are Phil and Bill, or Bob for that matter? One of them was Layton. He didn't feel they were getting very far and the only thing to do was to try and see if Morgan would talk to him. He tossed and turned for another hour until he finally fell into a deep sleep.

It was 7pm when he awoke, hearing Milly move around the bedroom, closing drawers quietly and putting more water by the side of the bed. He sniffed and she looked across. Sitting down she looked a bit more sympathetic than she had earlier, asking him how he was? He wasn't aching as much, and his head was not throbbing like a sledgehammer banging down on concrete. Milly offered to help him get up and come through to the sofa. 'I've got a nice salad on the table.' Jake coughed and said that nice and salad were not usually things that go together in the same sentence, but admitted he didn't really fancy much more than that. Milly also suggested that he could do with a shower, and he promised he would shortly. A couple more tablets and a little watch of Sky Sports News would come first. Milly debated whether to change the sheets, then decided she would sleep on the sofa again and change them tomorrow. Jake would no doubt be sweating again. He was enjoying this more, caring Milly, so decided he could get away with making out he felt worse than he did, at least for the evening. Her tolerance level would probably diminish soon after that.

The next day Jake had a full on cold, but the aches had gone, and his cough hadn't got any worse. He definitely felt better, just needed to keep the tissues close at hand. He got up, couldn't hear any other movement from the apartment, and went for a pee. He then walked out into the living room where sunlight was streaming in from the terrace window. Her duvet was still strewn across the sofa, and the remains of coffee in a cup were on the side. Jake decided to sort himself out, have a shower, get dressed and go back to the houseboat. He would then make a call to Morgan Ellis. But Amey first.

Amey had kept quiet for a few days, having not contacted Jake. She'd spoken to Jane Colton again, as well as a few others. She was keen to know what Greg Jones knew first hand, so would suggest to Jake that she would set up a meeting with him. As she was putting together a ham and mustard sandwich in the kitchen, her phone rang. It was Jake. She sighed and picked it up.

'Alright lad,' she said, walking away from the breadboard.

'Hi Amey, full of cold but not too bad. How's things with you?'

'Nothing much to report to be honest. Nothing of any use from the cleaners,' Amey hesitated, 'look, I was going to speak to Greg myself. Is that ok with you?'

Jake considered it momentarily, 'of course, I haven't really spoken to him for a while.'

'I was just thinking that maybe he's had time to have another think and I might be able to get him to remember something.'

'Sure,' said Jake, he hesitated and thought about mentioning her slip up with regards to not having met him before but decided to let it play out. 'For my part I'm going to try and set up a meeting with Morgan,' he stammered slightly and then blew his nose. 'Also, I was thinking it would be better if just the one of us saw him if he agreed to it.' There was a pause and Jake wondered whether Amey was still there.

'Fine,' she said, he was sure he detected a touch of petulance in the reply, 'if you think that's best. You'll probably be very lucky to get hold of him anyway.'

'Exactly. I know it will be a miracle, but

I'll give you an update straight away if we do manage to meet.'

'Fair enough lad. I'll come down to Lymford early next week and we can put our heads together.'

'Cool,' Jake said, a word that he knew would provoke a frown from Amey if he could see her, but he was feeling provocative.

Morgan was on domestic duties. The sun was warm and the limited grass they had at the back of the house badly needed its first cut of the year. Tomorrow he was in London, and then he had three days before the madness would completely take over. He would have little time at home for a while with *Death in the Afternoon* being premiered and released across the country, then all around the world in the next few weeks. The Leicester Square premiere was in nine days' time on Thursday the 16th of May, a date that had been etched in his memory for months, and one which he was feeling increasingly nervous about. He decided to just wear his shorts in the hope he got a bit of a tan before the event. He wasn't keen on any fake tan, although his legs were not going to be on display at the premieres. He knew he had succumbed to celebrity vanity.

Morgan sat down on the garden sofa, facing the house, and the familiar ring from his mobile phone cut through the peace. This one being the chime of an unrecognised number.

He picked it up and thought twice whether to accept before thinking there was no reason why he shouldn't. He just hoped it wasn't something that was going to ruin his day. The first thing he heard was a sniff, and a clearing of the throat.

'Morgan Ellis,' was the opening line that Jake heard. He suddenly felt very nervous that he was talking to a celebrity. He knew that Morgan had a good reputation so hoped he would find him approachable.

'Oh, hello Mr Ellis,' he had a moment's indecision whether to call him by his first name but decided that a little formality and respect would be wise. It is a wonder what thoughts can go through your head in a split second when the adrenaline is flowing. 'Please excuse me for calling, but my name is Jake Stone.' He thought for another split second he would mention that his partner was Milly Lucas, from The Crunch radio station, who interviewed him last year. He decided this would not add value, and Morgan may not remember her. Jake carried on, 'I know you're a very busy man at the moment, but I'm a private investigator and wondered if you could help me with something.' There was a painful pause.

'With what exactly Mr Stone?'

'Well, I think it may be better if we could meet up. I know you won't have a lot of spare time but it's very important.' Jake could feel his heart rate increasing.

'Well, you're going to have to give me a bit more than that.' Morgan replied, with just a touch of arrogance.

'Of course. Well, I've been enlisted by a chap called Greg Jones. His brother was Layton Jones. He was found dead in the New Forest in early 2012, murdered.' Jake waited a moment and thought he heard a slight gasp from the other end, he carried on, 'and it was never solved. I'm trying to get him and his family some closure, and you've come up as a person that could have some information to help with this.' Jake decided to leave it there awaiting a response from Morgan. There was further silence, and then he could hear a rustle as if he was moving around. When he finally spoke, his tone had changed, and he was almost whispering.

'I don't think I can.' Morgan said. Jake was feeling a bit more confident now that the opening exchange was done.

'I think you can Mr Ellis, and it's extremely important to the family. I also have a former detective helping me.' He knew this came across as quite bullish, but Morgan wasn't going to agree if it didn't come across that he somehow had a persuasive angle.

'Right…right, let me think.' There was a tremble in his voice now. 'I'm here on Thursday, and that's it for quite a while. My wife and daughter won't be here for most of the day. Can we meet here, say 11am. Do you need the address?'

'That's fantastic,' Jake replied, with as much enthusiasm as he could muster. 'I know where to come, my uncle and aunt live quite close by, you may remember them, Geoff and Fiona Boothroyd, live up at Micheldever.'

'Yes, yes……yes I do,' Morgan responded but sounded very distant.

'Well, thank you again, and I look forward to seeing you on Thursday.

Jake put his phone down on the kitchen table feeling like he'd scored the winning goal in the Champions League final. He punched the air several times and pranced around for thirty seconds. He knew it wasn't very cool, but he really didn't care.

CHAPTER THIRTY FOUR

Morgan looked at his phone, knowing this was the call he'd been expecting for twelve years. There was a tinge of relief in a strange sort of way. The question was how is he now protected? Jake Stone wasn't police; he was a private investigator. On his own he can't convict him of anything, but who's this former detective he's talking about?

Morgan wandered back to the sofa and fell into it. Anna knew about his past; he told her years ago when drunk one night. She was shocked, and for a while it could have been the end of their relationship, but once they'd worked that through, he'd felt so much better telling her. It was a huge relief, but it also meant that he would always have to trust her. They'd only talked about it twice since, but half-jokingly she reminded him that she had something on him for the rest of his life.

Morgan always reconciled with himself that he didn't commit any murders, he was in the dark about a lot of it, but he knew there was a rationale why they had happened. He wished Anna was here now so he could tell her about the phone call. He wondered whether this investigator knew about the other two murders. He held his hand out to pick up his coffee cup from the garden table, his hand was shaking so he decided to leave the cup there. As he stood up his legs also went to jelly. The watch on his left hand, bought from an expensive shop in New York, told him it was the 7th of May. Morgan thought he'd remember this date for a long time to come and decided that he would tell the truth on Thursday, as he knew it. He had to for his own sanity.

The M3 was getting busier. The weather was good, and the holiday traffic was increasing. Roadworks meant he had to drive through Winchester and the one-way system was a nightmare. Jake had a busy day. He'd arranged to see Sue in the afternoon at The Green Room, but wondered if this wouldn't be so crucial now that he was meeting Morgan first. He drove past it in the city centre on his way. It looked quite busy with a few people sitting outside having brunch. Coming back out of the city he knew where he was and parked outside Morgan's large wooden gate. He rang the buzzer and the door opened. He walked up the path to the front door. Morgan was waiting for him, looking shorter than he imagined, a little dishevelled, but Jake admitted to himself, undeniably handsome and much like he could be the man in the photo thought to be PC Joe Attwood.

Morgan greeted him with a handshake which was firm, and he then guided him through the house to the garden at the back. There was a pot of coffee on the garden table and two cups. As they went up the steps to sit down Morgan remarked 'that it wasn't very often they got the cafetiere out these days. We have got one of those all singing, all dancing professional coffee makers, but hardly ever use that either. It's the Nespresso we use all the time. Although I prefer tea most of the time, Anna never drinks it.' Morgan smiled weakly as they sat down. Jake was a bit nervous but could tell that the man three feet to his left was more so. He knew he needed to go through the usual pleasantries about it being a lovely home etc, and once that was done, and the coffee poured, he got out his notebook with his list of questions, and a pen to record their conversation.

'So, first of all thank you for seeing me. I realise this is not a great time for you with the film about to come out.' Morgan nodded. 'As I said on the phone, Greg Jones called me about Layton, so I'll outline what I know.' Jake then went through the details without mentioning Hayling Island at this stage. He talked about Karen, the fake policeman, and Amey and Matt turning up at the scene. Jake then asked Morgan directly what he could tell him about it.

Morgan looked down at the sofa and played with the fabric, pulling it between the thumb and forefinger of his right hand. He went to speak, but the incoherent first words came out as a squeak. He cleared his throat and started again.

'In 2012 I was very much a struggling actor. I couldn't afford to stay in London and came back here, dossing at one of my parents' apartments they owned in town. I did some bits and pieces, helping out Louise at Winchester Theatre School, which is where I started out. I helped out at local groups, did a small bit of acting with them, and even took up some gardening jobs.'

Jake interjected, 'I mentioned it on the phone, but at this point I have to declare a bit of a coincidence. My uncle and aunt are Geoff and Fiona Boothroyd, they live in Micheldever. I believe you did some gardening for them years ago.'

Morgan raised his eyebrows, the dark look on his face brightened, but only briefly. 'Yes, I remember them. Friends of my parents.' The dark look quickly reappeared. Jake sensed that Morgan seemed keen to tell his story, which relaxed him with the thought that this could go well.

Morgan carried on. 'One night, around October 2011 I got speaking to this bloke called James, he was working at The Green Room. Another struggling actor he'd been in Casualty for a bit, and Poirot, but he was out of work having given it up. I was on the verge of doing that myself,' Morgan looked up at Jake with a wry smile. 'Look at me now, just proves you've got to keep working at your dreams until there is no hope.'

Jake was scribbling away. 'Can I just ask, this James, do you think he knew who you were anyway, and deliberately engaged you in conversation?'

Morgan pondered for a bit, 'to be honest I couldn't say. That was a long time ago and I don't remember the exact circumstances. He could have done, but I was only really known for that chocolate commercial, so I don't think I was easily recognisable, but who knows?'

'I'm thinking that he knew you were an actor who was having a bit of a bad time and needed money?'

'With all due respect Mr Stone, you're running ahead with the storyline here. I realise your investigations must have revealed there was someone called James involved but let me tell you my version of events.'

Jake felt suitably chastised and apologised, allowing Morgan to carry on.

'So, we got talking and after a while he said that he knew how to make some good money, in a short space of time, and although what I may see wouldn't be nice my role would be observational. My first thought was no, but we talked more, and I liked him. He didn't seem like a crook. We were in similar situations and, crucially, he convinced me that there was no link to organised crime. Quite the opposite it would be doing a service to the country, and I would be fully protected.'

'What did he mean, did he expand on this?' Jake asked.

'Nope, I asked but he wasn't giving, I never knew any more than that. He was my contact, and I would get my instructions from him.'

'So, you agreed to go along with it from there?'

Morgan leant forward and tapped the table with his two forefingers. Jake could see a vein sticking out from his neck. He turned to look at Jake properly for the first time, putting his right leg flat on the sofa, foot tucked under his left knee, trying to get comfortable and relaxed.

'I concluded that whatever was going to happen was going to happen anyway, and my role was damage limitation.'

'An interesting perspective. It's still conspiracy to murder.' Jake exclaimed.

'I didn't really know that then, I was still young and naive.'

'So, what did you know before Layton's death?'

'Well, it was a while before I heard anymore. Then I was asked to meet with this chap called Bob in The Green Room. James worked there, and I went four or five times. This bloke had evil written all over him, really fucking nasty. He was always there with three others, but Bob was the one who seemed to be calling all the shots.'

'Did you know what they were meeting about?' Jake asked.

'Not really. I assumed they were some sort of secret group, and this was where they planned everything.'

'So, why did they want you to go there, what was the point? James was your contact.'

'I've thought about this a lot over the years. I think it was to scare me, make sure I complied and kept my mouth shut. They were warming me up, or rather Bob was. Later I realised they weren't what I thought they might be.'

'Did you know the names of the others?'

'Bill, Lucy and Phil.' Morgan replied.

Jake nodded; this confirmed the names on the WhatsApp group found on the phone in Hayling Island.

He cleared his throat. 'And did you recognise Layton from the three?'

'Yep. That was the shock when I saw the body, Bill was Layton so I couldn't figure out why he was killed. As far as I knew, Layton was part of them.'

'So, what were you being told when you met them?'

'Not a lot. Just to be ready, wait for James, it's important work etc.' Morgan paused and scratched his head as if he had fleas in his hair. 'Then I got the call in February 2012 to go down to the New Forest.'

Jake just nodded for him to carry on. 'I was told to get an authentic looking policeman's uniform, which I borrowed from Louise's wardrobe collection, to go to this spot in Brockenhurst and await a call, which is what I did. I was told that I needed to be first on the scene to make sure the body was dead, and try and clear up any loose ends, and then to get away before the real police arrived.'

Jake frowned. 'But how did they know that you could do that as soon as the body was found? Was somebody else watching as well?'

Morgan shrugged. 'The killer was there somewhere, whoever it was, but they knew that a woman went running past the spot every day at the same time, so she was innocently lined up to discover the body.'

'Karen Carpenter?' Jake said, which Morgan nodded to.

'And then that was my first mistake. I felt sorry for her, it was cold, so I gave her my jacket, then the police arrived, and I had to make a quick exit without getting the jacket back.'

'So, was it you that got it back?'

'Do you mind If I call you Jake?' Morgan asked, 'and call me Morgan.'

'Of course,' Jake replied.

'Jake, I was just told it had been retrieved. I

didn't have to do anything.'

'Did you know who and how?'

'No, but I really didn't want to know.'

Jake cleared his throat. 'What I don't understand is that Layton was seemingly tied to the branch, which broke, just before Karen came by. And one person alone couldn't have tied him up there?'

Morgan shrugged. 'I realise that, but the details I didn't know. I think, and I stress I only think, the branch breaking wasn't bargained for, it just came down coincidentally, just before Karen got there. The branch wasn't high, so they assumed she'd see the body tied to it.'

'But why?' Jake asked, his face screwed up so that his eyebrows were almost meeting. 'Why bother?'

Morgan shrugged again and said, 'because they were sickos, twats, idiots, scum. They were getting a kick out of it. I just don't know. By this point I was already regretting it. Madness, total madness.' He was looking distressed and upset. Jake allowed a pause for silence while Morgan composed himself. He looked at Jake and scratched his head then looked at his watch. Jake had so many questions and wondered whether he was going to be told that was it for now. Morgan stood up and reached for the coffee cups.

'I really want to tell you everything I know. I feel safe to do that, we have at least another hour before my wife is back, so another coffee?'

Jake nodded, 'Yes please. Americano if you're doing Nespresso this time.'
Morgan smiled and walked down to the kitchen. Jake could see him through the window making a phone call.

CHAPTER THIRTY FIVE

While Jake and Morgan were talking, Amey was on her way to meet Greg. She was keen to understand exactly what he knew about Layton's life, up until the point of his death. She pulled into the car park opposite a Starbucks, just outside Southampton. She hated Starbucks, felt they were a creeping stain across the country, trying to Americanise the country bit by bit.

Even she had given into the warmth and ditched her thick jumper for a thin green top and green cardigan. She wore a dark blue and green tartan skirt, so she looked as though she'd come straight off the farm, having shot grouse in the morning. Amey had never been on a farm in her life. She crossed the busy road and pushed the door open and saw Greg sitting by the window. He would have watched her coming in. She'd met him once before, as the family only came forward just before she left the investigation in 2012, but she recognised him from the files and Jake's description. He also knew her from the little information he had at the time, as being the DCI who first went to the scene of Layton's death. They both put their hands up and Amey mouthed that she would get a tea.

'Hello lad,' she said as she sat down. 'They tried to sell me a Chai Latte, whatever that might be. Just tea I said.' Greg smiled nervously, and agreed the choice could be too much.

'Anyway, we never really crossed paths to talk in 2012, did we? I spoke to your parents a couple of times, but, as you know, I'm now working with Jake Stone on the investigation. The one I never got to see through at the time.'

'Yes, he's been very good so far,' Greg said, brushing off the crumbs from his t-shirt which was white with a smiling yellow face emoji on it.

'We're getting there,' Amey said, reassuringly. 'What I want to go over is what you knew about the Albion Defence Group and who was in it?' She stirred her tea, took a sip, and grimaced.

'Nothing really. I'd heard of them, from the news and the demonstrations they used to hold, but until Jake told me about Layton's alleged association with them, I had no idea.

'What about Jane Colton, did she ever talk to you about them?'

'No. I didn't really know her very well. She did leave a message on my phone yesterday, but I haven't called her back yet.'

'Do you know what she wanted?' Amey asked, looking concerned.

'She just said to have a chat about how the case is going to find Layton's murderer.'

Amey pushed her tea to one side, deciding

it was undrinkable. 'Is there anyone that you know of from the time that Layton was in the ADG? Any names he mentioned?'

'No, it's like I said to Jake, he was pretty distanced from the whole family, and in hindsight it seems to be from the time that he really got in with them. I'm sorry I'm pretty useless, aren't I?

'No lad, you could throw that back at me and Hampshire CID for not finding his killer in the first place. It's just important we don't miss any tiny detail, that we understand who knew what, as well as what everyone didn't know. It's all really important.'

'There's one thing, and this came from my parents who are now in Australia. My mum said that Layton told her something once on the phone.'

'Go on,' Amey said, leaning across the table towards him.

'He told her that he may not always be good, but he was trying to be good now.'

'What do you think he meant by that?' Amey asked.

'Well, we thought it was to do with Jane, that maybe he hadn't been the model boyfriend and was trying to win her back, looking to demonstrate how he may have changed.'

'Well, maybe that was true.' Amey stated. 'What was he like as a kid?'

'Pretty gentle to be honest, but he could

be quite opinionated. His best friend was an Iranian boy at primary school, then when he was about thirteen they had a big falling out, and he seemed to start disliking any foreigners that were in the school. But then later he had a girlfriend for a while, and she was from Poland.'

Amey frowned at him. 'So white was ok but not black?'

'I don't know about that. I just never saw any real hate from him towards other races, he just didn't mix with them.'

After about twenty minutes Amey could see there was little more to be gained from the conversation so felt satisfied she'd got all the information they would get from Greg. She went back to her car quite happy that he, and the cleaners had no more to offer the case.

CHAPTER THIRTY SIX

Morgan came back out from the kitchen with an excited little dog following in his wake.
'May I introduce you to Lola, we've not had her long. We rescued her with the help of the Dogs Trust.' Lola wagged her tail and looked longingly at Jake. He reached down and gave her a stroke, then he put her head between his hands and gave her a little shake.

'She's lovely. What is she?'

'A Spoodle,' Morgan replied. He was smiling. The atmosphere had completely changed, and you could tell he loved that dog.

'Crikey, there's a cross breed for everything these days.'

Morgan smiled again, 'Crikey! That's not a word you hear very often these days.'

Jake laughed, 'well I've definitely been known to say stronger words, just ask my partner, Milly.' Jake suddenly realised he hadn't mentioned that Morgan and Milly met not long ago. 'Another confession I'm afraid. Milly is a presenter on The Crunch, she interviewed you last year.' Morgan thought for a moment and then his face lit up.

'Yes, yes, I remember, we had quite a laugh.

I love that station, always have it on when I'm down here. Now you come to mention it, she talked about you. Shit,' Jake could see a lightbulb go on, 'you're the bloke who was shot, found out you had a long-lost sister, and a dad who was killed in front of you. That's sick buddy.'

'She told you then?' Jake looked a little embarrassed.

'Yeah, she was telling me about it. We said it would make a good drama.'

'She wants me to do a podcast to talk all about it. Not sure I'm ready for that yet.'

'Oh, you should man, it sounded like a riveting story. You could write a book.'

Lola was still wagging her tail frantically and Morgan looked genuinely interested in what Jake had gone through. He had a feeling that people may be right, perhaps Morgan is the nicest actor in Britain, but he had a job to do. They settled back down but the ambience was just a little less forbidding.

Jake got his notepad ready again. 'Tell me about the woman in Hayling Island?'

'That was gruesome. So, after Layton, I went home and waited for James to contact me, which he did, and told me to hang on and wait for him to phone again. He gave me a bit of a telling off for the jacket but said that it was all sorted. A week or so later he told me to go to Big Lake Holiday Park on a particular day. I can't remember exactly what day it was. Basically, to mingle with the other policemen.'

'What about the shock of discovering Layton was one of the people you met in The Green Room. Did you mention that to him? Question it?'

'He just brushed it off, telling me not to worry about it, it was better I didn't know.'

'But it must have scared you?'

'Even more than I was already you mean!'

'Yes, I suppose so.'

'It did. I wanted to run away, deeply regretting getting involved, but I felt there was no choice but to see this through.' Morgan picked at the fabric of the sofa again. 'James was quite convincing at reassuring me I would be alright and doing my country a service.'

Jake was turning pages in his notepad furiously.

'Going back to Hayling, couldn't the other policemen have easily picked you out as someone they didn't know?'

'That was my worry, but apparently in major incidents like this the bobbies could come from a number of stations. Anyway, I got the call to go and join the others, but also they said that a phone had been dropped when the killer was getting away. He was nearly caught I believe. My job was to try and retrieve it, but there was no chance. I was shooed away by the DCI.'

'Amey Lorimer?' Jake added.

Morgan nodded. 'Best thing I could do then

was to slink away while no one was looking. I went back home again and waited for James to call. By this time I was bloody terrified and wanted it all to end. Then I heard the details of it on local TV and couldn't believe the way she was killed. No one deserves that.'

'I've seen pictures, it's truly shocking.' Jake was shaking his head. He tapped his pen on the notepad. 'Was Karen Carpenter anything to do with this?'

Morgan frowned, 'I really don't think so. She was used, but in a different way to me. But hey, what do I know?'

Dark clouds were lumbering across the skyline, blocking out the warm sun. Lola padded back indoors thinking this stranger is ignoring me now, so time for a little sleep.

'So Jake, you haven't told me how you tracked me down? I've always expected it, but I didn't know who they would be. I knew at some point this would happen.' Morgan looked almost tearful. 'It's been that monkey on my back for twelve years.'

Jake hesitated.

'It was Milly. She saw a photo from Hayling which you were in, not clearly but she thought it looked like you. Me and Amey did a bit of digging and convinced ourselves it was you. We had a little bit of help from the fact there seemed to be a Winchester connection through The Green Room.

Morgan was now visibly upset and Jake was now feeling quite sorry for him. 'I used to love that place, but I can't go there now. Too many bad memories.'

Jake pondered as he took a sip of coffee. Morgan was looking at him. He hadn't actually learnt anything much so far and couldn't decide whether he was holding back, or that he really didn't know much. He seemed genuine.

'Can I ask? You made a phone call when you went inside for the coffee. Who was that to?'

Morgan actually smiled. 'As you've gathered, I'm not very good at this deception game. Not clever to make a call when you can still see me.'

Jake raised his eyebrows.

'Well, if ever I was in trouble I was given a number to call, if I needed help and maybe had a situation where questions were being asked.'

'And?' Jake asked.

'And it went to voicemail, and I cut the call off. I thought I'd hear you out more first. I just have no idea what the best thing is to do, but don't forget James told me I would always be protected.'

'What exactly do you think that means?'

'James always assured me I'd be alright, no matter what happened. That's been the hope I've clung on to despite the guilt of it all. I can only think there were circumstances that I would never know about, which meant it was a good thing that they died.'

'Do you really think that?' Jake asked.

'I have to. I really have to.' Morgan replied, his facial expression was almost painful.

They both checked their watches and knew that time was running out.

'I may need to contact you again Morgan?'

'I get it, but time will be short, but you can always ring me.'

'Okay, a couple more things before I go. Any idea where James is now?'

'No, but he was very friendly with one of the barmaids in a pub in town, the Royal Oak. I think her name was Emilia, Spanish, from Menorca I believe. I met her a couple of times.'

Jake smiled inwardly. 'And was Lucy the woman killed on Hayling Island?'

'Almost definitely, from the pictures I saw on TV after her death.' There was a long hesitation as Morgan wrestled with his own thought process. Jake raised his eyebrows sensing this and waited for him to carry on. 'And Phil was the Andover one.'

Jake looked surprised. 'Andover! There was a third?'

Morgan just nodded solemnly.

CHAPTER THIRTY SEVEN

Not for the first time, Jake looked across to his left as he approached the village of Brockenhurst. Just over there, beyond a small car park, was where Layton was killed. He drove past it frequently, and each time he couldn't prevent his eyes glancing that way. It was twelve years ago but maybe some new evidence will miraculously appear through the forest of oak trees which dominated the landscape in this part of the forest. He felt the need to go back and have a look around, he wasn't sure which tree it was exactly so would try and get a better location from Amey.

He passed a large hotel to his left which was very close to the murder scene, set back from the road, he always imagined it to be populated by affluent Londoners wanting their spa break for the weekend. The New Forest was diverse, many born and bred locals were almost scraping a living in an expensive part of the country. Many other people had large second homes, or ones they've retired to, and these people supported the numerous Michelin starred restaurants that dotted the area. Jake felt just a little guilty, he came into money, moved here and lived on the coast in a town that was considered one of the most expensive in the country to live in. He was aware that many born and bred local young people could only ever dream of owning property there. Jake tried to support local charities so he could feel he was giving at least a little something back, but it was probably a futile attempt to ease his own conscience. This was probably another topic that could be covered in a podcast but would need to be handled sensitively.

Once again, the crossing barriers came down as he approached the railway line. Another five-minute wait while a train sped through to Southampton one way, or Bournemouth the other. His thoughts clicked back to Morgan, and the third murder, which he now knew had never been classed as a murder, or if it had, was completely hushed up. Bearing in mind where it happened this was unlikely. A busy office with loads of staff hanging around. This was Phil, so three of the four known by the staff at The Green Room as the Secret Friday club were killed in 2012.

He'd popped in to meet with Sue after Morgan, but her memory was not good. She remembered them, but descriptions were poor, and she clearly hadn't identified Morgan as the well-known actor he now was. Jake soon had the feeling that she didn't have any riveting revelations that she tried to pretend she had, so he made quite a quick exit, still reeling from Morgan's own revelation.

The barrier lifted and Jake drove on to Milly's. She wouldn't be back for a while yet. He'd more or less packed up the houseboat and lived in her apartment now. He was due to move into his brand new apartment next week. It wouldn't be easy to research Phil as Morgan had no idea what his real name was, but he knew it wasn't really reported at the time, and so it was assumed that he died of natural causes. He would call Amey about that as well.

The first drops of rain started to fall from a very threatening sky as Milly drove across the railway line at Brockenhurst, two hours after Jake. By the time she got to Lymford it was like a tropical storm, the raindrops bouncing off everything they fell on, creating little waves of wet that ran down the sides of the road in ever increasing depth. Jake saw her coming and poured a glass of wine ready as she came through the front door.

'Oh, you darling,' she said, throwing her shoes and coat off, and shaking herself.

Jake smiled and kissed her on the cheek. 'In the interests of client confidentiality I shouldn't tell you about my day…. but I can't help myself.'

'Let me sit down,' she said, 'I'm dying to hear about Morgan. How is he?'

'He remembers you and sends his regards.' They both sat on the sofa as the smell of homemade curry wafted through into the room, reheating on the hob. 'Have to say, he seemed like a nice bloke who got in too deep. He's now scared, in fact I think he's been scared for twelve years, and here he is, becoming a major star, and he wants to unburden himself knowing it could kill his career if it all came out, potentially leading to a prison sentence. I actually came away feeling so bloody guilty, and hoping he comes through this okay.'

Milly took a big sip and relaxed, her head settling into the back of the sofa. Jake told her about the third murder, which he'd got a bit of a quick result on.

'I traced the local Andover paper to late March 2012, and a report of a man dying from a heart attack at the offices Morgan mentioned. Only a short piece and the name wasn't known, but it confirms he was right. I'm sure a bit more digging will tell me who he is and I can join some dots together.'

'What about this James? Anything on him?' Milly asked.

Jake shook his head, I've got a description now from both Morgan and Sue, but that was twelve years ago so not sure it's going to be much use.' Jake got up and checked on the curry. After giving it a stir and putting it on the lowest heat, he plonked himself back down on the sofa.

'I just wish I could understand why they were killed?' Jake was feeling exasperated. 'It seems to me they were all probably members of the Albion Defence Group, and from what Morgan was saying it sounds as though it may have been an undercover job.'

'MI5 or something?' Milly suggested. Jake looked at her and raised his eyebrows.

'It's a theory. But why make it so messy? They would do it with the minimum of fuss.'

'I agree but might explain why the investigations never seemed to go anywhere. Hushed up.' Milly stood up to go and have a look at the curry in the kitchen. She stopped in the doorway. 'What if the three were ratting on the ADG, the ADG found out and killed them to shut them up?' Jake looked at her and frowned but started running the theory through his head.

'So, James was supposed to be looking out for them, working for the establishment, and Morgan was the lookout? No, that doesn't make sense because there would be no need to have Morgan.'

Milly came back into the room. 'That's true. So, Morgan was inadvertently working for the bad guys? Also, presumably was James?'

Jake nodded and ran both his hands through his hair.

'You know that James was also friendly with a Spanish barmaid, from Menorca, where Tommy Phillips ran his little show.' He got up this time, wandered around the room, before topping up his glass of wine. 'If they were moles,

I still would have thought the ADG would have wanted to do away with them, quietly.'

'So, you're thinking there's another dynamic going on, like some sort of serial killer?' Milly asked.

'Well, yes,' Jake was hesitant, 'Is it James?' That would kind of make sense. Morgan's there to clear up his mess.'

'Errr, could be,' Milly agreed. 'Not really the way a plain old simple serial killer works though, is it?'

Jake felt a bit worn out and started to wonder if he would ever get to the bottom of it. Amey worried him now, something there wasn't quite right.

'Right. Enough for today, I've got a call with Morgan in the morning then that's my last chance with him. He's going to give me more detail about Andover. Then I'm going to see Amey in Salisbury, give her the lowdown, and then we're going to work bloody hard in trying to trace James.'

'I wonder how this will all work out for Morgan?' Milly said, picking up the TV guide from the table. 'Look, he's got a feature in here, talking about the movie.'

'He's clearly a decent bloke,' Jake said as he prepared to put the rice in the microwave and get the naan bread out of the oven. 'I have a hunch he'll be alright, but if it all goes public then the world may well frown on it. He'll be tainted goods, no more Hollywood for him.'

CHAPTER THIRTY EIGHT

Jake put the phone down on Morgan after half an hour of talking. It threw more people into the mix. Who's the bloke known as Dan, who met Morgan at the offices in Andover? Now the death can no longer be considered natural causes, and he didn't have a heart attack. But, on the other hand he might be easier to trace and adding another character into the sequence of events opened up the possibilities more. Morgan was pretty sure that was it, there were three people as part of the operation, and he was then free to get on with the rest of his life. He'd done his bit and he got paid.

Jake was also pretty sure that the dead person here must be Phil, from The Green Room's Secret Friday Club, and so that would link everybody up. If the fourth person was Bob, then what exactly was his role? Was he a friend to them, a colleague, a comrade? Or was he setting them up? Jake suspected the latter, so he and James were coordinating their demise. Morgan had kept an eye on the local papers and the internet afterwards and didn't find any trace of what happened in Andover. This seemed odd, you would have at least thought there would be a mention of someone having a heart attack in such a public place. Again, it was unfathomable why you would kill someone there, with potentially dozens of witnesses. Just like last year, Jake felt he was treading on the back of a big story that didn't want to be revealed. The stakes must have been high.

He checked his watch. He'd agreed to see Amey and give her a full update face to face. He was going to meet her in the Cosy Club in Salisbury and got there promptly at 2pm. With it being a Friday there appeared to be several people who had finished work for the week. There was a boisterous group sitting close to the bar. Five men in their fifties, and two younger ones, from the conversation he could hear they appeared to be the sons of one of them. One bloke was lamenting the state of 'Broken Britain,' and eulogising on the need to get the current government out of power. Another was talking about the new neighbours who had moved in, and how they weren't going to fit in. One thing was clear, this group weren't on their first pints of the day, and they were enjoying themselves. Jake hoped he'd be doing that in twenty years' time.

Amey suddenly appeared on his left shoulder.

'I'll have a glass of Chardonnay lad, as it's Friday,' she said, taking off her familiar brown mac, 'and I'll grab a table over there, in the corner.'

'Ok, ma'am,' Jake replied, feeling he knew how Matt Boyle must have felt when he was working with her.

Jake ordered a shandy and brought the drinks to the table. He put them down and quickly grabbed a tissue from his pocket.

'The dregs of a cold,' he told Amey as he sat down. She looked particularly stern today.

'Well, I've got some big news after my visit to Morgan.' He sat back, sniffed again, and filled her in on his last couple of days.

'Well, that's an interesting turn of events,' Amey said, looking puzzled.

'Isn't it?' Jake thought she'd be more enthused.

'Have you found anything out yet on this Andover murder?'

'No, haven't really had the chance yet. That's a job for later.'

Amey looked thoughtful, then said, 'I'll do that. Why don't you concentrate on James, and maybe this girl from Menorca he was seeing?' I think we've exhausted other people. Not sure anyone's got any more information to give from the New Forest and Hayling Island ones.'

Jake looked at her. Don't forget this Dan character? 'If you don't mind me saying, you seem a little defeatist. Not the usual Amey Lorimer?'

'I'm sorry lad, just a few things on my mind.' She let out a small chuckle but didn't say anything else. Jake decided he would take the opportunity to ask her a little more about herself.

'So, tell me. How long were you a detective?'

'Oooh,' she said, looking slightly taken aback but quickly composed herself, 'about fifteen years, came down from the Met in 2008. Joined Hampshire but decided to live over the border here in Wiltshire.'

'What made you come down here? I mean it's lovely as I discovered, but life in the Met would never be dull.' Jake thought about last year. He knew there were good people there, Steve Crumpler and Jenny being ones he met through his own family investigation. However, the Met had been through a bit of a rough time and didn't have such a great reputation.

Amey sighed. 'My husband, Adam, was killed. He wasn't in the force but was walking home late one night and just one bullet killed him. Severed his jugular. Half an inch to the left and it would have flown straight past him without touching.'

Jake shook his head and let her carry on. 'He was an accountant, boring dull accountant, he'd got off the tube at Clapham after a few drinks with some colleagues, came across two gangs having a bitch with each other, gun went off and Adam was the one hit. He'd even crossed the road to avoid them.'

Jake let out a gasp of air. 'Anyone ever charged?'

'Nah. We knew who they were, but everyone clammed up so there was no bloody evidence.'

'So, you got a transfer?'

'Yep. Although Hampshire's not as sleepy as we like to believe.'

'In what way?' Jake asked, loving the opportunity to get under the skin a bit of local crime.

'Look where it is. Close to the capital, on the sea. Ideal for drug running as there's plenty of harbours and expensive yachts that go under the radar. They're not all pleasure crafts, some of them have specific jobs to do.'

'Like Lymford?' Jake ventured.

'Like lovely little Lymford. Believe me, any seaside town on the south coast has its secrets.' Amey said this with more than a touch of bitterness.

'Any children?' Jake asked. Amey seemed to consider this before replying.

'No,' she replied, rather emphatically.

Jake took this as a cue not to ask any more personal questions. He'd got her to open up a bit but thought he'd reached the limit for today.

CHAPTER THIRTY NINE

Stacey had the task of keeping an eye on the investigation down in Hampshire. Old dirt was being dug up and turned over. That was okay, it wasn't a problem so far, and it may never be, but this Jake Stone was getting just a bit annoying. She knew they had him to contend with nearly a year ago. Private investigators were such a pain in the arse. Stacey turned the camera off that was hidden in Milly's apartment and waited for Jake to get back in his car so she could listen to any phone calls. Morgan Ellis had been very forthcoming, and it was good work that they'd managed to get the two tiny cameras in the house and garden of his home while the family were all out two weeks ago. The first audio device had been planted in Jake's office a few weeks ago when they were alerted to his meeting with Greg. They'd managed to get one of their own operatives to help deliver a new sofa to the office, and the device was underneath it and gave crystal clear sound every time he was there. Stacey sent an email to her boss with an update. Bhavin would take over later and she could finally get some fresh air, or as fresh as it got near Vauxhall. As a star struck film buff, she thought that Bhavin would probably be concentrating on Morgan's house rather than anywhere else. He was very excited that Morgan Ellis was now on the radar.

Jake had a quiet drive home, reflecting on what Amey had said. He always sensed there was a certain sadness about her. She was probably lonely, but would never admit it, but he still had reservations about her.

According to the radio forecast we were about to enter an early summer heatwave which Jake was happy to hear, he switched the radio over to Spotify via Bluetooth. 'Move any Mountain' by The Shamen came on, which got him singing along.

Back in his office he started some research on the Andover murder. He was looking for the reason Phil was at the offices on that day, what was his role, who was he meeting there? The country had been winding up for the London Olympics and the bank where he went was a major sponsor. He wondered if that could have anything to do with it. Morgan hadn't known. He stopped himself as he promised to leave it to Amey who was keen to pick that up. He spun around in his chair, tapping the arms with his hands, thinking it would help him, but he wasn't sure where else to go with James, and felt the only lead he now had was the Menorcan girlfriend. Maybe it was a good opportunity to contact Cesar again. He sent out an email before deciding to leave for the day. He had an important date with Milly where he really wanted to get the cards laid out on the table. He was treating her to dinner at The Pig in Brockenhurst so his bankcard would get a bit of a hammering.

Hi Cesar,

Hope you're all well out there. Hope to see you soon. This is a bit of a longshot but I'm trying to trace someone called Emilia who comes from the island, used to work here in Winchester in 2012, not sure of her age but I reckon she'd be in her mid to late thirties now. If my thoughts are right she may have had some connection to the Red House.

All the best
Jake

CHAPTER FORTY

'You look gorgeous,' Jake said, just as Milly opened the door before he put his key in himself.

'Why, thank you kind sir,' said Milly, giving him a twirl. She wore an off white, V neck blouse with long tight cuffs, and a tight-fitting knee length dark skirt.

'I could just eat your bum,' Jake smiled as he came through the door.

'Maybe later darling, if I'm not too full. Seriously, you look very handsome yourself Jake. I almost wish we weren't going out.' He'd put on a royal blue suit, white shirt and matching tie. He'd put a small amount of gel in his hair to keep it in place, had a fresh shave and polished his shoes.

'I can cancel?'

'No way, I've been waiting to go to The Pig for years. I've said I'll do a review for my new podcast. Hang on, I need to take a selfie.' Jake reluctantly smiled at the camera. Milly was venturing further into the world of Instagram and LinkedIn. She was threatening to try TikTok. Jake reminded her he was thirty-five going on sixty so don't expect him to be doing the same thing.

It was only a ten-minute drive to the restaurant, tucked away in a large mansion, which was now called a boutique hotel, on the edge of Brockenhurst. They were guided through to their table in a large conservatory which was festooned with plants and greenery. The waiter quickly came over and introduced himself as Georgio, and paid Milly special attention.

'Isn't he lovely?' Milly said as he walked away, having handed a food and drink menu to them both.

'Just doing his job,' Jake replied dismissively. 'Fuck, look at the price of the wine.'

'Don't worry, I'll do you a deal, you pay for the food, and I'll pay for the wine.' Milly said, leaning forward and grabbing Jake's hand.

He looked intently at her. 'Well dearest, I'm driving so you'll be drinking most of it! No, I'm paying for everything, you deserve it.' Jake smiled but switched to a more serious look, 'after what you went through.'

Milly sighed heavily, she felt very nervous but knew she had to address the elephant in the room. Something she'd avoided for the last few weeks, and these were cards that Jake wanted to lay on the table.

'Seriously,' she started but then paused, just to make sure Jake understood that she wanted to be serious. 'I think this is the right time to ask you this, it's really important for us and our future. Have you ever wanted children?'

This time Jake sighed, loud and long. Milly had dealt the hand before he had a chance to pick up the cards. He'd known since they first became a couple this had to be discussed, and what happened recently just made it more important. He also thought about his recent conversation with Fiona.

He took a deep breath. 'It really is the time to be honest, isn't it?' Milly nodded at him, 'but I know it sounds wrong, and we've touched on it already, but no I don't. I can't tell you why, but I can't see them as part of my life.' Jake suddenly became scared of what Milly might say next, but it needed to be settled.

Milly put her head to one side slightly and half smiled. 'Nor do I. I just don't feel the need to be conventional. I've always felt that I should, it was the normal, right thing to do, but I don't want to. I made peace with myself a couple of years ago and stopped beating myself over it.'

'Can I ask, because we've never discussed your ex-husband much. Did this contribute to the ending of your marriage?'

'Mostly,' Milly responded. But it seemed she wasn't going to expand on this.

It was like the sun going behind clouds on a hot day. It was a relief. Jake kissed the back of her hand and felt a bit of a sting in his eyes. Milly smiled. 'I've had a long chat with Isabella about it, and how you might feel. I think she's my new best friend.'

'That's rather lovely,' Jake said, amused, and pleased that his new sister and girlfriend were becoming close.

'And,' Milly added, 'she's coming over in a couple of weeks. She told me to let you know. She'll stay at mine.'

'Whoa, 'Jake said, 'I'll be in my new swanky pad by then, she can stay with me.'

'No, we can have girly chats about you.'

Georgio returned and asked what they would like to drink.

'Champagne,' Jake said without hesitation, 'and we'll catch the train home.'

The alcohol from the night before was still weighing heavily on Jake's body as he put the key into the lock of his office door. He'd grabbed a couple of Portuguese tarts from the bakery assuring himself they would be a good hangover cure. The steps sounded loud as he laboriously climbed them, sending minor jolts through his head each time his feet hit the next step. He opened the windows as the early summer heatwave was arriving, the room felt very stuffy, although he wasn't sure if that was just the hangover weighing his body down. He wouldn't stay long. It was Saturday after all, and a Bank Holiday weekend.

Jake picked out a bottle of water that was in his small fridge tucked into the corner of the office. Half of it was gone within ten seconds. He gasped and flopped into his chair behind the desk, which looked remarkably tidy. He wondered why he'd put his jeans on this morning when it was already twenty-four degrees outside, jeans were going to make him sweat even more than he already was. Jake had seen from his phone that he had an email from Cesar. He opened the laptop to read it better. For some reason he always felt more comfortable reading important stuff on the laptop.

Hi Jake,
You've not given me a lot to go on but I'll ask around and look through our records. As you know we're not a huge island so I'll trawl through and see if I can find someone of the right age. Things are pretty quiet here still so I've got the time.
Love to Milly and see you soon.

That's good, Jake thought to himself. Now he needed to give Greg an update, so he gave him a call. It took a while, but he eventually answered and after speaking to him for about fifteen minutes Greg seemed satisfied that some progress was being made. They discussed his meeting with Amey and her asking him about the ADG. Jake knew Greg didn't know about them, and he'd told Amey that he didn't, so why did she ask him again?

What next? Jake's head was still a bit muzzy, and he thought about going home to his houseboat and getting some more packing done, but just as he stood up his mobile rang. It was Morgan.

'Hello Morgan, thought you'd be pretty busy now?'

'Hi Jake, man it is hectic. I'm recording for Sky on Monday, to be broadcast on Friday. I've got two other interviews to do with Lily James later today.'

'Lucky you,' Jake said, feeling just a little jealous.

'I called because there was something I remembered from the Andover case. James told me, and he said that he shouldn't have mentioned it afterwards, the bloke killed was in some way organising the Olympic torch relay through the town. I think he must have been on the council. They were at this bank place because they were sponsors of the Olympics and had a big presence in the town.'

'I did wonder about that myself, whether there was a connection,' Jake replied. His mind was drifting, and mainly to himself he said, 'what had he done that warranted him being killed?'

'That's over to you, my friend. Look I've got to go, I just thought that might be useful.'

Jake hesitated. 'Yes, yes, it is. Thanks for calling....and by the way, good luck, hope you smash it.'

'Thanks man,' Morgan said, and ended the call.

CHAPTER FORTY ONE

Bhavin was nearly asleep when he heard the feed coming through from Jake's office. He sent another email to his controller. Jake was getting closer, and he knew they would need to be doing something soon. It wasn't going to disappear so he expected they would pay Amey another visit. He hoped he would be included. After a few minutes all went quiet in the office and Bhavin knew that Jake had left the building. All was quiet in Milly's apartment as well, so he may have a long boring day ahead.

The rest of the weekend was very domestic for Jake. Once he'd locked the door to his office, he walked up the road to the letting agents where he picked up the key to his apartment. This now felt quite final and this time next week he'll have handed over the keys to the houseboat. He would miss it, but it was no longer practical for him to keep going, his life had moved on since he came to Lymford eighteen months ago as a complete stranger. Life since then had been eventful, and mostly very good. He went on to the storage unit on the outskirts of town, to start emptying his container which had been stacked with all his possessions that he couldn't get into the houseboat when he moved to Lymford. Luke had hired a van for him and turned up on the dot at 2pm. They made two trips to the apartment and arranged various bits of furniture, including his 50-inch tv and L-shaped light grey sofa. At 5.30pm they decided enough was enough and retired to The Seafarers for beer and food.

'What's it to be?' Luke asked Jake as they came through the door of the pub.

'Well, I actually think it's the day for a quick cider, followed by a lager. So, it's an Aspalls and Moretti, but I'm getting them.'

'Four pints to order then?' Luke said smiling. 'I'll have the same.'

Jake checked his watch, Milly was going to join them around 6pm as well as Luke's boyfriend, so a good hour of just them, a chance to talk to Luke about his plan for the future. They walked out to the garden at the back of the pub for the first time this year. The sun was still quite high in the sky, and it was tricky to get a bench. Jake hovered near a couple who looked like they were leaving but were taking their time about it, making sure they had their phones, that someone else knew where they were going, and all bags and jackets were taken. Jake sat down getting impatient.

By Monday he'd decided to move everything into the apartment and hand the keys back on the houseboat. There was no point keeping it on for another few days so Milly got busy adding the female touches that Jake wouldn't. Flowers on the dining table, arranging the kitchen for practical use rather than just shoving things in any old drawer and cupboard, and generally sorting things out. Jake felt that she was constantly one step behind him, moving anything he put down to somewhere else. By 8pm they both sat down and decided it was time to christen the new pad. By 10pm they were both fast asleep.

The heatwave was short lived and by Tuesday morning thunder was rumbling around Lymford. Jake looked out from his large living room window, in his shorts and dressing gown, and felt like some Lord of the Manor. Down below the tide was out on the river revealing dark swathes of grey mud with old boats marooned waiting for the tide to come back in. Looking to his right the ferry was loading up for the trip across the Solent to the Isle of Wight, where flashes of lightning could be seen despite the daylight. Finally, a train rumbled across the bridge on its way north, probably to London, carrying late commuters who would be miserable that the weekend was over. Jake felt so lucky.

'Do you fancy scrambled eggs?' Milly said from behind him.

'It's food isn't it? Am I going to say no?' Jake said, turning round with a big grin on his face. 'And you make the best scrambled eggs.'

'Well, give me time to work out the bloody hob unit. It's like an airplane instrument panel.' Milly wandered across the room and stood next to Jake.

'You know …. when we do move in together…. I reckon it should be here. The view is so much better.'

'I agree,' Jake said smiling, as a flash of lightning darted across the sky and the lights went out.

CHAPTER FORTY TWO

In Salisbury the rain was just steady. No thunderstorm here but Amey was going to have to be a little more determined. Hopefully, Jake will stay away from the Andover investigation and leave it to her to uncover the truth. Or not.

She was going to have to step up her game a bit or he might get a bit too close to it himself. His chat with Morgan worried her, but in reality, he knew very little about why he was doing what he was doing. He could identify James though, or that was the name he knew him by. Amey would ring James later; she was aware that she should have spoken to him a few weeks ago but didn't want to alarm him. He was shaken by the events of 2012 and wasn't the strong character he was back then. She was always going to try and handle Jake, and she wasn't on her own, but it was better James knew there was a bit of heat on and got his head out of the sand.

She sat down at her large oak table and took out her notes to ponder on what's next. The cleaners, Jane Colton and Greg Jones won't be able to provide any more awkward information, she can keep Dan out of it and Karen Carpenter was dealt with. Emilia was a bit out of reach, but she didn't expect her to be a problem. Matt Boyle was unpredictable and a bit of a maverick, but he knew what was best for him.

She realised that she couldn't trust Jake to leave Andover to her, if he did then it was a piece of cake, but she knew that he was pretty persistent. She'd come across private investigators before and, in her opinion, they were lazy, just doing what they needed to do so they could get the bucks at the end. She knew some blatantly lied because they were bored with a case, just to get it over with. She knew one in London who was on a missing person case and literally could not find anything on the whereabouts of a twenty-four-year-old kid. Within two days Amey had traced him to Inverness but the parents had already paid out a tidy sum for the work the PI had done. His conclusion was that he'd been lured across to Russia as he had a friend who came from Moscow. There was no way he was going to get any confirmation from the Russian authorities and 'one day I'm sure he'd return home.' The parents weren't satisfied but they were naive and believed him. Amey heard about it and took it on herself to investigate free of charge. She found the lad working in a hotel under a false name, and so let the relieved parents know. He just wanted to escape for a while from a family that wouldn't really let him grow up.

Jake was different. He wasn't driven by

money as he had plenty. He just loved the investigation, picking things over, probing and prodding, and he had a real determination to get to the truth. She admired him if she was being honest with herself, but she needed to kick him off course, but she wasn't sure how to. She was loving what she was doing as much as he was, he just didn't realise that her intentions were a little different to his own. She knew she could undermine anything he found out about James.

Brad Swinburn checked his time. He'd just completed the Auckland parkrun in just under twenty-five minutes, very close to his personal best. After a few congratulations all around and a swift bottle of water he made his way back to his car. As he got in, his phone woke up, displaying 'Annie' on the caller display. He pulled a face as he knew that it must be coming from the burner phone which was rarely used. Something was up. His normal mobile would come up with 'Amey.'

'Hello,' he answered tentatively, 'what's wrong?'

'A bloody private investigator is what's wrong lad.'

'In what way?' Brad said, with a sinking feeling.

'A bloke has been hired by Greg Jones to look into Layton, and the bad news is he's making some inroads. Don't worry, I'm on it, he thinks I'm helping him but obviously I'm handling it without raising suspicion.'

'So, what does he know?' Brad felt a rising sense of panic which he was trying to control. He already knew he was going to need to go and see his counsellor next week.

'Look, you know the arrangement, you know what the deal was, he's spoken to Morgan.'

'Shit, shit shit!' Brad blurted out. Amey carried on.

'It's okay, you know what Morgan knows, and it ain't that much, so they had a nice chat, but he couldn't give him any usable intel. Okay, he found out about Andover, but I've told him I'll look into that, so hopefully he'll keep his snout out of that one.'

'It was always going to happen at some point.' Brad's voice was breaking up a bit. 'Who would have thought that innocent lad, who wanted to be able to trust everyone, would become a major superstar. He must have grown some balls since we knew him.'

'I know, I know.' Amey said. 'I just wanted to let you know, and not to worry, we're dealing with it and you're a long way away. I'm pretty confident the machine will get behind it and Jake Stone will be put back in his box.'

'Thank you,' Brad said, sounding weary, he then perked up. 'I've got some other news though.'

'Go on,' Amey said, a little impatiently.

'Shannon has finally agreed to marry me, after six years of me asking I think she trusts me. I told her everything about my past and she understands. It was a massive relief.'

Amey sounded cautious. 'Not sure you should have done that lad. We always said damage limitation.' Amey suddenly changed her tone, 'Ignore me, that's good I'm sure…. congratulations! We'll speak soon.'

Brad put the phone back in his glove pocket and pulled out his old driving licence and looked at the name.

James Lorimer
Born London

He sighed, wishing he'd never got himself mixed up with his uncle, Tommy Phillips. James had to leave his mum on her own in Salisbury, both of them hiding their pasts, and he wondered how Emilia was doing.

CHAPTER FORTY THREE

Amey sighed and just quietly said, 'fucking hell.' She missed James and he'd had a rough time. He'd been in New Zealand for the past eleven years, forging a life on his own until he met Shannon. Tommy had manipulated him, and James wasn't as strong as he liked to think he was. His head was turned, like her own, when his father was killed in London, up until then he'd had little to do with Tommy as he was known as the thug of the family. Tommy grew up moving from gang to gang and never worked an honest day's work in his life, or the forty-two years he actually lived.

Tommy slowly seeped himself into James's psyche, like he did with many people, until James hated anyone who wasn't Anglo-Saxon white who could prove they were born in the UK. Before long he was joining Tommy in Menorca plotting all sorts of things to disrupt society. Amey pulled open a drawer where she had some photos. She pulled one out which was a recent picture of him and Shannon, looking happy eating ice cream on the waterfront somewhere in the North Island. Shannon was mixed race, father from Kenya, mother from Canada, living in New Zealand. Amey had wondered at times whether he was trying to atone himself, but he genuinely seemed to be in love with her, and the fact that she was half-Kenyan didn't seem to matter. It demonstrated to Amey the lengths that Tommy had gone to, and how influential he was. Getting away from the UK was the best thing James could do, but it was also the only thing he could do, an offer he had no choice but to agree to.

She flipped over a few pieces of paper and wrote 'Phil' at the top of a fresh clean page. What will she be telling Jake? Well, she'll say that she spoke to a few people, members of staff, who were at the building in Andover, but they couldn't have much information. All they really saw was a dead body, Morgan, who they hadn't taken much notice of, and the paramedics. Nobody had recognised Dan so he could disappear into oblivion, but she knew that she wouldn't get away with not getting Phil identified, one of the Three Amigos. He had been on the local council and not too much digging by Jake would find there was a councillor who died of a heart attack in March 2012, although publicity was minimised at the time. She cursed Morgan for telling Jake about this one, but it was inevitable. If Jake ever got to James, then she knew he would crack. His head wasn't in the right space to carry on lying so she wanted to protect him as much as she could. Being on the other side of the world was helpful.

Amey scrawled straight lines across the paper, partly in anger, partly in frustration. She felt things were coming to some sort of climax but wasn't really sure what the ending would be, her enjoyment of the case was now hitting some sort of reality which she may not have any control over. She decided that next time she spoke to Jake she would identify Phil by his real name, which was Roger Jenkins, a single man, but with two children that lived with their mother in Reading, while he lived in a nice four bedroomed house in the attractive village of Chilbolton. Roger had a big secret that he'd managed to conceal from almost everyone. He was also a member of the ADG, but Amey, at least for now, would deny that she could find a connection. She needed to get him down blind alleys until he could go no further. If she could.

Power was off in Lymford for an hour while the storm ebbed and flowed outside. Eventually it moved off in the direction of Southampton, following Milly as she drove to the studios. She was working on her latest podcast today with Elias, and this was about a Swede moving to the South Coast and the challenges he faced. She decided that she loved human interest stories.

Jake now had an office, which was the spare room, but he needed to decide whether to keep the office in the High Street going. He quite liked it, separating work from home, and it was better to see people there. He quickly decided that his home office was not to be his main place of work. Nevertheless, he would get it equipped. He didn't seem to have his mojo for investigating today. He was still enjoying the new apartment and there were little jobs to do, put up a few shelves, hang some pictures, move a couple that Milly had put up. At lunchtime he made himself a sandwich, cheese and beetroot with a bit of salad thrown in, and sat out on his balcony, which had dried out already. He'd just put the last corner of multigrain bread in his mouth when Amey called.

'Hiya,' he said, swallowing hard.

'You eating lad?'

'Literally just finishing my lunch. I moved into the new apartment yesterday.'

'That's nice,' Amey didn't sound very sincere. She went on to explain her investigations into Phil.

'He must have had something to do with the ADG, otherwise I don't see the connection?' Jake said, a little incredulously.

'I'm not saying he hasn't, I just haven't found it yet, but leave it with me.' Amey sounded like a headmistress.

'I'm taking a day off today anyway,' Jake replied, 'but it doesn't stop me thinking.'

'I don't doubt it.'

'I was screwing a clock to the wall, and I thought.... no, I didn't think.... I'm convinced that there's another level here.'

'What do you mean lad?' Amey sounded cagey.

'I experienced it last year when looking into my own family. Some sort of cover up. Not sure if I told you but I worked in the civil service in Whitehall for a few years before coming here, so I know what they can do. The civil service and the security services are often in bed together, as well as at each other's throats.'

'So, what are you actually thinking?'

'I don't know. There was some conspiracy to get them killed. It was planned by mysterious people in grey suits, who walk down sunny corridors overlooking the Thames.'

Amey wasn't sure what to say. After a few moments she spoke.

'No, I don't believe that. Don't forget I worked for the Met, I rose through the ranks to DCI, and I don't believe for a moment they would get involved in such awful crimes.'

Jake grunted, he thought that sounded a strange thing for her to say, like it was rehearsed. He thought not to question her.

'You may be right, but it's either the ADG killing their own, or it's another group of people who think they're invincible. I'm pretty sure that's what Morgan thought, although he didn't come right out and say it.'

Amey felt a little backed into a corner and spiralling a bit, she knew she would need to come up with another theory. She felt she was the one going down blind alleys now and what was her way out?

'Look, Morgan knows jackshit and we both know it. I'm going to have to go but I reckon we need to be careful of conspiracy theories.'

'OK, ma'am.' Jake said obligingly.

Stacey and Bhavin were working together today. They were able to bug Jake's new apartment thanks to a storage warehouseman who got into Jake's container and planted two devices, one under the sofa, and one behind a mirror. The same operative who bugged his sofa in the office. With Jake being on the balcony the sound was a bit muffled, but they heard enough today that would mean a visit to Room 222. This was Laura's office, but they knew this wasn't her real name, it was above their pay grade for them to know who she was.

CHAPTER FORTY FOUR

Jake found his poster of Gianfranco Zola, a picture he'd had since he was about twelve years old. He decided that Milly wouldn't appreciate a poster of the great Chelsea legend on his bedroom wall, but he decided to put it up for the reaction. It would be worth it. She was a Frank Lampard fan, or had been. He switched on the TV and relaxed back on the sofa just in time to see Morgan interviewed on Sky News. The big premiere was in two days' time in Leicester Square, Jake thought he looked a bit tired. It seemed that his publicity machine had gone into overdrive in the last few weeks and his was a name that all the media seemed to be talking about. Jake really hoped he would come through the attention, and the murders, unscathed.

    Jake jolted awake, he was dribbling down his chin and his neck was stiff. He checked his watch, it was 3.30pm and he'd fallen asleep on the sofa for an hour. Morgan had been replaced on Sky News with a piece about the impending death of the Conservative Party. Lots of talking heads were giving their opinions with just one saying they were 'regrouping,' and would 'come back stronger than ever.' Jake pressed the remote to turn the TV off and walked over to the radio to listen to Milly on The Crunch. She was playing 'House of Love' by East 17, although Jake knew she wouldn't have had any say in the playlist. She then started talking about her podcast, chatting to Elias about the content. Jake felt proud.

He pottered around but realised he didn't have anything else to do, so he went into the spare bedroom and opened the laptop. He got his pad out and flicked through the notes he took when he first spoke to Greg. Was there anything he'd omitted to pick up on? The family? The people he knew? Nothing was obvious, but he decided he needed to think a bit deeper. He wished he had the mind of Cormoran Strike and read into things that aren't immediately obvious. The complex nature of piecing things together, joining the branches of a tree to the trunk, until you get to the root. Something was nagging away at him, like a boil that wouldn't burst, and he couldn't quite put his finger on it. He thought about Amey and how much had she contributed to the case recently? It occurred to him that her investigations hadn't really resulted in anything constructive. He would wait to see what she came back with from the Andover murder. He wondered if he was totally wasting his time, and that he just wouldn't be able to get to the truth. He still hadn't worked out what Bob's involvement was in all of this, was he a coordinator for whatever the other three were doing? Was he an informer? Was he the killer? Was he Dan? Jake finally decided he would do his own investigation into Phil's death, but not tell Amey he was doing it.

He got himself a cup of coffee and got to work. He looked for local councillors that had died in 2012, it didn't take him long to find Roger Jenkins, who died of a sudden heart attack, but there was no mention where. He found a number for the leader of the council, someone called Jim Trussler to ask him whether he'd worked with Roger and remembered him. Jim knew of him but hadn't known him personally. He gave him the contact details for a Melissa Dugdale. She'd been in the council for years and had known Roger, so Jake sent her an email. He then traced Roger's partner. She now lived in Bournemouth, married with two sons aged seventeen and fifteen. Her phone went to voicemail, so he left a message just asking her to call him when she had a moment. He then saw an email pop up from Cesar.

My friend, I have news. There weren't that many Emilia's who matched that age group coming from the island. But I traced an Emilia Fernandes who lived here in Es Castell. She works in one of the bars down at Cala Fonts and I realise I know who she is. What would you like me to do?

Jake pondered for a while, rhythmically tapping a pencil against his front teeth. She was clearly friendly with James and if she comes from Es Castell there must be some link to the red house, but he wouldn't expect a Spanish woman to be involved in a British right-wing group who were against any foreigners in the country. He picked up a paper clip and twisted it through his thumb and forefinger.

Good work Cesar. I think I just want to know at this stage whether she worked in England in 2012 and who did she know? I reckon she would at least know who Tommy Phillips was. Thanks for your help, it's much appreciated.

Jake was satisfied he'd made some progress this afternoon so decided to take himself off for a run. Milly was playing football this evening, so he called Luke but he was busy. He thought he'd try Pierre because he knew that Pierre wanted to talk to him about ideas for his website, and more worrying, ideas for him on social media. Jake had been avoiding this but realised it was a step he needed to take. Pierre picked up almost immediately and was delighted Jake was thinking about it, so he bit the bullet and arranged to meet him, but it would have to include another visit to the pub.

Stacey and Bhavin knocked on the door of Room 222 and a loud voice bellowed out for them to come in. They were both just a little excited, but there was also a little trepidation of the woman they were about to talk to. Only seen briefly sweeping through the corridors going from one room to another, not really talking to the lower grades. The mystical Laura had an awesome reputation.

Her body defied her voice. She was actually relatively short, at 5ft 2 inches, slim with shoulder length curly blonde hair. Bhavin thought she was probably mid-forties but definitely had an air of authority about her. She gave them cups of coffee without asking whether they wanted them, or how they'd like it. They decided to accept gratefully. Laura sat behind her desk pulling open a file that just said '2012 ADG' on the front.

'Now then. Tell me what you've seen and heard.'

Stacey cleared her throat and put her cup on the table, she wasn't sure she could hold it steady.

'Well, Jake is coming to the conclusion that there is some other involvement. We didn't realise,' she looked at Bhavin, 'we didn't realise that he used to work in Whitehall, so he's got a little bit of an insight. He's not put off easily, he's definitely like a dog with a bone.'

'To be expected.' Laura was brusque. 'What did he say exactly?'

'He was talking to Amey Lorimer over the phone and said that basically he smelt there was something else going on. She was trying to deflect him by saying not to get wrapped up in conspiracy theories.'

Bhavin interjected, 'I'm not sure we can rely on her to get to the point of making Jake drop everything.'

'Are you sure Morgan Ellis is okay? He's pretty watertight, yeah?' Laura's face softened, 'he's now got a lot to lose?'

'One hundred percent,' Bhavin replied. 'He only knows what he's been told, and he's freely discussed it with Jake. At the end of the day, he doesn't know the background. He's fine.'

Lewis then walked into the office. He was Stacey and Bhavin's boss.

'Lewis,' Laura said as if she was about to tear him off a strip. Lewis was tall, overweight and bald, a complete contrast to Laura. 'What do we think Jake Stone would do if he knew the whole truth?'

'Well, that's our dilemma. I'm not sure it's clear. He's a man of principle, he likes the truth, and we know he's not overly fond of the establishment.' An ironic smile briefly appeared on Laura's face. 'He told us that when he left the civil service. But it's like we've always said, what does he really gain from it apart from letting the family of the three know what really happened to them, and who killed them.'

'Pretty strong motive,' Stacey added, looking between Laura, Lewis and Bhavin.

Laura stood up. 'Trouble with you Lewis

is that sometimes you don't have an ounce of human emotion in you. We can't always put procedure and our own dogma ahead of the natural human sense of what's right or wrong. In fact, we have to consider this to get things right.'

Lewis shrugged and looked a bit embarrassed. Bhavin contained a smile, but it was a sentiment that gave him a warm glow. He'd never got on with Lewis, and seeing him put down by The Boss was enjoyable.

Laura started pacing around her office, her hands clasped together as if she was about to pray. 'It wouldn't be so bad if that second killing hadn't been so brutal. There was no need for it. We had to literally build another Chinese wall to keep that one quiet.'

'Ma'am,' Stacey spoke, actually putting her hand slightly in the air. 'May I make a suggestion?'

'If it's a good one,' Laura replied.

'Why don't we go straight to Greg Jones. Tell him it's in his own best interests to drop it. Straightforward as that. He tells Jake to leave it alone.'

'Lewis has said that on numerous occasions. I must admit I've dismissed it right from the start. No, I still think it's a ridiculous idea.'

'But why?' Lewis asked, 'I still think it's the simplest and most reasonable solution. I don't get the impression he's a particularly strong character who would fight us and want to battle on.'

Laura looked daggers at Lewis, he could feel the forks being pressed into his eyes. She moved to a long wooden sideboard that stretched the width of her office and sat down on it, swinging her right leg over her left, revealing shoes that were hand made in Italy.

'What you three need to remember is that there are three families here. Now one is completely ignorant to a murder, the other, that nasty bitch in the caravan, won't be so easy to keep quiet if they think they can get more money out of it. They all hated her, but they've done nicely out of her death. They were like flies round a pot of jam when we came calling. They'll do it again if they think it's reared its head again.' Laura shook her head looking down. Without looking up she said, 'Get back to your desks and give me an update tomorrow.'

All three filed out with their heads bowed. Laura sat back down and tapped her desk with a pen. She knew Stacey and Lewis had a point.

CHAPTER FORTY FIVE

The date was Wednesday 15th May. Morgan Ellis lay in his plush suite in The Savoy, a super king size bed with all crisp white linen. Anna was back home in Hampshire and would join him later today. It was the day before the big premiere for Morgan, his biggest film, a potential role that could parachute him to huge things, maybe into super celebrity status. He was confident it was a good film, the early 'behind closed doors' reviews were good, but his previous confidence had ebbed away. Seeing Jake had brought him back down to earth. He loved acting to the point where it gave him immense joy when he had a good part and he knows he's given it his best, but he wasn't in love with the Hollywood merry go round. He could never live there on any sort of permanent basis, and he always mixed with other British and European actors in the US. Generally, they had a bit more realism about them and kept their feet on the ground. To go to a party in LA and have a chat about *The Great British Bake Off* was almost a joy, and to sarcastically take the piss out of each other was something few Americans understood. He wasn't sure he wanted super stardom. If it happened to him, he vowed that he would want to commit to doing as much work in the UK as possible. Fortunately, films being made in the country were at an all-time high with technicians and the studios well respected around the world. Their technical abilities meant that many of the big films were, at least partly, filmed in the country. If *Death in the Afternoon* was a success, then choices would open up for him. In theory.

The truth was that Morgan wanted to go away and hide, let the movie come out without him having to attend the parties and relentless interviews where he's asked the same questions again, and again. Life was really imitating art now, with the film having strong echoes of the 2012 situation which had come back to haunt him at the same time. Once he knew that would go away, he could relax again. He sat up and rubbed his face in his hands. He hadn't touched drugs for over a year now but if he had some to hand he would probably take them, just to get him through the next couple of days. He closed his mind to that thought because he could easily get some, but he was strong enough to remember the slippery slope it had taken him on previously. He laid back down again with his hands behind his back. He must trust what he was told in 2012, and no matter what happened he would be alright, it was what James told him and he believed James was coming from a good place. He had to believe that was true. It scared him that he'd put so much faith in what one man told him.

Meanwhile, in Lymford, Jake was in Sainsbury's doing a general shop for the apartment. His phone buzzed in his pocket just as he was about to get in the queue. He hadn't got round to setting himself up with Smartshop, and as he had alcohol he was going to get a real live person to serve him. He pulled the phone out and checked who was calling, it was Matt Boyle, which was a bit of a surprise.

'Hello Matt, how are you doing?'

'Not too bad thanks,' Jake could tell that he sounded serious and even a little earnest, so he pulled himself off to the side of the store to try and get a little privacy. A little hesitation and Matt continued. 'Can I come and see you? I haven't told you everything I know about what happened with those murders.'

'Oh okay,' Jake said, more than a little intrigued. He could feel his heart miss a beat at the thought of new information. He could do with it.

'Let's meet somewhere a bit neutral. How about meeting somewhere, out in the open?' Matt said, clearly on edge.

'Sure. When and where are you thinking?'

'How about tomorrow if that suits? We could meet in the car park just outside Lyndhurst, on the Ashurst road?'

'I know it,' Jake replied, 'what time shall we say? 10.30am?'

'Yes, yes, that would be good, I'll see you then.'

Matt rang off without a goodbye. Jake joined the queue, feeling quite excited. His first thought was to tell Amey, but something inside him said not to. In fact, he wanted to avoid her altogether now.

Amey was in a bad mood. She'd just spent thirty minutes getting around Salisbury with the ring road full of cars, motorhomes and caravans on their way to the coast or the West Country. She was on her way to Waitrose but when she got there it had been closed due to a water leak. She then had to come back round to Tesco, which she could have gone to in the first place and saved herself at least twenty wasted minutes. However, what she was mostly in a bad mood about was Jake Stone edging closer to the truth. The one person who he didn't really know anything about was Bob, the link between James and the three people killed, the one who met them in Winchester at The Green Room, gained their confidence and then lied to them. She didn't know who that was, but knew that the Hayling murder revealed a complete psychopath who clearly must have revelled in the opportunity to murder someone in a barbaric manner. That had shocked her, and she didn't expect it. All she really wanted to do was protect herself, and James. She hadn't gone through those hours of interrogation twelve years ago to have it all come back now. She'd cleared her name and thought that was the end of it, the corruption that Layton's family, Lucy and Phil were involved in would keep them quiet, but time had resurrected Greg's need to know exactly what happened to his brother. She knew that money had kept Lucy's family quiet, as well as the threats.

She sat down with a thump in the chair, dust flying up and circling in the sunlight shining through the side window of her living room. She was pretty sure that the London team will feel she's blown her chance to steer Jake away, and if she fails in this they may, which she was now admitting to herself, drag her into it again to act as their scapegoat. If this all blows over, she would go and live abroad somewhere and forget the past. She wished that Tommy Phillips had never been born her brother.

Cesar didn't waste any time. It was lunchtime and the restaurant *Miramar* would now be open. It should be quiet so he would check if Emilia was working. There was a gentle breeze blowing through the harbour area of Cala Fonts giving a slightly cool feel still, the inhabitants of this Menorcan town still awaited the heat of summer. Tourists were still quite limited although it would be busier by the weekend. He saw Emilia Fernandes immediately. She was smiling with a group of locals who were sitting down with their tapas. There was no one else in the restaurant, either inside or out, so he approached her as she walked away from them. She turned and saw him coming.

'Ah Cesar, what can I do for you? Are you eating?'

'No, not right now. I have a couple of questions for you?' Cesar said. 'Can we sit down for a moment?'

Emilia pulled out a couple of chairs under the awning facing out to sea.

'I'm doing a bit of work for a private investigator in the UK.' Emila's face immediately dropped, her olive skin seemed to grow suddenly paler, she shook her long dark hair.

'Not the police?' she questioned.

'No, not the police. The private investigator is someone called Jake Stone. What he wants to know is if you worked in a pub, in a place called Winchester, back in 2012?'

She now bit her lip, and he could see she was deciding what her answer would be. After a pause she nodded, barely moving her head.

'Is that a yes, Emilia?' Cesar leaned forward to ask her.

'Uh huh, I was there for a few months. I nannied for a while and worked behind the bar of a pub called the Royal Oak.'

'And did you meet an English bloke called

James?'

'Yes, I did. He was lovely to me, but also a bad person.'

'In what way?

'He was mixed up with that lot that lived over the water.'

'You mean the red house on the hill, Sant Phillippe?'

'Uh-huh.'

'That's a coincidence, isn't it? Did you meet by chance?'

'Yes, I've always thought so.'

'So, when did you know he was a right wing extremist?'

Cesar was being very blunt and not pulling any punches. Emilia was looking very uncomfortable and picked a tiny breadcrumb off the tablecloth, flicking it to the ground.

'When he said he had to leave the UK.' Emilia wasn't looking at him. 'He then told me all about what he'd done, he was in some way connected to the deaths of three people and needed to get away.'

'And you believed him?'

Emilia now looked up. 'We had become very close, so yes I did believe him.'

'Okay,' Cesar leaned back and pondered whether to ask anymore. He decided that he would need to go back to Jake before leading her anywhere else at this stage. Cesar was pretty sure she'd not told him the whole truth.

CHAPTER FORTY SIX

It was the day of the premiere and Jake heard Morgan being interviewed on the radio in the Showbiz News section. He was incredibly excited and couldn't wait for the movie to open this evening. Jake bit off a slice of toast which was inch deep in peanut butter, smiling at the superlatives celebrities are compelled to say in these circumstances. He drew the blinds across and looked out of his window. All was quiet. Milly had got him an Oodie for Christmas, but he was yet to wear it, preferring straight forward boxer shorts and a t-shirt to wander around in after getting up. He padded through to the spare bedroom grabbing a cup of coffee on the way, opening up the laptop to check emails. He was interested to see one from Cesar already.

Good morning Jake,

News from Menorca, I've met Emilia and she admits to working there and knowing James. She worked as a nanny for a few months. I didn't probe too deeply but she was clearly nervous. She claims it's a coincidence that she met James and that they both had a connection to this area, but I don't believe her. She says they were close and doesn't believe he used her in any way. I know the Fernandes family and they're no angels, lots of petty crime etc. Let me know if you need me to do more.

Cesar.

Jake tapped his finger against his chin, wrote this down in his notes and replied thanking him but not to do anything else. He may have to fly over again himself.

Stacey and Bhavin could tell Jake was on his laptop, but they couldn't see what he was doing exactly. This was frustrating as they needed more visual aids to piece everything together. Lewis entered the room and asked if they had any updates, but they just shrugged and shook their heads. He mumbled and then seemed to speak to the middle distance, muttering something about it being time to actually do something. He went back out and the two of them just looked at each other.

At 10am Jake got in his car and headed towards his meeting with Matt Boyle. He pulled into the car park and could see Matt sat on a bench about fifty metres away. It was one of those designed to spread your picnic out on with benches either side of the table. The weather was fine, so there was no need to worry about rain spoiling the setting. They both exchanged pleasantries and sat down to talk. Jake thought he appeared different in some way, maybe more confident.

Matt cleared his throat and spoke. 'First of all, I have a confession to make. I led you a bit of a merry dance last time we met as it was a bit of a surprise when you contacted me. My real name is not Matt Boyle, but I'm afraid I'm not going to reveal my real name. It's best I keep that quiet. Secondly, we haven't had this conversation. I will deny it if ever I'm asked. Thirdly, can you just check all your pockets, make sure there's nothing that could look like a listening device. I doubt there will be, but I need to be sure.'

Jake looked more than a little surprised but did as he was told. He only wore jeans, a t-shirt and a pair of deck shoes, so this didn't take long. He sat back down and looked across at Matt, nodding as if to encourage him to now talk.

'Right then. What I'm going to say,' Matt now looked intently at Jake, 'I'm only saying because I felt let down in 2012 and want to have my say. You've given me that opportunity.' Matt paused again. 'Can you just tell me what you've found out about the murders from that time?'

Jake was hesitant, unsure that he should divulge anything to this man who, it seemed, wasn't necessarily who he thought he was and sounded as though he may have an axe to grind. He decided to be a little economical, saying that he knew there were three, they were linked to the Albion Defence Group and the famous Morgan Ellis was involved, albeit maybe a little innocently.

Matt managed a rueful smile. 'Poor Morgan, he's been absolutely shitting himself, but I spoke to him this morning and assured him what he said to you is fine, and that he doesn't need to worry about anything. Enjoy his fame and fortune and his name will never be connected to the deaths.'

Jake was frowning. 'So, who are you?' He asked.

'I'm police trained, I'm intelligence trained, I'm not as dumb as I may have been made out to be.'

Jake could tell this wasn't the slightly bumbling chap he met previously working in Sainsbury's. There was silence while a young couple walked past hand in hand but taking no notice of the two men sitting on the benches. Matt waited for them to get out of earshot.

'Well in 2011 the Albion Defence Group were getting quite powerful. Tommy Phillips had mobilised a lot of people and he had his inner circle of around eight generals, as he called them. Tommy Phillips genuinely wanted a white Britain, the irony being that he based himself in another country. Spain, or Menorca to be precise. I'm sure you have found that out.' Jake nodded at him in agreement. 'I'm sure the reasons were that there would be less heat on him if he went abroad to direct his operations.'

Jake spoke. 'So, what were his operations exactly, what did he want to do?'

'To disrupt the London Olympics. With the world's attention on this country, he wanted to create maximum publicity for his cause. The bloke had an ego the size of Russia. I think he loved to be hated, as long as he could get himself in the spotlight. That was his intention.'

Jake thought about this. 'I think I'd only vaguely heard of him though. He wasn't well known at that time, as far as I can remember.'

'No, but he would have been.'

'So, what's your part?' Jake said, a bit abruptly.

'I was undercover. There's a section of the intelligence services that few people know about. Again, I won't say what they're called but I was parachuted into Hampshire Constabulary as a detective.'

'Why there?' Jake asked, frowning again but having a heightened sense of intrigue, he felt he was getting close to some real answers.

'Amey Lorimer,' Matt said defiantly, 'she's the sister of Tommy Phillips. They were quite close, or so it was believed, and I was to try and find out what I could about her and what she might know about the ADG. Ideally, get a sense of what Tommy was planning.'

Jake didn't express much surprise at this, he'd sensed something about her that he couldn't put his finger on. It confirmed some of his doubts about her that had surfaced recently.

'And did you get anything from her?'

'Not a lot to be honest.'

'So why did the murders happen, and why in the way they did?'

'They were a surprise because they were members of the ADG, and I don't have all the answers. First of all, I thought we did it but that didn't really make sense. Once I saw the Hayling murder of the person we know of as Lucy, I knew this was the work of a true psychopath. This brings you back to the ADG. They attracted those sorts of people. An idealism which gives them a cause to follow which they can almost hide behind.'

'So, what did Amey say about them?'

'I think she was genuinely shocked. She knew that her son, James, was involved and that concerned her. As I said before, I quite liked her. She got caught in other people's webs.'

Jake looked surprised for the first time. 'James is Amey's son? He's the one that controlled Morgan and worked at The Green Room?

Matt nodded. 'I knew PC Joe Attwood wasn't who he said he was straight away, but I couldn't work out what he was playing at. You remember that I was only ever told what I needed to know. There were things happening which always meant I didn't have the full picture. Amey became quite…. erratic, shall I say.'

'So, she was taken off the cases?'

'What I know is that they, and when I

say they, I mean my bosses in the section, wanted to get things closed down. They wanted the murders to go under the radar, and so Pat Tweddle was brought in to take over from Amey; he'd been lurking in the shadows at Hampshire for a while. Amey went off on sick leave so between us we got the investigation wound down.'

'As instructed?' Jake questioned.

'Yep. It meant my involvement came to an end. Tweddle barely talked to me after that, and I was completely out of the loop. Eventually they took me off and I was effectively kicked out from that job without any real explanation, so I was left feeling a little bitter.'

'Now working in Sainsbury's using the same name?' Jake questioned, thinking this a little odd.

'Like I say, there's only so much I can tell you, but it's an identity I could keep.'

Jake now felt a little exasperated, he thought he would know more from the meeting. It put a few things together in his own head but still didn't get him nearer to knowing who exactly killed them.

'Tell me, will I ever find out why they had to die, and who did it?'

Matt pondered this. 'Possibly not. They may decide to tell you, but then I don't know what's happened in the last twelve years. Tommy dying effectively killed off the ADG, which must have been a relief to many many people. I think he was so dominant that there wasn't a proper deputy, or someone that could organise them in the same way as he did.'

'What about Morgan? How can you be so sure he'll be alright?'

'I had a phone call yesterday, and all I was told was to let him know that what happened then would never come back and bite him. Your movements will have been monitored in the last few weeks, and at some point, I suspect they will intervene.'

Jake thought about this. 'Am I wasting my time then?'

'That's up to you. You're an investigator. I'm sure you like investigating and so would like to get as far as you can, even though it may not end in a conclusion.'

'Umm.... I think you're right.' Jake looked up and took in a good view of the New Forest from their slightly elevated spot. 'Will I have been listened to? Bugged?'

'I'd be surprised if you weren't. That's why I asked you to check when you arrived. I expect they'll have got into your house and office.'

Matt stood up and so Jake took his cue that he'd said enough.

'There's not much more I can tell you, but you know where I am. He managed a half smile. Jake deduced that there was a story behind him currently working in a supermarket. They shook hands and both wandered back to the car park.

'One thing,' Jake said as a thought came to his head. 'Did you see Morgan Ellis at the scene of the second murder in Hayling Island?'

Matt smiled properly this time. 'Oh yeah. Amey didn't recognise him, but I did. He's a much better actor now.'

CHAPTER FORTY SEVEN

Jake's mind was wandering as he drove through the New Forest on his way home. He didn't look left at the first murder scene as he approached Brockenhurst, but nearly hit a pedestrian who decided not to look closely for incoming traffic before crossing the road in front of him. He should have asked a bit more about Karen and the jacket, did he know Emilia? He was intrigued why he was in Sainsbury's, what were they up to, or who working there was trouble that needed somebody to be undercover? Matt didn't actually confirm he was undercover in Sainsbury's, and he didn't find the reason he had an axe to grind convincing enough.

    He could feel a headache coming on, he had to stop at the level crossing so popped open his glovebox and rummaged round for tablets. He found two left in a blister pack and threw them into his mouth. The barriers lifted and he drove his Audi on to Lymford where the welcome smell of sea air wafted across as he got out of the car. He felt mentally weary, feeling that he could be just wasting his time, but he couldn't help thinking what Amey was trying to do by joining the investigation. Surely, she would want to put him off the scent? Come to think of it, she hasn't contributed a lot, so what does make sense is that she was getting involved, saying she'd speak to people instead of him, and so closing down these lines of inquiry. He was supposed to trust her rather than go looking and asking his own questions. The information she got from Jane Colton, Layton's girlfriend, was useful but then she'd have to show she was providing something. She needed to keep close to it to see where he was going, probably so she could protect James as much as she could. He started to feel angry at the thought of it and knew he would need to confront her.

He got inside his apartment and just slumped in a chair by the window. If there were bugs in this place, then he needed to start looking for them. The sky was leaden grey which seemed to match his mood, he opened the patio door a bit to let some air in. He felt the need for some mindless TV, even though it was still early afternoon, but couldn't be bothered to get up again to fetch the remote. He felt his eyes close.

He woke with a jolt and checked his watch, it was 4pm and rain was battering against the windows. There were small puddles right across his small terrace, a couple of chairs he'd left out there were sodden, so he quickly opened the door, closed them up and laid them against the wall, slightly protected from the rain. He then went through to the bedroom and changed his clothes. He wasn't going out again so shorts and t-shirt would do, he put on a pair of white socks as it was now feeling a bit chilly, but he certainly wasn't going to put any heating on in May. He grabbed his laptop and brought it through to the living room, made a coffee, and sat back down in the chair. Jake opened the lid and fired it up, but instead of going to his notes on the case he decided to Google Matthew Boyle. The first page was dominated by information on a professor at Oxford University, and a young footballer who had tragically died. He kept scrolling, not finding anyone who resembled the one he'd just met. He didn't really know what he was looking for, or what he expected to find. He was about to give up but clicked on images to see if there was a face he recognised. Halfway down the page he saw the Matt he'd been talking to earlier today, smiling at the camera. He clicked on the image, and it revealed him with a woman at a Food Fair in Romsey. The picture was from the local paper and just showed the woman biting into a pie, so she was slightly obscured, but Jake was pretty sure the woman was Karen Carpenter. What the hell did that mean? He ran his hand through his hair, cupped his hands and rested his head on them. He got up and started searching for listening devices. After an hour he didn't find anything.

Milly turned up just as Tomasz

Schafernaker was presenting the weather on the BBC at 6.30pm. She wasn't stopping as it was the last Lymford Ladies football match of the season. They were playing Ringwood Town, and this was a title decider. Jake recalled the events of the day as Tomasz was telling them that the grim weather we had at the moment would be better by the weekend.

'I knew there was something not quite right about Amey.' Milly sounded a little triumphant. 'I wish I'd met her. I would have sussed her. The trouble with you men is that you lack a woman's intuition. You're a good PI Jake but you'll never have that.'

'I feel a little offended,' he replied, with a half-smile.

'It's not just you, none of you men have it, but in your defence you're generally more rational than we are.' Milly was smiling.

'So, with your female intuition, can you tell me what's Emilia's involvement, what was her connection with James?'

Milly sat down and examined her right hand. She needed to redo her nails at the weekend. 'Two things. She either just met James in Menorca and it was an innocent relationship. Or, she was a link between the ADG and James, passing on messages.'

'Not sure that's particularly insightful. You're saying she either was, or wasn't, part of ADG, but either way they were involved? Well done Miss Marple. You need to join Cormoran Strike and kick out Robin.'

'Ooh, somebody's a little tired?' she replied, mockingly.

Jake put his hand through his hair again and hung his head. 'Sorry, I am a bit, I think I'll have an early night.'

'Well, I'm off to win a trophy so I'll see you tomorrow. One last thought though. 'If Matt Boyle is still with the same secret employers now, as he was in 2012, why did he speak to you?'

Jake frowned. Milly grabbed the door handle of the living room to go out. 'I mean, did he really want to help out of some sort of grievance, or is he leading you on as well?' She smiled again and said, 'good night.'

He stood up and let out a groan of frustration. He looked across at a photo of him with his parents in London when he was twelve. A picture that Milly liked and put on a bookshelf in a corner of the room. He idly spoke to the picture, 'I just want to know who actually killed the three of them, that's all, and now it seems everyone is lying,' He turned away and went to a bottle sitting on the kitchen worktop. A glass of Merlot was needed, and an episode of Grantchester.

Matt Boyle felt better, better that he could honestly tell someone what happened to him. The true story. He lived in a nondescript nineties-built house on the edge of Eastleigh, never married, his life just wouldn't support it, but he yearned now for some normality. As soon as he got close to someone that would mean being honest, and honesty wasn't something he could do. He knew people who could, their work and their home life were all based on concealing the real person. Matt Boyle was born Tony Campbell on the 24 July 1987, in Newport, South Wales, son of Gwyn and Mair Campbell. He was an only son, and his parents were killed in the 2004 tsunami in Thailand, the whole family were holidaying in Phuket, and they were swept away by the tide that devastated their beachside hotel. Matt clung to a pillar just inside the hotel, but his parents' bodies were never found. He was seventeen and was lost for a number of years. He eventually found himself in London working for the Met and was 'recruited' in 2010. He became Matthew Boyle, working undercover as a detective in Hampshire, his job was to monitor Amey Lorimer who was a 'person of interest,' due to her family connections with the Albion Defence Group. This came to an end in 2012 and he was reassigned. His problem was that the top dog in the organisation gave him no recognition for the work he'd done, in fact he was criticised for not being as diligent as expected when the first Hampshire murder took place. Admittedly, it may have been a little unprofessional to then have a relationship with the woman who discovered the body, but she wasn't a suspect. It was decided that there was no need to change his identity, which Matt was a little uncomfortable with, but he was then asked to infiltrate a Greenpeace group in Devon before returning to Hampshire and working for Sainsbury's, where a drugs ring was suspected to be based. It seemed unlikely and indeed he had found nothing. He was disillusioned and ready to give this life up and have a normal life with a regular job.

CHAPTER FORTY EIGHT

Laura called Lewis, Stacey and Bhavin into her office. She'd made a decision, and she needed them to sort this one out and reach a conclusion. She had six different situations on the go and this one needed to be concluded. It was dragging on too long and was like a splinter in her finger that she couldn't prise out. All three of them looked nervous as they were ushered into Laura's plush office which had an enormous window overlooking the Thames. She was in full power mode and Lewis knew this was the time when you sat and listened.

'We've dragged our feet over this one and I probably should have intervened sooner.' Laura took off her glasses and leaned forward in her chair, then abruptly got up and walked to the window. 'Lewis, I want you and one other, you choose, to go pay Jake Stone a visit. The other one of you I want to go and see Amey Lorimer.' There was a pause while the three sat down and waited to see whether she would carry on. 'I want you to take non-disclosure agreements with you to see Jake Stone and give him the whole story.'

'Really?' Lewis said, sounding a little incredulous.

'Yes, really Lewis,' Laura turned to him and glowered.

'You mean everything?'

'Look Lewis, I think we have to. How long have I been in this role? I'll tell you, it's been two years. And who was my predecessor?' This time she was waiting for one of them to answer.

'Oh yes,' Bhavin chipped in.

'Correct Bhavin,' Laura looked at their faces with some amusement, as the penny dropped. Stacey spoke.

'He was in charge for something like 20 years, wasn't he?'

'Correct again.' Laura walked back to the table and sat down opposite them.

Lewis spoke this time. 'And he was overseeing the events of 2012? Fully involved and making the decisions?'

Laura nodded. 'You three go away and decide what you're going to do and make the calls. I'd like this cleared up within a week. Only I was here then so we don't have the baggage, but you've all done the research.'

'What exactly do we say to Amey Lorimer?' Lewis asked.

'Tell her that her work is done and get back to her knitting, or pottery, or whatever it is an old lonely woman does.'

They looked at each other, stood up and filed out of the room.

'Come and see me when you're done.'

Laura shouted out as the door closed.

CHAPTER FORTY NINE

Milly called Jake as he was just sitting down behind his desk in his office, in Lymford High Street.

'Have you seen the reviews for *Death in the Afternoon*? They're really quite good overall. The Guardian has given it five stars.' Milly was quite excited.

'No, I've not seen them yet. I'm pleased for him.' Jake was distracted as he could see that he had a missed call from an undisclosed number. It was probably another potential client. There was a voicemail so he would listen to that shortly.

Milly lowered her voice, 'I've got something to talk to you about tonight. Are we seeing each other?'

'Hey, it's Sunday night. You know I never go out on a Sunday night, so yes. Do you want to come round to me? I'll cook.'

'Great. Are you in the office on a Sunday afternoon?'

'Yep, I've only really popped in but got waylaid looking at an email. It looks like Cesar has been ferreting around in Es Castell and found out a bit more about Emilia.'

'Maybe you need to set up an international

office?' Milly joked.

'Makes you wonder, eh? Anyway, he's found out that Emilia was working for the ADG as some sort of secretary. Her family would do anything in the name of crime if they got something out of it. He reckons that she was probably helping James back here, and like you said, passing messages between him and the ADG in Menorca.'

'Wow, it does get more complicated,' she responded, 'look. I'm going to have to go and get some food in for Isabella's visit. I'll see you around 6pm.'

Jake wandered to his window on the High Street, noticing the large number of day trippers that seemed to be aimlessly wandering up and down, pointing at things in shop windows and shaking their heads. Lymford had some expensive shops. He put his phone on speaker and listened to his voicemail.

Hello Jake Stone. My name is Lewis Carter and it's of the utmost importance I speak with you. Please call back on this number.

He looked at his phone with some alarm. His first thought was that somebody he knew was ill, or perhaps dead. But that didn't make sense as he thought they would have said something like they were sorry to tell him that they had some bad news. Instinctively, it was something to do with his investigation. Jake phoned straight back.

'Hello, Jake Stone here.'

A strong, confident voice was on the other end.

'Thank you for calling back. I haven't got time to mess around, especially on a Sunday, but myself and a colleague urgently need to come and see you,' he paused, 'there's no time to lose. We want to see you in your office on Tuesday.'

Jake was taken aback but could tell he wouldn't have a choice.

'Yes. Can I ask what this is about?'

'You can, but I won't be saying anything over the phone. Needless to say, I need to rely on your silence.'

'Okay then.'

'We'll be there at 9.30am. One other thing can you make sure your girlfriend, Milly Lucas is there, and we'll ensure Greg Jones is also attending.'

Jake felt vaguely scared and intrigued at the same time. Clearly, he knew what this was about, so he phoned Milly straight away. Her reaction seemed more enthusiastic and mentioned that 'it sounded exciting.' Jake sensed that he would be wasting his time with any further investigation, and that by the end of Tuesday he probably will have finished with the case. At least he may finally get the answers, and more importantly so would Greg.

At 3pm the next day, Monday, Amey's doorbell rang. She was just potting a plant in the kitchen sink, and so tutted as she shuffled to the door. There was a smart young man in suit and tie on the doorstep who introduced himself as Bhavin Hariharan. No warning phone call for Amey to say he was coming. He held up some ID.

'May I come in Mrs Lorimer?'

'Do I have a choice?'

'Not really,' Bhavin replied. He was clearly on a mission, and she had a good idea what it was going to be about. Amey ushered him into the living room and told him she'd make tea. Bhavin was nervous but thought he was doing a good job of hiding it. He had rehearsed what he would say and had volunteered to do this particular visit on his own. Under the circumstances, he felt there would be some irony in that, as an Indian born employee, he should make the visit to someone connected to the Albion Defence Group. Amey came back five minutes later having put tea bags in the cups, and milk. Bhavin wasn't really going to have a choice how he wanted it, or even if he wanted it. Which he didn't. His plan was to get out before the tea was cool enough to drink.

'I'm sure you know why I'm here, and who I represent.' Amey nodded, a very severe look on her face. 'My message is quite simple, you knew the arrangement twelve years ago and it still stands. You need to go back to your sedentary occupations, knitting, WI, breadmaking, or whatever it is you more mature people do when retired, and forget about your involvement with Jake Stone. We're seeing him tomorrow, along with Greg Jones. Do you get me?'

Amey screwed her face up. Bhavin could see a wave of different emotions run through it. Anger, shame, incredulity. Bhavin was pleased.

'You know I was just trying to put him off? Just to keep James out of it.'

'We do.' Bhavin replied but didn't elaborate.

'I was trying to put him off the scent, but I also couldn't be seen to be doing nothing to help him.'

Bhavin just nodded. He looked around the living room, then spoke.

'This house, in this situation, in this city, couldn't have been cheap. I'm sure you wouldn't want to jeopardise your nice comfortable life, would you?'

'Pfft,' Amey responded, 'I was a good detective. I earned it. I didn't need your money, or your threats to have this.' She picked up her teacup and drank noisily from it.

'So, we have an understanding. You will not contact Jake again, you will not speak to anyone, ever again, from the ADG or the victims' families from 2012. Life will go back to its status quo?'

Amey almost slammed the teacup down.

Bhavin got up to go.

'I'll see myself out.' As he got to the living room door he turned to Amey, who was scowling at him as if she was putting a curse on.

'We've allowed you one concession. We know you've been in contact with Brad Swinburn, and we'll let that go. And to show we're not completely heartless he'll be okay as well. However, one further step out of line from either of you and we'll make it difficult for him.'

Bhavin walked out the door, down the path to his car and looked out over Salisbury. He climbed into his brand-new BMW feeling pleased with himself, and waited for the sweats to diminish.

CHAPTER FIFTY

It was 9.15am when Jake heard the first ring on his doorbell. He walked down the stairs and opened it. Greg was standing there looking very white, Jake invited him in, glad that he was there before Lewis.

'Milly's here as well,' Jake said as they walked up the stairs. He opened the office door, and she was arranging the chairs in a circle. She'd bought two dining room chairs with her as she calculated they would need them. This was going to be serious, so having someone sit on the sofa didn't seem quite right.

'It's like Poirot,' she said, where he gets everyone together to announce the killer.

'Yeah, but I don't think our little grey cells are going to be wanted.' Jake was now trying to make the best of it. He was hoping they would find out exactly what did happen in 2012, although he was also dreading that they were in some kind of trouble, they'd upset the authorities, and this was going to be a reprimand. He didn't know what power these two people had who were visiting. The coffee was brewing, the tea bags were ready, and the biscuits laid out on a plate. The doorbell rang again, and they all looked at each other. Jake walked downstairs and opened the door to Lewis Carter and Stacey Peck, as identified on their passes. The passes just indicated that they were members of the UK civil service, nothing more than that, so Jake led them upstairs and introductions were made. The tension was palpable, it was hanging in the air like a thick mist, swirling around but not clearing.

The first thing Lewis did was sit on the sofa and reach underneath, he fiddled around with the fabric and then pulled out a small black disc and held it up to show them.

'My sofa was bugged?' Jake exclaimed. 'Is that legal?'

'No,' Lewis said, 'but I'm sure you won't want to make an issue of it.'

'Are there any more anywhere?'

'We'll take care of them tomorrow.'

Jake looked at Milly who was biting her lip. Lewis had a flat black case with him and pulled out three sheets of paper. He looked at them, scanning his eyes from one to the other as if he wanted some dramatic reaction.

'What I've got here are non-disclosure agreements, commonly known as NDA's.' He held the papers up and Greg reached out to grab one. Lewis pulled the papers back to keep hold of them. Jake was already disliking Lewis; he clearly enjoyed the drama of what he was doing. Stacey spoke for the first time. She had a much more, 'girl next door,' look about her. Shoulder length mousy coloured hair, pleasant smile and dressed in a regular smart blouse and trousers. She looked at Lewis as she started to speak, as if for approval.

'We will tell you everything you want to know about the deaths in 2012, but in return we would like you to sign these agreements, so that you never talk about them again to anyone else. I'm not exaggerating when I say it's of national importance. The tensions we have in our society today would be stoked up if this became public. You all watch the news. We're living in dangerous times.' She looked at them, seemingly wanting them to understand and agree.

Jake found he wasn't surprised by this. He rationalised that at least this would be a job done for him and Greg would know the truth. Judging by the look on Greg's face he thought he would be thinking the same thing. Milly seemed a little more outraged.

'But what gives you the right to listen into innocent citizens' private conversations, without their permission?' She looked at Stacey.

'When it's in the national interest,' she replied, raising her eyebrows at Milly, in a slightly condescending manner. Possibly not the girl next door, Jake thought to himself.

Lewis took over.

'Look, we're not going to negotiate with you, sign the agreements, or...?

'Or what exactly?' Milly asked, but calmer this time.

'Mrs Lucas. We're actually being quite generous here, by giving you the opportunity to hear the truth.' Milly realised that they had done their homework. It wasn't very often she liked to be referred to as Mrs Lucas, her married name, even though she'd been divorced for five years. It was still her legal name. Milly backed down and Lewis pulled out a pen, making an audible click, four times, ready for their signatures.

'What do you think Greg?' Jake asked. Greg nodded slowly. 'I think you're the one who needs to be happy with this.'

He cleared his throat. 'At the end of the day I'm going to find out what happened, and no disrespect to you Jake, we'll probably find out more than you ever could.'

Stacey was already pulling out a clipboard and placing the NDAs on it. She grabbed the pen off Lewis and passed it to Greg. He took each of them off the clipboard and passed one each to Jake and Milly, for them to read. After a few minutes of silence, he signed his copy and passed the clipboard and pen to Jake. They did the same and passed all three signed NDA's back to Stacey.

Lewis spoke. 'Right, let's get this over with.'

CHAPTER FIFTY ONE

Jake looked at the clock he'd recently put on the wall. It was 9.45am on the 21st May 2024. He was thinking this could be a day to remember.

'Okay then,' Lewis started. 'Let's go back to 2007, this is when we first became aware of Tommy Phillips and his activities. He was an extremist and basically wanted to drive all non-white, non-British-born people out of the country. That was his ultimate aim. He wasn't a terrorist as such, but he was dangerous. Over the next four years he gradually rallied his followers and formed the Albion Defence Group.'

'Hang on a minute,' Jake interjected. 'Who exactly are you? You've not really explained that to us.'

'I'll come on to that a bit more later. Suffice to say, we're a small unit that very few people know about. The PM doesn't know we exist, and quite frankly we can't trust them, as they change so quickly these days.'

Milly's eyes widened and her mouth opened, but she closed it again. Lewis carried on.

'Tommy knew the heat was on him a bit and so he moved his sordid little operation to Menorca in 2011, and that's also when we infiltrated the group.'

'Anyone we know?' Jake asked.

'I don't think so, so I will keep his identity quiet,' Lewis was clearly getting irritated about any interruptions to his story. 'Anyway, we found out they were planning to be a bloody nuisance and demonstrate at pre-Olympic events, as well as when the games were on. As you know this was a huge deal for the country and we were desperate for it to go well. There was a will to make sure that it was successful at any cost. You may remember we were only just starting to get over the financial crash of a few years earlier.'

It occurred to Jake that they didn't realise he already knew most of this, thanks to Matt Boyle. They didn't know about that conversation from last week, which explained Matt's caution about checking for any hidden devices, and the open-air setting.

'Layton Jones, Roger Jenkins and Barbara North were all members of the group, and they'd been assigned tasks while in Menorca which they were to carry out back here in spring and early summer 2012. They were showing signs of nervousness about the actions planned.'

Jake interrupted again. 'And they were Bob, Phil and Lucy, respectively.'

'Yes, as you discovered in the WhatsApp messages.' Stacey chipped in.

'Well, Amey Lorimer discovered them.'

'We'll come on to Amey in a minute.' Lewis now looked annoyed that Stacey was contributing. She was clearly there for the experience and not to necessarily say too much. Milly felt the irrational need to slap his face, but she drank more coffee instead and picked up a bourbon, biting into it loudly.

'Our informant,' Lewis was back in charge, 'managed to persuade the three of them that this was a step too far and as patriots they wouldn't want to see their country tarnished in this way. This was quite a dangerous move but proved successful. The three of them agreed to feed back to us what Tommy was planning to do, and so started working for us. In the meantime, they were meeting the bloke known as Bob in Winchester to arrange trouble. I have to say they were actually very brave. Unfortunately, they got found out.'

Jake looked puzzled. 'So why not just kick them out of the ADG and get somebody else to do their dirty work?'

'That's underestimating the evilness that had pervaded Tommy Phillips, and in particular this Bob chap. They both wanted them killed for their treachery and deceit, and we knew it was time to get our man out of there. So, Bob killed all three of them. He was a confident psychopath who thought that he could do what he wanted. He decided to have fun and vary the killings. It was only then we realised how truly awful the

ADG had become.'

'But he staged them so elaborately.' Greg now spoke.

'Impressive, wasn't it?' Stacey added.

Jake wasn't going over this in his head. 'Can I ask, was your infiltrator James Lorimer?'

Lewis asked for another coffee and Greg got up and poured some out that was left in the cafetiere. He offered everyone else, but they were okay.

'No, it wasn't. James was a bonafide ADG member, but he was also having doubts. He was under orders to supervise the tasks that the three were going to carry out from The Green Room, but with Bob in charge. Our man tried to suss out whether James could be turned but decided it was too much of a risk to approach him.'

'What were the tasks?' Milly said.

'They were all going to cause trouble when the torch relay went round the country. The one which David Beckham started by flying into Cornwall with it.' Jake, Greg and Milly nodded, thinking back to when it was televised live on TV. 'Later on they planned to go to the stadiums and protest. They were getting supplies of teargas and truncheons ready, as if they were the police, so this was serious.'

Jake didn't want to say that he'd had a further discussion with Matt Boyle, so asked how Amey Lorimer might have fitted in. Lewis looked slightly surprised.

'Well, being the sister of Tommy Phillips she was always on our watch, and her son James was obviously involved. We got Matthew Boyle in there to watch what she was doing. I think she was torn as she definitely had sympathies with the organisation, but she was still a good detective. Getting her suspended would raise questions. I don't think she knew the killings were going to happen but she wanted to protect James.' Lewis paused, looking a bit unsure how much he should say. 'We wanted to close this all down, so she was replaced with Patrick Tweddle, and we used Matt to help with this.'

'Are you saying people were paid off?' Jake asked.

'Oh yes, quite a few people. Amey, James, and a few others.'

'What about Morgan Ellis?' Milly questioned.

Lewis smiled. 'He's still a little in the dark, and it's best that apple cart is not upset.'

'In what way?' Milly was going to persist.

'He was brought in by James to do his role, whatever you'd call it, clear up, observe, whatever. Importantly, he thought there was some warped good to it as James told him it was for the good of the country, and he would be protected.'

Jake spoke. 'I think he really does think that…or he desperately wants to think that, and it's the belief that he's holding on to.'

'Bottom line is, he was working for Tommy Phillips and the ADG. They paid him. You could say the ADG kick started his acting career. It helped him get some one-to-one coaching and a better agent.'

Milly looked at Jake and said. 'He must never know that.' Jake agreed

It was now 10.45am and they all needed a break. 'How long have you got?' Jake asked Lewis, who said that they weren't on a schedule today, apart from getting this wrapped up. They would return to London at the right time. Jake said he would pop downstairs and get cakes from the bakery below. Greg and Stacey were now sitting down on their own, next to each other.

'Can I ask,' he said tentatively, 'had Layton changed by the time he was killed, was he regretting what he'd done, by joining this idiotic group?'

'From what I know, bearing in mind it was before my time, all three of them did. The one we're not so sure about is Barbara North. She was having an affair with Tommy and when he found out she was double crossing him he wanted her killed in that gruesome manner. He just asked Bob to do it, and he did. She had a small family, and nobody really mourned her death. However, there is a suspicion that she was going to rat on the other two, but Tommy didn't wait to check. Don't forget he was away in Menorca and relied on what he was being told.'

'So, who told him they were having doubts and were now informing on the ADG?'

Stacey looked up to see where Lewis was. 'We're pretty sure it was James.'

'But then he regretted it?'

'It seems like it. Yes. He got himself into a bit of a mess and so it was decided that a new identity in New Zealand would be best for him.'

Greg let out an exasperated sigh and sat back in his chair.

CHAPTER FIFTY TWO

The others came back and sat down. Jake had managed to chill Lewis out a little bit as they briefly had a conversation about getting through the New Forest in the summer. Lewis had a cottage by the sea at Mudeford.

'I don't think there's much more to talk about, so any questions from you three?' Lewis asked.

Jake spoke. 'Matt Boyle. Would I be right in thinking he knew what Morgan Ellis was doing? Did he recognise him at the scene of Layton's death?'

Lewis gave a wry smile. 'You are correct Mr Stone. He'd never met him before, but he had a description and knew what his role was. We were kind of looking out for him as well, so when he gave Karen Carpenter his jacket, Matt sorted it out, so it went missing. Amey had no idea, but Matt was prepared to take the wrap from Amey for seeming to lose it.'

'In a way both sides were looking after him?' Jake asked.

'You could say that. He was a bit of a pawn in a deadly game, but thankfully he came to no harm.'

'Was Matt pushed to one side?' Jake sounded a little defensive.

'He started an affair with Karen Carpenter, and that was unprofessional. We had bought her silence and both of them should have stayed away from each other. You know she was having an affair while planning her marriage to another man?' Jake raised his eyebrows, thinking about when he first visited her.

'It seems to me that a lot of money was paid out during all of this?' Milly now asked.

'It was, and it wouldn't happen now, but the Olympics was huge, and we didn't want any sort of scandal rearing its ugly head. You may remember at around this time there was starting to be a little dissent over London staging them, and so the pro-Olympic publicity machine was in top gear.'

'And what a success it was in the end. The country was the most positive it had been in years. There was a real feelgood factor going on.'

'Yep,' said Lewis, it's been all downhill since then.

Jake was tapping the side of his head. 'So, these three were killed by Bob?' He looked across at Greg, 'Sorry mate.' Greg nodded to acknowledge that was okay. 'Various people are paid off to keep quiet, what about Bob?'

'He very quickly disappeared abroad. We know where he is. He can stay there and won't cause us any problems.' What Lewis wasn't going to admit was that Bob had been permanently silenced in Istanbul ten years ago.

'Will I also not be hearing from Amey anymore?'

'You won't. Our colleague visited her yesterday. She really just wanted to monitor what you were finding out and do what she could to safeguard James.'

'The killing of Roger Jenkins,' Jake was thinking again, 'that was a tricky one. Who was Dan?'

'If I'm honest we don't know what happened to him,' Stacey now spoke and Jake thought she was as well versed on the subject as Lewis was, and she was keen to have her say. 'He literally disappeared.'

'What were they going to meet about that day? He was killed at the banks' offices, although everyone thinks it was a heart attack.'

'That was a meeting to talk about the torch relay going through Andover. It was to stop at the offices for a while and as Roger was on the council he was going to both arrange it to happen…but also to arrange for it to be disrupted. With him swapping sides he was going to report back, and we would work out a plan to stop the disruption without it looking like him.'

'Gets complicated.' Greg said, with his head in his hands.

Silence returned. Lewis and Stacey started to make movements to go.

'One last question,' Jake said. 'You really didn't have to tell us all this did you? I mean you could have just told us all to back off, maybe pay Greg a few quid and he tells me to drop it?'

Lewis and Stacey looked at each other. They had expected there would be a need to add this last comment.

'Jake. We know about you from your, shall we say, troubles last year with your biological family. Your adopted father.' Lewis paused and looked Jake directly in the eye. 'Your father, Isaac Stone, was head of this unit shortly before his own death.'

Lewis let that sink in and watched Jake's face turn to complete disbelief. Milly grabbed his arm and gasped. Greg stared at him. Lewis spoke more:

'We felt we owed you a full explanation because Isaac was in charge in 2012 and knew exactly what was going on. He made a lot of the decisions that led to us ending up where we were. In our eyes it was a successful operation.'

'Wow,' is all Jake could say. He was looking stunned and couldn't collect his thoughts into one coherent response.

'So, did he oversee the end of the ADG? Because I don't remember hearing about them after that.' Milly said. She knew that would be a question Jake would ask once he'd recovered himself.

'Pretty much,' said Lewis. They dispersed knowing they were a spent force and then Tommy got what he deserved. Cancer a few years later and dying a lonely death in Menorca.

Everyone got up and Lewis and Stacey said their goodbyes. Lewis looked at Jake and said that he may have more questions, and he could contact him if he wanted to. As they went out the door Jake asked if he could know the name of their unit.

Lewis realised they hadn't said much about them, and he didn't want to.

'Every country has their more secretive teams. Ones working for their country's defence and security. We are one of those.' He hesitated before pulling out his notebook from his case. 'I can't say it out loud, but I'll write it on a piece of paper. We changed the name two years ago and only twenty people know that we even exist, so destroy this paper straight away. He handed it to Jake.

On the paper was written the word STONE. Jake's mouth opened wide and closed again. He looked at Lewis.

'In honour of my dad?'
Lewis nodded. 'A great man.'
Jake felt his eyes water.

CHAPTER FIFTY THREE

It was Thursday 20th June 2024. A General Election was looming and there were political posters everywhere. The day was sultry with a heat haze rising above the ground, shimmering and distorting everything at ground level. Jake, Milly and Isabella stood outside The Green Room trying to gauge how many people were inside. Isabella had come back to Lymford after only being away for a week. She said she wasn't going to miss this. Jake grabbed Milly's hand and pushed the door open. There was quite a cacophony of noise as they stepped in, a few people in suits but most had taken the advice of the invite and dressed smart casual, or just casual. They manoeuvred themselves towards the bar, Jake checking that Isabella was behind him. The drinks were free, so Milly and Isabella had Prosecco, while Jake ordered an Estrella. He could see Sofia busying herself behind the bar, but he doubted she would remember him.

They moved carefully through to the back until they could finally see him, sat with his family, in a raised area where there was a bit more room. Morgan saw them and beckoned them forward to come and sit with them.

Morgan hugged Jake like a long-lost friend and kissed the ladies on both cheeks. He introduced everyone to each other and looked like the cat who had got the cream.

'I'm so glad you could make it,' he said, pulling chairs out for them. 'The fact is I don't know who most of these people are, but I'm loving it. Just loving being back here again after so long.'

Two weeks ago, Jake had managed to see Morgan just as he was coming back to earth after the premieres. They sat in Morgan's back garden as they had a few weeks previously. Jake had assured him that the investigation was dead and buried, it would never be raised again, but most importantly he told him that, although it may not have seemed like it at the time he had discovered that Morgan had done his small bit to help the country, and he was, and always will be, protected. Jake concluded that was not actually a lie, but it was the best thing to tell him. They then spent another hour finding out they had quite a lot in common and bonded unexpectedly. Jake drove back to Lymford wondering how he'd just become a friend of a major film star.

A group of Winchester councillors and business people wanted to celebrate Morgan's success and so contacted him to discuss where. He was unsure about The Green Room, but it was Jake who persuaded him. He needed to lance that boil.

'You were right,' Morgan said to Jake, 'it's so great to be back here. I'd forgotten how much I liked it. Sofia wants to put a picture up on the wall of me, Anna and Isabel here tonight. She's already taken a photo.'

'You've arrived, mate.' Jake laughed. 'From Hampshire to Hollywood.'

Morgan was in good spirits; he couldn't stop grinning. He was now speaking to Louise, his old teacher from the Winchester Theatre Group. She was telling him how proud she was. Morgan turned to Milly. 'And I'll come back on your show for an interview again.'

'I'm afraid you won't,' she said, 'I'm leaving.' Morgan looked aghast. 'It's all changing there so they don't want me, but I'm branching out into podcasts. How about doing one of those with me?'

'Sure, why not,' Morgan replied, still grinning.

Jake looked across at Isabella who was now sat amongst a group of mainly men. He smiled and nudged Milly.

'Look at the cougar, she's being chatted up by a bloke at least ten years younger than her.'

Milly looked and laughed. 'Look at him though he's gorgeous. Isn't it Austin Christie, plays for Southampton? He's got lovely milk chocolate skin, dark eyes, nicely trimmed beard. I'll tell you what, he's my free pass.'

'Only if I say he is,' Jake retorted.

'Well, I'm telling you.'

'Look at my sister, can't take her anywhere. Don't think you've got a chance Milly Lucas.'

'I'll make do with you then.' Milly laughed.

Jake was now on his second Estrella, 'I'm quite a catch you know.'

'Only cos' of your money darling.'

'And my father saved the Olympics for the country. 'Jake winked at her.

Milly laughed again, 'oh my god, you're going to keep reminding me of that aren't you?'

'Yes, my little cupcake, because it's only you I can mention it to!'

Jake looked around the bar, at Morgan now showing someone pictures on his phone, him with Lily James in Leicester Square. Isabella giggling like a schoolgirl with her footballing suitor, and Milly as happy as he'd seen her for a while. He had a feeling this was going to be one of the best evenings out he'd had for a long time.

ACKNOWLEDGEMENTS

Thanks to Brenda for her diligent and honest feedback during the writing process. Nicola for the book title when I was struggling with one, and Laura for her proof reading.

Special thanks also to Richie from More Visuals for the cover design, and to David and Nicola for the use of their home!

A final thanks to all my friends, family and colleagues who have kept asking me when my next book is coming out. It really does inspire you to keep going.

JAKE STONE INVESTIGATIONS

Jake Stone is a new private investigator having left London, and the civil service, for the South Coast. His new job brings him in contact with dangerous gangs, corrupt policemen, and revelations about his own life.

Don't You Want Me?

Murder Never Dies

Printed in Great Britain
by Amazon